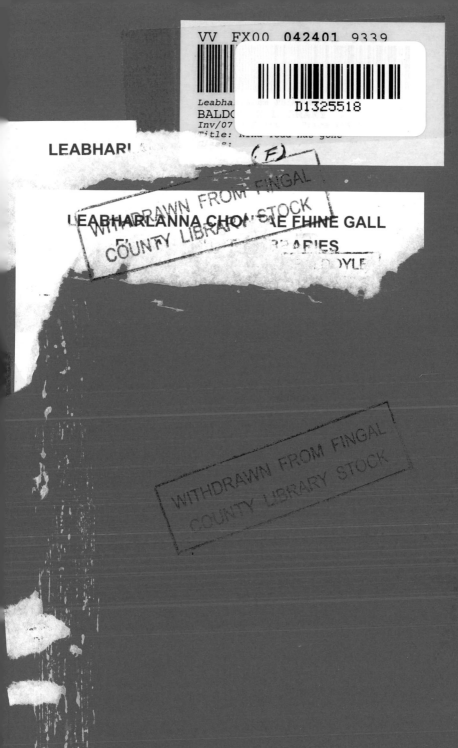

NINA TODD HAS GONE

NINA TODD
HAS GONE

LESLEY GLAISTER

BLOOMSBURY

First published 2007

Copyright © 2007 by Lesley Glaister

The moral right of the author has been asserted

Bloomsbury Publishing Plc,
36 Soho Square,
London W1D 3QY

www.bloomsbury.com

A CIP catalogue record for this book is
available from the British Library

ISBN 9780747586944

10 9 8 7 6 5 4 3 2 1

Typeset by Hewer Text UK Ltd, Edinburgh
Printed in Great Britain by Clays Ltd, St Ives plc

The paper this book is printed on is certified by the © Forest Stewardship
Council 1996 A.C. (FSC). It is ancient-forest friendly. The printer holds
FSC chain of custody SGS-COC-2061

ACKNOWLEDGEMENTS

With thanks for their help to Alexandra Pringle,
Bill Hamilton, Julian Broadhead, Clare Barstow,
Josh French, Katrina Dexter and Andrew Greig

To Andrew

~

The memories of her birth mother are rare and faint. The first is of sitting close to the bars of an electric fire, the hot orange burning her face as they shared a bag of chips. One for you and one for me and licking the vinegary grease from the paper. When the chips were gone she chewed the paper into a gummy wad. She went to sleep still chewing and in the morning the paper came out grey and printed with ridges from the roof of her mouth.

She slept under Mum's coat, hard scratchy material, and woke with a button pressed into her cheek. Nothing to see in the night but a dot of orange growing and shrinking. It was Mum's cigarette in the dark and she liked to watch it and sniff the mothery smell.

Once they were thrown off a train, but this may have been when she was older, on a visit. When the ticket-man came round, Mum's face was blank as an egg as she searched her pockets, but he didn't believe she ever had a ticket and they had to get off at the next stop.

'Fuck you,' Mum said and made a V-sign. Her face was red but when they got off she laughed and they swung hands and sang the yellow-taxi song.

One cold day they sat on a park bench. She was cosy in jeans and a warm coat but Mum's legs were bare and grey as porridge and the skin on her heels stuck over the backs of her sandals like old cheese. A man came up and sat down with them. He made Mum laugh and they smoked a cigarette and he came back to Mum's room.

Lots of men loved Mum and cuddled her and bumped her against walls and on the floor like that. She would draw pictures and try not to look at their faces and sometimes she would put her fingers in her ears.

Afterwards it was good and always chips.

Then one day a lady with cold hands came and took her away.

*

L isten. You should always trust your gut feelings. They are a gift from your subconscious to your conscious mind. If only I had trusted mine.

I was sitting in the lobby of the Hotel Astoria staring into a coffee-spoon. Not mine. I was drinking wine. The convex side of a spoon reflects you the right way up but flip it over and you're upside down. Did you ever notice that?

I picked up my glass. A girl in a nylon overall cleared away the cup and spoon, emptied an ashtray into a plastic sack. She gave me a pitying look. Soon I'd go up in the lift, back to my room and lock the door. But not till Charlie called. My phone sat on the low glass table in front of me, silent.

The girl came back to polish the table, squirting it with lemony spray. She snapped her bubble-gum and gave me that look again, *All on your own?* I swigged back my drink. Now I'd have to get up and walk through the bar where everyone else was partying. Or I could just sit there clutching my empty glass.

I should have followed the advice of my gut and gone back to my room. It was only meanness that made me stay. There was a free drink on offer. I checked my phone again – and saw that someone had stopped beside me. I ignored him for as long as seemed normal and then looked up and up his long legs and body to his face.

He was the most handsome man I've ever seen in real life. Black hair, fine features, deep dark eyes. I pretended to drink from the empty glass. Such beauty was superfluous and almost aggravating. There was no call for it. Not on a wet Tuesday night in Blackpool.

'May I?' He gestured to the space beside me on the sofa. I shrugged. He sat down, crossed one leg over the other and sank back, the leather exhaling beneath him. 'Long day,' he said. I winced an agreement.

I picked up a brochure about local attractions and pretended to read. I thought he'd take the hint but then he spoke again.

'Drink?' I looked up sharply. Did he mean me? Was this a pick-up? He leant forward and tapped my empty glass. 'Refill? I've got half an hour to kill and I hate to drink alone.' Maybe it was the surprise, or maybe the wine I'd already had that made me nod.

I watched him walk through to the bar. Long, long limbs – he must have been six foot three or four – in a black moleskin suit, perfectly cut, just a little creased. I glanced around the lobby and met the eyes of the cleaner, who was polishing the reception desk. She raised her eyebrows at me and blew a pink bubble. I looked away. He came back with a glass of white wine, much better than the free stuff, and a Scotch for himself.

'Business or pleasure?' He relaxed back into the sofa.

'A course,' I said.

'Yes?'

'A load of rubbish,' I said. 'It's about self-esteem.'

'Is that something you lack?'

It seemed almost dangerous to look directly into his face. When I did he smiled, and with the gleam of his bright brown eyes I was dazzled. I sipped the wine and looked down.

4

'Nervous?' he said, nodding at my jiggling foot. I can't help it. Charlie puts his hand on my knee to stop it if we're in the cinema or watching TV. I uncrossed my legs and pressed both feet flat on the floor.

'I'm on Marketing Strategics,' he said, 'and ditto.'

'Ditto?'

'Load of rubbish.'

A laugh crawled out of me and I told him about the getting-to-know-you exercise. Standing in a circle, tossing a beanbag between us, whoever caught it had to shout out their name and something wonderful about themselves.

'Like what?'

'Like, I'm Sally and I'm very punctual.'

'Sally.' He extended his hand.

'No, no,' I said, 'that was someone else. I'm Nina. Nina Todd.'

'Nina.' His fingers closed round mine. 'Nice. Are you?'

'Nice?'

He laughed and I looked away, blushing right down to my toes. I focused on a waitress carrying a platter of chicken wings towards the bar.

'I meant punctual!' he said. 'What did you say . . . when the beanbag came to you?'

I shook my head.

'Go on.'

'OK then. "I'm Nina and I'm good at spelling." '

He snorted. 'Well anyway it sounds more fun than Marketing Strategics. All pie charts and jargon. Have you eaten, Nina?'

'No.'

'Not joining the party?' In the bar the laughter had been replaced by a buzz of conversation and the chink of cutlery on plates.

'I'm not a party person.' I got up to go. 'Thanks for the drink.'

'Nina,' he said. 'Would you have dinner with me? Looks like I've been stood up.'

'But I don't even know your name!'

'I can soon put that right. Promise not to laugh?' He bit his lip and pulled a face. 'It's Rupert – and no bear jokes, please.'

I looked down at him and I didn't laugh. 'Rupert's OK,' I said.

'I've grown into it,' he said. And then wrinkled his nose and growled. It was stupid but it made me laugh again.

'You said you had to wait half an hour,' I pointed out. 'It can't have been that long.'

He shrugged. 'Quiet dinner. Two strangers away from home. No strings.' He opened his palms.

'I've got to make a call,' I said.

I took my phone and went to stand by the big revolving doors. As people swished through I caught a whiff of raw sea air. If Charlie had answered I'd have said no to Rupert but he didn't answer, neither on the landline or his mobile. I knew where he'd be – round at his brother Dave's, who was depressed.

Suddenly I felt reckless; what the hell, I thought. Why not? What harm could it do? Two strangers away from home. It would be a consolation. That was when I got the gut feeling that told me *Don't*, that told me *Walk away and don't look back*. I went over to Rupert and said, 'All right. Thank you. Yes.'

I thought he meant that we'd eat in the hotel restaurant but he knew a good place ten minutes away, he said, and how about some sea air to give us an appetite? My jacket was too flimsy for the rain and wind. My thin shoe soles picked up the chill of the promenade as we walked along under the coloured lights. Red and yellow smeared and glittered the wet concrete. The sea was invisible except for a breaking edge of white but it moaned and swooshed and I

6

felt it in my stomach. A gust of wind rattled the lights above us and Rupert took my arm.

'Don't want you blowing away, do we?' he said.

The restaurant was warm and dark with candles flickering on thick white linen cloths. A serious grown-up restaurant. Charlie would have walked straight past and headed for an Indian or Chinese. I wanted to check the prices on the menu. But before I had a chance to look, while a waiter was still helping me out of my jacket, Rupert ordered a bottle of champagne.

'I'm sorry,' he said, as we were shown to our seats, 'I should have asked, do you like champagne?'

'Who doesn't? But—'

'If you're worrying about the cost, please, this is on me.'

'I can't.'

'No strings. I can afford it. Let me treat you.'

I breathed in the rich foody scents and wavered like the flames of the candles. 'OK then, ta.' People were looking at him, and looking at me with envy because I was with him and no one else looked half so good for miles and miles around. I told myself to relax. What would be the point of not enjoying it now?

During the blue-cheese soufflé and the monkfish skewers, between the glasses of champagne and then Chablis, I did relax and gabbled on about the other people on the course, like the woman who'd said, 'I am wonderful because my breasts are still pert after feeding two babies.'

'That *is* wonderful,' he said, a little quirk to his lips. He leant forward and looked at my eyes.

'What?' I said.

'Eyes are the windows of the soul,' he said.

I shrank back when he said that rubbish. Eyes are just balls of muscle filled with water, nothing to do with souls at all. I felt like getting up and walking out on him, but then he changed the subject and I forgave him his cliché.

He drained the wine bottle into my glass and returned it upside down to the ice bucket. I sneaked a look at myself in a polished spoon.

'What are you doing?' he said.

I told him about the reflections and he tried it for himself and then . . . I don't remember more of the conversation, or leaving the restaurant, though I do recall floating through the wind tethered like a balloon to his arm. And I do remember a kiss, under a lamp-post, the taste of the inside of his mouth, the smoothness of his tongue.

His room was bigger than mine, with a wider bed and a window that in daylight would have shown the chilly acres of the sea. He pulled the cord and drew the curtains against the dark. He opened the mini-bar and poured us each a cognac. Inside the fridge was a toy bear with white plush fur. It had a sign round its neck beginning, 'Missing a Loved One?'

I remembered then. I should have gone back to my own room then and locked the door. But instead I watched myself be kissed and though I knew that this was cheap behaviour, cheats' behaviour, the moment when I could have called a halt had already passed. Maybe it was the drink. Maybe it was . . . I don't know. I don't think I even want to know.

As he undid the buttons on his linen shirt, I saw that they were the skinniest mother-of-pearl. His chest was neatly furred with ferns of black hair, his belly was taut, a trail of tendrils leading down. He pulled me up against him and I could feel hardness through the soft black moleskin of his trousers. And once we'd gone that far there seemed no point in stopping.

But there was no tenderness or even the pretence of it. While he was inside me I caught sight of us in the mirror, my white legs hooked crablike round his back, and was engulfed in such a wave of dread and sorrow I thought that I would drown.

After he'd rolled off I lay numbly beside him for half an hour while he stared at the ceiling. And then said something about his wife. I thought it a fine time to be mentioning a wife. Had I mentioned Charlie? Of course I had. The wine made sure of that.

Rupert turned over and ran his finger from my shoulder down to my hip. 'Smooth skin,' he said. Goosebumps followed his finger down and I pulled away. Skin is the largest organ of the body, packed with nerve-endings, sweat glands, hair follicles; so much more complex than it looks.

I got up and began to pull on my clothes, tripping with one leg in my tights that twisted and tangled round my knees.

'You don't have to go.' He leant up on one elbow watching me. I hate anyone watching me dress. Even Charlie. Even at the best of times.

'Toothbrush,' I said.

'Use mine.' A shudder ran through me at the idea of scrubbing my teeth with his brush, the thought of mingling all those particles of food and plaque. Dirtier, more personal, than sex.

'And I need to phone my husband.' The zip was sticking on my stupid skirt and I wrenched so hard there was a sound of ripping.

'You didn't say you were married.' He grabbed my left hand. 'As I thought. I'd have noticed a ring. That in your room too?'

'Don't wear one.' I snatched my hand away. 'Don't like rings. And anyway you never mentioned your wife till just now.' I didn't bother with my bra, stuffed it in my handbag, buttoned my blouse up wrong and pulled my jacket over it in a panicky rush. I couldn't get out of there fast enough.

*T*he first time she had sex she was twelve. The foster parents then were Christians and she had to go to a church youth club called the Fellowship. 'Nothing like a bit of good clean fun,' the foster father liked to say.

It was on Wednesday nights and there was a table-tennis table, magnetic darts, board games and a counter selling bottles of limeade and cherryade, crisps and Wagon Wheels. She didn't like the Fellowship and didn't much enjoy the good clean fun. She didn't find it easy to mix or make friends. She preferred to stay at home and watch telly rather than bat a ping-pong ball about and finish off with prayers.

She used to volunteer to work behind the refreshment counter. It was better than leaning against the wall on her own. Gideon was a tall boy three years older than herself. He was the minister's son and nice to chat to while he helped her arrange the bottles of pop at seven o'clock and pack them back into a cardboard box at nine.

At Christmas there was a disco. Pop songs from a tape-recorder; cheesy Wotsits, Pepsi and a lightshow that swirled peppery lights around the walls. There was no refreshment stall that evening, everything came free along with the love of Jesus. She'd pretended to be ill. She wanted to stay in and watch The Two Ronnies' Christmas Special *but her foster dad had rubbed his hands and said, 'A good night out will do you wonders.'*

And in a way he was right.

Gideon asked her to dance with him to 'Uptown Girl', then he took her into a little side-room and locked the door. He talked gently all the time he lifted up her skirt, pulled down her knickers, opened up his trousers and did it to her. The only nice thing about it was the way his arms wrapped round her. Nobody ever held her tight like that. For a few moments to him she was important. The most important thing.

I t came out of the blue, after all the years of waiting. It was
an ordinary Wednesday morning in September. I lay in late
as usual. I was out of work. What's the point of work when
you've got all the money you need? Dad calls me a lazy arse,
strong stuff from him, and Mum does her sniff when the
subject comes up but that's because they don't understand. I
haven't been idle since leaving school; I've been waiting.

Sausages for breakfast reading the *Mail*, Mum's paper,
which I know is looked down on in some circles but doesn't
stink like Dad's. He takes the *Telegraph* to the lav first thing
and smokes while he's waiting to go and it picks up the
smells. Funny thing though, reading about a murder, girl
found in field, usual sort of scenario, made me think of her.
Not that I haven't thought about her every day since it
happened.

There was an ad for a holiday that caught my eye. Mexico is
where I'll head for. I like the food. When I cook I buy those
burrito kits or sometimes enchiladas. Not really to Dad's taste
but it's good to ring the changes in the kitchen. Extend the
palate, you could call it. Reading about the holiday gave me a
feeling of restlessness. When the time is right it'll be look out
Mexico here I come. Heat and guitars and chilli peppers,
señoritas with their long black hair.

The furthest from home I've ever been is Scotland – where our last family holiday was spent. We toured about on the west coast, final destination Isle of Skye. Isobel's choice. 'A romantic name for a romantic place,' she said.

I remember going up a mountain. It was hot, and hard-going scrambling up the loose grey bits of stone. We stopped to eat our picnic on a patch of scrub. I was below Isobel on the slope and the way she was sitting, I couldn't help but look up her legs. She was wearing cut-off jeans with a pair of Dad's thick socks tucked into her walking boots. I could see stubble on her shins, also in the gap between her shorts and her thigh on one side, a strip of white cotton and a wisp of private hair.

It's only natural for a boy to watch and see and try to learn the mysteries of women. Nothing perverse about it. Ask any adolescent boy with a sister if he's never looked at her that way. She was wearing a white baseball cap, a little twig of heather or something caught up in her hair from where she'd flopped down earlier. I can see her clear as a picture. We had egg sandwiches. Mum had put chopped capers in them. Hard to credit the flair she had in those days adding that extra flourish to everything, even to egg sandwiches! I was complaining and spitting bits out and Izzie said, 'Jesus, Mark, grow up,' but smiled at me in the way she had, nose wrinkling.

I'd finished my sausages and folded the *Mail* when the phone went. Dad was upstairs with Mum. It was Detective Inspector somebody or other asking to speak to Mr Curtis. As well as Dad, I am also Mr Curtis, of course, so it was not a word of a lie to say, 'Speaking.' He went on to inform me that under the Victim's Charter 1990 we had the right to know that Karen Wild was due to be released from custody in the month of October into the city of Sheffield. 'Thank you,' I said. He also told me that she'd changed her name by statutory de-claration although he was not at liberty to divulge said name.

I put down the phone. It was like an explosion in my head and I had to wait for the dust to settle. Too much to take in just like that: that this was *it*. All systems go.

My gut feeling was not to tell them and I should have stuck to it, but it was too big a thing to keep bottled up inside. And she was their daughter; they did have the right to know. I went up to the bedroom where Mum was watching telly in bed while Dad tidied up around her and I came straight out with it.

Dad reacted with silence but Mum knocked the biscuit tin to the floor in her rage. She said all the things that are obvious but true, like: 'That monster alive and kicking while our beautiful girl is dead and gone.' Nothing you wouldn't expect a grieving mother to say.

When I was younger Dad said I shouldn't take Mum's coldness to heart, that she had a kind of illness and I should try and understand. 'One day she'll snap out of it,' he used to say. 'Be patient. Give it time.' But he stopped saying that somewhere along the line.

To get away from the atmosphere in the house I drove to Felixstowe. When I was younger I'd go there, push through the shrubs and stare at the hole in the ground, locked securely now that it was too late, surrounded by DANGER signs. But before long, the council, admitting some liability in leaving such a hazard unattended, cleared the area and created – Dad's idea – an ornamental pool.

Isobel loved fountains; she said when she grew up she'd have one in her garden. She loved the noise. She tried to explain something to me about it standing for life, always falling, always rising. She had that imaginative, arty streak in her. The fountain was in the middle of a round blue pool, quite a tall spray that, when the wind blew, would sprinkle your face. People took to throwing coins in the water as they do and making wishes. But over the years it got neglected and now the fountain's nothing more than a feeble bubble. When all this is over and done with, I'll give money to the council for its restoration and bring Mum and Dad here just to see the look on their faces.

I called round to see Karen's foster parents. Dad said he felt sorry for them bearing the brunt of her behaviour like that and her not even their own flesh and blood. They took her in out of the goodness of their hearts and look how she repaid them. It tore their lives apart.

When Dr Merriam opened the door I was taken aback by the mess of the house, the grime, the garden all overgrown, a huge monkey-puzzle tree blocking out the light. When I said who I was he sighed and asked me in. To tell the truth I wasn't too keen on going in, what with the state of the place.

'My wife's out,' he said and offered me sherry, which came in a tiny sticky glass. The room we went in was a tip, piled with plates and papers and suchlike. We had a bit of preliminary chit-chat, then I told him Karen Wild was going to be released. He nodded and said, 'Well, she's done her time.'

I had to count to ten then. I sipped the sherry, which was sickeningly sweet, until I could speak in a level voice. 'So she'll be free to live her life,' I said. His eyes were nearly hidden under big ledges of white eyebrow but he gave me a sharp enough look.

'Poor girl,' he said and it was all I could do not to choke. 'She wasn't all bad, you know, not through and through.'

I looked at the floor and saw a cup clogged up with mould. 'I wonder what she'll do,' I said.

'There's the bit of money Joan and I put away for her,' he said. 'We'd intended to fund her through university . . . but it turned out the state was to shoulder that expense!' He gave the wheeze of a laugh. 'But we put it aside for her all the same, to give her a start when she comes out.'

'Will she come and see you?' I said.

'We cut off contact when she went inside – a mutual decision. So no, I don't expect so.'

'If she does,' I said, 'would you let me know?' I took out my notebook, ready to leave my number, but he shook his head.

'Take my advice and let it go, son,' he said. 'Let it rest its ugly head.'

*

I went back to my room, fumbling the key in the lock. There was a sick, scummy sensation in my heart. I put out the DO NOT DISTURB sign, locked the door and stood with my forehead against the Fire Safety Procedure notice. It was cool against the hot of my skin. I stood back and read about emergency exits, wishing there was such a thing for me.

I didn't even want to be there. I'd only moved in with Charlie four months ago and had had no intention of leaving him even for a single night. But then this course, Women and Self-Esteem in the Workplace, had come up. There was only one place and everyone wanted it – Christine was mad keen – but it was me that Gary summoned to his office.

'How would you like to go?' he said.

'No ta.'

His chair squeaked as he leant forward. The face of his wife beamed at me from a square of sunshine on his desk.

'It would do you the world of good,' he said. 'You've been here four months and I'm delighted with your performance.' He raked his fingers across his head and a fair hair fell out and fluttered to the desk. He beamed at me expectantly. 'Go on, Nina,' he said, 'it'll be the making of you.'

I gave him a sickly smile.

'Good girl.'

And he wasn't much older than me.

I trudged back to my desk where Christine was bursting to know what he'd wanted.

'You!' Her voice squeaked when I told her. 'But you're *new*. I've been here since school.'

I shrugged.

'You don't want to go, do you?' she said.

'No.'

'It seems silly you going when you don't want to.'

'When you do?'

'No.'

'You do.'

The phone rang and I answered it. Christine rattled away at her keyboard, sighing huffily. Mid morning she usually fetched me a cup of coffee but on that day she didn't.

'I don't want to go,' I said when she came back ostentatiously brandishing a single mug. 'It's all Gary's idea. I'm sorry.'

'You've got far more self-esteem than me,' she said, 'than anyone.'

I stared at her but she was quite serious.

'Why don't you have a go at Gary then?' I said. 'I wish you would.'

'Haven't got the self-esteem.' She sucked a point of her colourless hair. 'I could of just done with it.'

'Sorry.'

'Oh, it's not your fault,' she said. 'I'll get you a coffee.' And off she went, Dr Scholl's slapping against the soles of her feet.

Now I sat down on my smooth hotel bed and looked at my phone. I'd switched it off in the restaurant, childishly, to pay Charlie back for not calling. I wished I hadn't. If I'd spoken to him earlier then . . . But there are so many ifs in life, irritating little sneezes of fate: if this, if that, if not, if only.

Now I couldn't bear to switch it on and hear his voice. I

needed to shower. How could I even think of talking to Charlie with the smell of Rupert still on me? If there'd been a scrubbing brush I would have scrubbed my skin off. I stood for ages letting the steaming water pour over me but it didn't stop me feeling like a whore.

I took the little photo of Charlie from my purse and stared at his dear face. It was done in a photo booth at the station, on impulse, while waiting for a (delayed) train to London. His hair looks darker than it is and there's a line of brightness running through him where the curtain wasn't properly closed, but I like the smile, the straightness of his look. Standing outside the booth waiting for the damp strip of pictures to issue from the slot, I'd said, 'Can I move in with you?' The question had just popped out of my mouth. I hadn't meant to ask him yet. We'd known each other only a few weeks, but when it's the right person you do know. There's no point wasting time.

He hadn't answered immediately. We'd taken the strip of photos and had a coffee while waiting for our train. If he'd said no, I don't know what would have happened, but after a bit of thought he said not yes but, 'I don't see why not.' That is so much a Charlie thing to say. Understatement is his thing. We'd held hands all that day, on the train, walking by the Thames, sitting in the theatre watching *Les Misérables*. I have never felt so close to anybody, or so happy, in my entire life. In his wallet is a picture of me, cut from the same strip.

As I sat on that hotel bed and looked at his level eyes, my heart was crushed inside me with the force of what I'd done.

I had to see him. First thing, I'd go home. Sod the course. I couldn't face another day of it – my self-esteem a lost cause now anyway. We'd go out to dinner, my treat, and then home to make love and then – but at the thought of dinner I had to go and lean over the toilet. I forced my fingers down and scratched the back of my throat. I wanted to spew up the dinner and the evening. I wanted to spew up my whole self.

I was shivering as if I was getting flu. I huddled in a towel and opened the mini-bar to find water. A pair of eyes met mine. I slammed the door and then thought, come on, get a grip. It was only a toy bear, identical to the one I'd spotted in Rupert's fridge, a poor cold bear with the same sign around its neck.

Missing a Loved One?

Send them me!

I'm only £9.99

Including P&P.

Cynical marketing tactic, Charlie would have said, *preying on people's loneliness.* Or guilt, he might have added. I took the bear out of the fridge; I couldn't stand the thought of it banged up in there.

I lay awake for the rest of the night. I'd never told Charlie a lie, except about things that happened before we met, but everyone does that. I thought I'd tell him this and keep everything clean and shiny new between us. *Come clean* they call it and that's a good expression. It would be the only way to lose the filthy feeling. But, then, as I lay waiting for the hours of the night to creep past, I began to wonder if telling him would really make me clean? Maybe it would only make him dirty too. Would it be better to be strong and deal with it myself? Which would be the better thing to do?

At last it started to get light. I heard a comforting creaking of feet in the corridor as newspapers and early breakfast trays were delivered, and then, with the relief that night had passed, I fell asleep. When I woke I lay in a horrible hungover blankness till it all came crashing back. I crawled out of bed, boiled the kettle and made a cup of coffee before I called Charlie.

'Had your phone switched off?' he said.

'It's gone a bit dodgy,' I said, 'battery or something. I'm coming home.'

'What's up?' he said and I said nothing, nothing, nothing. Only that I'd missed him.

'I've promised to go round Dave's tonight,' he said.

'That's OK,' I said.

'And Nina, I've got to go to Bradford tomorrow – I'll be back late.'

'Good job I'll see you tonight then,' I said.

'See you later.' He cut off the call.

A door banged in the corridor and someone coughed. I phoned reception and asked for a taxi. I switched on the TV while I dressed and stuffed everything in my bag. It was the news: guns and tanks, the birth of a panda, the weather, clouds and sunbeams on a chart.

Passing Rupert's room on my way out, I caught sight of myself in a mirror, picking along on pantomime tiptoes. I made myself walk properly but my heart was thumping because, of course, he would be in there still, sprawled out on his wide bed, sleeping the sleep of the sated male. Bitter coffee crawled up my throat with the shame but as I got into the lift and left him behind I breathed out. It had been stupid but it was done. I'd never have to see him again. All over and done.

∧

I put off the move north till after Christmas due to Dad's accident. He fell off a stool changing a light bulb and broke his ankle, so I was required to man the decks till he was back on his feet. It was frustrating, I was raring to go – but there it was. No question of leaving them in the lurch.

By December, Dad was up and about though he still had his outpatient appointments so I agreed to stay on until after Christmas, which is a painful time. The year Isobel went missing, we'd gone through the motions. I don't know why. Is that the strange thing to do or the normal? There were presents under the tree for Izzie that have never been unwrapped and they're still in a box in the attic now. From me, a manicure set in a leather case. I'd agonised over the choice, pink or white. She liked to do her shopping in a rush on Christmas Eve. 'That's half the fun,' she said. So there was nothing from her. And I'm glad. How would we have coped with opening her presents?

Our table was square, unless you pulled out the leaf, which we only did when we had company. That Christmas we had none. 'Just us,' Isobel had begged. She'd been homesick at university, and now she was home wanted to be the centre of attraction. Christmas before the tragedy used to be fun, at least it used to seem fun to me then. Family jokes and treats;

Cluedo; Monopoly – and the most terrible recorder consort. Mum bought us all a different pitch of recorder and about once a year we'd squeak and splutter our way through a book of Christmas carols. The female contingent were musical but Dad and me had cloth ears.

That last Christmas Mum laid the table for four as per usual. It was a gesture of faith. We all hoped above all hope that she would waltz in through that door. But her place stayed empty, her cracker unpulled, the recorders in their boxes where they've been ever since. And ever since they've set a place for her at Christmas. Every year I buy whisky for Dad, bath stuff for Mum and they give me money, which I don't need. I'm better off than them due to Grandad's will. We do turkey and the trimmings, a glass of something nice, try to put a brave face on it, reading the cracker jokes and suchlike, but after lunch it all dies off. A space yawns open between us. This year, Dad spent the afternoon under the bonnet of his car, Mum watched a film and I went through my scrapbooks.

Said my goodbyes on the twenty-eighth. Wanted to be settled in for New Year. Stayed in a B&B in Sheffield while I looked for digs. New Year's Eve I went downtown and got on the edges of a throng, music pounding out and fireworks at midnight. When twelve struck people started reaching out and kissing. I scarpered off out of it then. Who would want the wet lips of a stranger on their own?

Found a place, self-contained on top of a house near the park where you look out over the tops of trees. Landlady a nice sort and keeps herself to herself down there which is just as I like it. For a day or two I was heady with excitement. Independence at last, at twenty-seven! A trip to Tesco, it's amazing all the things you have to buy, not just food and that but washing powder, bleach, cleaning stuff, lav paper and so on ad infinitum.

And I began to search. Of course in a city such as Sheffield, population 500,000, it was unlikely I'd spot her right off – not that I didn't try. I went to all the places that girls go: Next, Marks and Spencer's, All Bar One. I joined a couple of gyms, the bigger types. I tried to put myself in her shoes, just out of prison, a bit of money in the bank, what would she do? Self-improvement, I thought, hence the gyms. I kept my eyes peeled as I worked out and swam looking at the fair-haired girls. And as the weather warmed up there they'd be sprawling on the grass, shoulders, midriffs, bare thighs on show. I walked about among them looking. Some of them would glare back or get uppity but only because they didn't understand.

I would be looking for the blondes but also there were the dark girls that sometimes caught my eye, the angels, the Isobels. Fair girls are ten a penny, most of them bleached, but girls with sleek dark hair, caramel eyes and rosy cheeks like Izzie, that colouring is rare.

On the fourteenth of January, the anniversary of the day that she was found, I do my ritual, allow my fantasy. All the better in my own place with complete privacy. A bottle of champagne – Dom Perignon. When she was sixteen, at a wedding, she took one sip of it and said, 'One day I'll drink nothing else.' So I drink it in her honour, always raising a private glass to her. I had that and some burritos, extra chillies from a jar. It's normal practice for a man to fantasise, particularly someone such as me with his love life put on hold.

I lit candles and put the music on – Isobel's favourite Mozart Horn Concerto no. 4. I wore her dressing gown, which might seem strange but it is not feminised in any way, it's just a plain blue silk kimono type thing with a red bird on the back. I took it from her room the day her body was found. Nobody ever missed it. I can see her in it after a bath, hair up in a towel like a turban. You could see the shape of her breasts. They were middle-sized. I couldn't stand great big suffocating ones but you do want something to get your hand round. A flat chest is a letdown for a man, say what you like. It smelt of her then and still does faintly, the scent she used, and a little old whiff under the armpits. I kept her bottle of scent and put a dab on my wrist now and again.

In the fantasy they are both there, the brunette and the blonde: the good sister and her killer. The hair gets tangled together and – some things are best kept for the dark.

C harlie was still at work when I got in and I was glad to be alone. I threw all my clothes into the washing machine and ran a deep hot bath. I stared in the mirror and there was no difference in me that you could see – except, maybe, an extra slippery brightness to the eyes.

I booked a table at the Mumtaz. My treat. It was actually a few days short of four months since I'd moved in, but Charlie would never know the difference.

I ironed the dress that he liked best, dark red with pearly little buttons down to the hem, and I mixed martinis, the proper way, to surprise him. I felt like one of those American wives who greet their husband in a negligée. When he got home I put my arms round him and felt the familiar meeting of our body surfaces, the way my nose is the exact height of his shoulder, his musky end-of-a-workday smell.

'I only wanted a cup of tea,' he said, but laughed and took the chilly glass – and once he'd had a sip, perked up.

'You look nice,' he said, taking in the dress and the way I'd spiked up my hair.

'I've booked us into the Mumtaz,' I said.

'But Dave . . .'

'We can go to Dave's any night,' I said. 'This is our anniversary. Four months since I moved in.'

He blinked. 'Is it?'

'Hasn't it gone quick?'

He swilled the drink around his glass, put his fingers in to catch the olive.

'I feel bad about Dave though.'

'He won't mind. We'll go tomorrow. Maybe drag him out to the cinema or something.'

He knocked back the drink. 'Ring him then, will you? I'll grab a shower.'

But Dave didn't answer his phone. If he had, I don't know what. He had a very unfriendly greeting that put you on the defensive: *Can't speak now. Leave a message if you think it's worth it*. So the message I left may have been a bit brusque, but it was nothing meant.

I hadn't noticed before the smell of grease that hung in the air outside the Mumtaz. It was all right when you got into the red dimness and the curry smell, but the grease did catch in your throat. We ordered the Feast for Two. The tablecloth was scattered with the crumbs of someone else's poppadum, but it didn't matter. We ordered pints of beer and tucked into our samosas but I couldn't think of anything to say.

'So why did you leave?' Charlie asked, scooping up dahl with a bit of chapati.

'It was just a load of rubbish,' I said. 'It was a waste of time and I was missing you too badly.'

'What did you do?'

I could have told him all about it, I could have made him laugh about the pert-breasted woman, but I couldn't bring myself to say the same things to Charlie as I'd said to Rupert. The food on the table between us seemed huge and too complicated to eat, with the different colours and textures, the craggy bhajis, the snarling naans.

At the next table there was a birthday party going on with party poppers and lots of flesh on show and raucous shrieks of laughter. I felt sorry for the quiet and dignified waiters in their attempts to get any sense out of the revellers. I watched the man with a big badge that said 'Birthday Boy' on it unwrap his present while his friends screamed and whooped. It was a blow-up woman. They spent the rest of the evening passing her round and trying to inflate her. There was so much noise we couldn't talk and didn't stay for the kulfi or a coffee. It was only nine-thirty when we left so there was still time to see Dave.

His bedsit was in the attic of a house beside a roaring road. You had to climb over a pile of junk mail and go up three flights of stairs, holding your breath against the reek of dirty people and their dirty minds. Dave opened the door to us without a word and let us in. He'd been smoking dope and reading the *I Ching*, which was his way of divining the way forward. But it held him back, I said that to his face, but his face shut off to me.

'Had anything to eat lately?' Charlie said, though of course he hadn't. Charlie went out to get him some fish and chips and some beer for us all and left me with Dave. We'd hardly spent any time, just the two of us. He continued to throw his coins, crouching on the floor and peering at his book by the light of the gas fire – the light bulbs had gone. I offered to read it out for him, just to be friendly. I stood by the window where enough streetlight came upwards for me to see. He threw the coins and it made 33 TUN, which is Retreat. I read it out to him: '*The first line divided shows a retiring tail. The position is perilous. No movement in any direction should be made.*' This is what I mean by it holding him back.

'You can't run your life by this rubbish, Dave,' I said again. 'You should get out more.'

He peered at me in his moleish way between curtains of greasy hair. He had a look of Charlie but with the features scrunched together on his face while Charlie's is wide open.

'Shall I make you a coffee?' I offered, but on the way to the kettle I nearly fell over a bicycle pump. He had hundreds, collected since childhood. I picked it up. It was shiny green with something purple on it. 'Nearly broke my neck,' I said and handed it to him. He took it from me and weighed it in his hands.

'Why bicycle pumps?' I said.

'Because they're beautiful useful things,' he said, his voice coming alive for almost the first time since I'd known him. 'They marry simplicity of style with efficiency of action. Look,' and he pumped it at me fiercely until I backed off. Who is to say what is beautiful and what is not?

Charlie came back with the beer and Dave's supper and also a light bulb, which Dave wouldn't let him screw in overhead but only into a lamp with a thick wicker shade. The light sieved through in slivers on the walls. There was only one armchair. Charlie sat in it and I perched on the arm while Dave, who preferred a squatting posture, picked at his cod and chips.

'Been keeping your appointments?' Charlie asked him but Dave's mouth was full. 'Been doing any painting?' This was a stupid question, he hadn't painted for years, but it was just Charlie trying to get some sort of conversation going. Sitting in the squalor of Dave's bedsit, I got a sudden vision of white tablecloths and candlelight and blinked it hard away. How could I have done that? The light made wavery patterns on my dress and Charlie's hand, resting on my knee. I took his hand and squeezed it.

'Fancy the pictures tomorrow?' I said to Dave.

He shook his head.

'Or maybe a drink. Get you out of here.'

But he only shrugged.

'I'm worried,' Charlie said, as we walked up the hill towards our home. 'He's getting worse. He only eats if I take something round. Could you pop in tomorrow night, make sure he's OK?'

'You saw his reaction.'

'But you could try,' Charlie said.

'You should stop him doing that *I Ching*,' I said.

When we got in, I showered but couldn't wash deep enough to feel that I was clean. Charlie was waiting when I got into bed.

'Four months, hey,' he said and we kissed.

'Why have you got this on?' he said, kneeling up to pull my nightie over my head but I tugged it back down.

'I feel a bit offish,' I said.

'Dodgy curry?'

'Dunno. Just . . . can we just . . .'

And so we lay in each other's arms, his heart beating against mine, and I felt his body soften into the heaviness of sleep while I stayed wide awake.

~

A fter Gideon, she'd have sex with almost anyone. She became known as a slag but she didn't care. It was something to be known as. It was better than nothing. With a pair of strong arms round her she felt grounded, even safe, amidst the different sets of foster parents, the spells in children's homes. The changes were not her fault. It was just the way the cookie crumbled. Some case-worker put that phrase into her head and it made her life seem not much more than a trail of crumbs.

But when she was fifteen, life changed. This was her chance and she knew it. She was fostered by a pair of doctors – Joan and Roger Merriam – and taken to live in Felixstowe – away from her whorish reputation – in a big house near the sea. The doctors gave her their grown-up daughter's room. They let her choose new wallpaper and curtains. She had her own view of the long front garden: a lawn and flowerbeds, a gravel path, a monkey-puzzle tree.

The doctors paid good money to send her to a private school; told her repeatedly how bright she was, how pretty. 'The world can be your oyster,' they liked to say. They helped her choose her GCSE subjects and even talked about university. Joan went to school functions, discussing her progress with the teachers, seeming to care as much as if she was their own. But she was bright enough to know that she was a project, something like a rescue dog. They were liberal and charitable and though she was grateful it annoyed her sometimes. But she knew she must take this rope she had been flung.

She was bright and she was pretty and before long she had a boyfriend. Jeffrey Stern was the son of some friends of the Merriams, a couple of retired professors. He was not good-looking and there was no competition; she would never have expected a good-looking boy to take her seriously. He was seventeen, tall and stooped; with hair the colour and texture of old rope. He played the piano and had the longest fingers she had ever seen. His glasses were perpetually smeared but the eyes behind them were sweet hazelnuts, the way he looked at her soft and shy and she wasn't used to that. She wasn't used to the touch of gentle, tentative fingers, the soft experiments of his kisses.

The first time he kissed her they were in the kitchen washing up after a Sunday lunch. He'd been drying the same glass for a couple of minutes gabbling something about Bartók and then he'd lunged at her, the kiss missing her lips at first until she turned her head and let him have her mouth. The glass had dropped from his hand and smashed. After the kiss, they'd stood looking at the shiny curves of broken glass and he'd said, 'I hope that's all right with you.'

She'd smiled and leant up to him for another kiss. And she'd done something she'd been itching to do ever since they met – remove his glasses from his nose, breathe on them and rub them clean.

They went to the cinema together and his hand snaked across the back of her seat and cupped her shoulder. The innocence of it made her want to howl. They walked on the beach and he gave her his hand when she jumped off the breakwaters on to the crunchy shingle. They kissed in the salty shadows between the beach-huts until their lips were chapped, his specs clutched in her hand, and always she would clean them before she let him have them back.

∧

S topped shaving soon as I left home, let my hair get long, a
disguise for the preliminary stages. After a couple of
months I took a job as a milkman. One thing I've learned
since leaving home is how innocent I've been re the cost of
living. Life is steep. Couldn't afford to eat into my reserves
before I'd got her in my sights. Also I needed something to get
me up of a morning, get me out and about, and the advantage
of the milk round was that it left the afternoons free for my
enquiries.

But week by week, nothing happened and I could see I'd
have to up my strategy. Looked in the Yellow Pages for
detectives and found hundreds of them offering all sorts –
absentee searches; marital decoys; bugging; surveillance –
some of them quite dodgy or at least what I'd call underhand.
'Don't Get Your Hands Dirty,' one said with a sinister ring. I
chose a firm with a discreet logo and no outrageous claims.

Mrs Chivers didn't look the part – I wasn't expecting a
woman, for starters. When I went in the office I thought she
was the secretary. There were flowers on the desk and a
calendar with kittens on the wall. I was expecting to be shown
through but she got straight down to it asking me to outline
my request. Private *investigator* not detective, she soon put me
straight on that point. She looked more like a head mistress.

Grey hair neat to her head like a swimming cap, business-like approach, handshake almost like a man's. I showed her the newspaper photo of Karen, the famous 'angelic' one.

'How long has she been in the city?' she asked.

'Since October, as far as I know.'

'You say she's using an alias? Any ideas?'

I shook my head.

'You should have come at once, when she was still a stranger in town,' she said and I felt stupid then because of course she was right. What had I been thinking, expecting to manage this on my own?

'Before I proceed with this case,' she said, 'I must be assured that if I locate this person it will not lead to the committing of any crime.'

'Nothing like that.'

She pressed her lips together and gave me a dubious look. 'And confidentiality is assured in both directions?'

'Yes.'

'Five hundred pounds,' she said, 'two fifty up front, the balance when you get results.'

I took out the money. I had it in cash, which seemed more fitting than a cheque. As I peeled off the notes I couldn't help feeling it was money down the drain.

'Call back in a fortnight,' she said.

It was time to get serious and into role. Rupert would be charming and suave in his style of dress but a bit vulnerable too, something about the eyes. When I was thirteen, after the thing with the girl who'd been Isobel's friend had happened (and got blown out of all proportion), I was sent to a specialist school where they did drama therapy. And that's when my talent came out. Role play – be a victim was the main one – and also the school plays. I learned lines easily but it was more than that. It's simple, a trick, to turn a role on and off, just pretend hard enough to be another person, hard enough to see

34

through their eyes, feel through their skin and know the voice growing in them, and you are them, as long as you stay in control. What they call staying in role. I can't see what the fuss is all about. I was lead in every school play till I left. And then, in the best performance of my life, I was Rupert.

*

On Monday morning there was a package waiting for me on my desk. I picked it up and gave it a shake – something light. I peeled off the brown paper and found a box with the logo of the Astoria embossed on it in gold. Inside the box, in a nest of tissue, was a white bear. The fur was shaggy and the paws were velvet brown. It squinted up at me with eyes like apple pips. Out of the box came a vague smell of fridge that made me shiver.

Christine came in and stopped to balance against my desk while she changed her shoes.

'Aaah . . . isn't he cute?' She picked it up and I heard its stuffing rustle.

'Have it,' I said.

'I couldn't!'

'I don't want it.'

'Why not? He's so cute.' She snuggled it up to her cheek.

'I'm not into toys.'

'Where's he from?'

'Free gift,' I said. 'I'm only going to chuck it.'

'Oh she can't do that, can she,' she said in a diddums voice. 'I'll call you Mr Snowy and you can live on my desk. Ta.' She smiled. 'My horoscope said look out for an unexpected gift. Just goes to show, doesn't it? What are you again?'

'Sorry?'

'Like, I'm a Gemini?'

'Got to see Gary,' I said and bolted for the Ladies'.

An hour or so later, as I was working through a pile of order forms, the phone rang and I picked it up and said the usual: 'Green's Robotics. Nina speaking, how may I help you?'

There was a silence. I waited, tapping my pen, and repeated the greeting.

'Don't you like him?' said the voice.

At the inside of my wrist I could see the blue flicker of my pulse.

I had to clear my throat. 'It's not that.'

'What then?' He waited. 'You want to draw a line under it, is that it?'

'Yes,' I said. 'It was a mistake.'

'A mistake is when you forget to post a letter or miss a bus,' he said. 'Not this.'

Christine's face appeared from behind her computer, eyes wide.

'Sorry,' I said.

'Sorry?'

'I've got work to do.'

'Meet me.'

'No.'

I put the phone down. The palm of my hand was wet and I wiped it on my skirt.

'Nothing,' I said to Christine. She gave a sarcastic chuckle and went back to her keyboard. I could see the white smudge of fur propped up on her desk. The big hand of the wall clock, always three minutes fast, jerked forward.

'So how's your self-esteem now then?' she said after a while. 'What did you do? What was the hotel like?'

'OK,' I said.

'Just OK?'

'Just OK.'

'I bet Gary gave you a bollocking?'

'Not really.'

'He was pissed off that you left before the end. I said you should of sent me and he said maybe I should of.'

'You're right. He should have,' I said. I got up and went back to the Ladies'. I ran my hands under the cold tap, squirted out a worm of soap and rubbed it into suds, watching my face in the mirror. I roared my hands under the drier and flattened down my hair. It needed a cut and the pale roots were growing through. I keep it short and dark. Charlie's hair is longer than mine. He's the one with the curls.

Back at my desk I saw a sticky memo on my monitor. *10.30 Rupert??? Will ring back.*

Christine gave me a minute to take it in, then, 'So, spill, who is he?' She took a nail file out of her desk and rasped away at her thumbnail, a tiny sound that put my teeth on edge.

'No one.'

I trawled through my emails. When the phone rang I answered calmly, the standard greeting, and it was only a customer with a simple enquiry. But the next caller was Rupert. Christine had gone to get the coffee so I was able to give it to him straight.

'Listen. I'm sorry and all that. But there's no way—'

'No?'

'Thanks for the bear but please don't ring again.'

'Meet me at lunchtime,' he said.

'What are you doing in Sheffield?'

'Business.'

'What about your wife?'

There was a silence.

'I can't meet you.'

Christine came back carrying two mugs, a packet of Garibaldis jammed under her arm. 'The park gates near your work, one o'clock,' he said.

'How do you know—' I started, but the phone went dead. I opened my drawer and looked at the photo of Charlie. I keep it in my desk because Charlie is my business and no one else's – though Christine knows his name. I took the photo in Blackpool the day we met. Funny, I've only been to Blackpool twice and both times I've met a man.

I signed my flexi-time form at twelve-fifty and left the building. The park was ten minutes away and Rupert was already waiting by the gates when I arrived. I'd forgotten how tall he was and the bright brown of his eyes. He held out a paper carrier bag.

'Sandwiches,' he said, 'and a drink.'

We walked in silence past the swinging kids, past the café with its man-sized ice-cream sign, and stopped at the duck pond.

He nodded at a seat in a puddle of sunshine. 'Shall we?' he said. Ducks, spotting the paper bag, surged towards us quacking. There were ducklings and a moorhen chick like a ball of dust flitting on the surface of the water. All those ducks and coots and moorhens with the hearts beating inside them, intestines coiled and packed, little sets of livers, kidneys, lungs.

I looked at the ground and noticed Rupert's boots, conker brown, gleaming. His trousers were soft pale corduroy and his jacket buttery leather. It struck me that everything he was wearing, and that I'd ever seen him wearing, was brand new.

'What are you doing here?' I asked.

'I said. Business.'

'How did you get my number?'

'Child's play.' He smiled sideways at me, the tip of his tongue resting on the centre of his upper lip. There was a flip in my chest like a fish jumping and I looked away quick. He opened the bag and took out two wax-paper wrapped sandwiches. I recognised the wrappings from the expensive place that did brie and grape rather than cheese and pickle, but I wasn't interested in sandwich fillings.

'I'm not hungry,' I said. 'Look, this can't happen.'

'Drink then.' He took two small bottles of champagne from his bag – Dom Perignon – and before I could object he popped the corks. He stuck straws in the necks and handed me one. I almost laughed. If there ever was a champagne moment this was not it. But I was thirsty. A woman with wild pink dreadlocks walked past, saw the bottles and grinned. I waited till she'd gone and took one.

'OK then,' I said. 'Since you've gone and got it. But I haven't got long.'

'Bacon and avocado or mozzarella, rocket and roasted tomato?' he said. I noticed the length of his lashes, a pinprick mole at the corner of his eye. 'Or shall I throw it all to the ducks?'

My stomach growled. I could faintly smell the bacon through its waxy wrapper. I sucked a strawful of fizzy champagne.

'I'll have the bacon one,' I said. It seemed stupid to go hungry. The bread was thick-cut, soft, speckled with walnuts. I tore off a crust and a chunk of avocado slid out. The ducks quacked and squabbled round our feet.

Rupert wasn't eating his sandwich, just picking at the crust. We sat there quietly for a few minutes.

'Sounds interesting,' he said, in the end. 'Robotics.'

'Not really. It's just components for some industrial thing.'

'Been there long?'

'Look. Thanks for the lunch but look . . . I'm sorry. And what about your wife? We must both forget it.' I threw a bit of avocado in the pond and a crowd of ducks splashed in after it, jostling and quacking.

'I don't expect they get much avocado,' he said.

I could feel the worms of champagne trickling through the

straw, wriggling in my veins, and I had to fight not to smile. I took another bite of the sandwich, delicious mixture of textures and tastes: soft nutty bread, salty bacon, avocado velvety smooth.

'Do you always do that?' he said, nodding at my waggling foot. I uncrossed my legs and put my feet together, squeezed them flat against the ground. Fidget Breeches someone called me once, and it's true.

'Tell me about your husband – Charlie, is it?' Rupert said and to hear that name on his lips quenched any chance of a smile. 'Do you love him?' he said.

'Of course.'

'OK, what is it about him that you say you love?'

'None of your beeswax.'

'Go on.'

'Not just *say*, *do*,' I said. I took another suck of champagne. Now it was starting to work its way to my brains and I had to be back soon.

'But what does that mean?'

'What?'

'Love.'

'Love?'

'Yes. Love.' He looked genuinely puzzled.

'You know,' I said.

He frowned down at his sandwich, his black eyebrows drawing together, and when he looked up there was an unreadable sheen across his eyes. 'But what is it about *him* that you love?'

I thought about it. 'That he's himself. He's . . .' I struggled to put it into words, 'good,' I decided at last, though I knew it sounded lame.

'*Good?*' Rupert said. He was tearing off little bits of bread and tossing them into the water. 'How would you know?'

I shrugged.

'How do you define good?' he said.

'Getting a bit deep, aren't you?'

He blinked at me and I sneaked a look at my watch. Ten minutes and I'd be off.

'OK,' I said. 'Well for a start he's unselfish. He wouldn't hurt a fly.'

'Faithful?'

'Yes.'

'Sure?'

'Yes.'

'But not you.'

'I won't do it again.'

'Sure?' His eyes found mine.

'Sure.'

He sighed. 'Do you really think there's such a thing as good?'

'Of course.'

'And yet you are not it.'

'I do my best,' I said.

I sucked at the straw again but it made an empty slurping sound.

'More?' He offered me his bottle but I shook my head.

'It was a lapse.'

'A lapse,' he repeated, thoughtfully.

The glint of the water, the light swaying in threads through the leaves of the trees, the quacking of the ducks and the ludicrous conversation were making my head spin. He put his hand on my knee. A tremble passed through me at the weight and warmth of it.

He leant close so I could feel his breath on my ear. 'You and I both know,' he said, 'that there is no such thing as good.'

'I've had enough of this,' I said, getting up. But he caught my hand and tugged me back down. My knees were weak and foggy from the champagne. A guy walked past, gave me an odd sideways look and my heart went cold. Was it someone Charlie knew? I don't go out much but when I first knew Charlie we'd go to the pub together, there were lots of faces, he had a lot of friends. Was this one of them? I didn't recognise him but if it was . . . I felt sick.

'For instance, my wife is not good,' Rupert said.

'No?' I took my hand away. The guy had gone now, but anybody could walk past on such a lovely day.

'She's a bitch.' There was a choked sound in his voice.

'I'm sorry.'

'I just thought you might listen,' he said. 'After the time we spent together. There is a connection between us.'

'I'm going.' I stood up.

'See the birds,' he said. 'Are they good?'

'What?'

'They'd kill each other for a beakful of bread.' I was startled by a roughness in his voice but then he shrugged as if to say, what can you do? And smiled at me, a long dimple slanting on his cheek. He chucked the rest of his sandwich in the pond and there was a mayhem of feathers, mothers shouldering off the chicks, males snapping at females in their greedy panic.

'Well, they seem to like mozzarella,' he said. 'Meet me tonight?'

'Sorry.'

I started to walk away.

'Please.'

'No.'

'Just to talk. Wouldn't Charlie understand?'

'No.'

'Even though he's so good?' He caught me up.

'Can't you talk to someone else?' I said.

'There's no one.'

'Try the Samaritans.'

We were walking faster and faster back towards the gate.

'Leave me alone,' I said, but he just smiled and tried to take my arm. 'Get away from me,' I shouted. There was a woman coming towards us with a pushchair and I wanted her to hear, I thought he'd stop if someone was witnessing it, but she bent over to fuss with her child, pretending not to notice.

I speeded up almost to a run. I realised I was still clutching the bottle in my hand and threw it towards a bin but it smashed on the ground.

'Dangerous,' he called after me. 'No need to run.'

∧

A fortnight later I called back to see Mrs Chivers. I was
ready to be disappointed, or for her to demand more
money up front, or to say we needed to widen the search to
nationwide or somesuch – so I was taken aback when she
handed me a photo of a complete stranger.

'Here she is,' she said.

I took the photo from her and my heart sank. This was a
woman in about her mid-thirties with short dark hair, and a
thin angular face.

'Karen Wild,' she said, 'also known as Nina Todd. Works at
Green's Robotics as a clerical officer.'

I stared at the face but it gave nothing up to me. Maybe a
trace of familiarity there, but not of Karen.

She handed me another photograph of the same woman
getting into, or out of, a car, a man there too . . . *he* did look
familiar. Then the woman again, standing on the doorstep,
and I got a shiver through me then and almost laughed,
knowing where I'd seen them. They were on my round!
Forty-seven Chestnut Avenue.

'That's not her!' I laughed. 'These are customers.'

'Customers?'

I didn't have to explain myself to her. 'You've made a
mistake,' I said.

Mrs Chivers put the full-face photo of the stranger on the table beside Karen's and tried to convince me, pointing out the proportions of the features, but I wasn't buying it until, 'Watch this,' she said. She scrolled through the documents on her computer and brought up the face of Karen. Gave me a shock seeing her there large as life scanned in and enlarged on that screen.

'This is extraordinary technology,' she said, 'it's made my job a lot easier I can tell you. Now,' she clicked on a menu, 'we'll age her fifteen years – or we could make it twenty . . . life's hard inside.' As I watched, something happened to the face right in front of my eyes – the cheeks slimming down, the jaw sharpening, a girl's round face changing to a woman's. 'Now,' she said, 'put yourself in her shoes. If you had long fair hair and you wanted a different look?'

'Short,' I said.

'Spot on. Short and dark.' And the face of Karen mutated into the face in the photograph, the woman I'd met on her own doorstep and never given a second glance.

'There's one difference,' she said, but I couldn't see it, not till she pointed out the different length of the nose. 'You'd see it more in profile. You said she had some money. If you were intent on changing your appearance and you had money, what would you do?' She sounded pleased with herself. 'On the fourth of October last year, less than a week after her release, Nina Todd booked into the Bartlett Clinic for a nose reconstruction for which she paid two thousand six hundred and fifty pounds.'

She put the photos and information into an envelope. 'I wish all my cases were as straightforward,' she said.

I paid the balance and left. That was that: a fortnight, five hundred quid and the search was over. It was almost too easy and the shock of it sent me into a spin for the rest of that day. I'd actually been face to face with her. Maybe only once or twice – it was usually the bloke who came to the door on Saturdays. But still, I'd been that close, close enough to sniff her, to look hard into her face, and never had a clue.

Kept on delivering that week: one full cream; one semi-skimmed. All fingers and thumbs, dropped a pint on the path when I got near her door. Then it got to Saturday. A later start and I call at each house for the week's money. Some leave it out in an envelope, which is a risk I personally wouldn't take. Chestnut Avenue is what you'd term a 'nice' street and number forty-seven is a white semi, bay-windowed, chestnut tree outside. I sat in my float getting psyched up. The curtains were open but there was no movement. Then the old woman from the bottom flat came out. She came through the gate right up to me.

'I've been waiting for my cup of tea, young man,' she said, 'while you sit there twiddling your thumbs. You can cancel the full cream from now on, I'm fetching it from the shop.'

'Sorry, madam,' I said. 'I'm not feeling too well. Needed a minute . . .' I wasn't sure if the 'madam' wasn't overdoing it but she didn't seem to think so.

She looked at me. 'Oh well then, I'll take it from you.' I hopped down and got her a pint from the back. 'And you should get home and put your feet up.'

'I'll do that,' I said.

She took her milk and went back round the side of the house. I went through the gate, broken as long as I've been calling, to the front door and rang the bell. Nothing at first though I could hear a radio on in the distance, hear the nine o'clock pips. Then footsteps, the door opening and the bloke standing there. Mr C. Martin, as he's listed in my order book, in a dressing gown.

'Milk,' I said.

'Yeah, cheers, hold on.' He left the door open and went back into the house calling, 'Nina? Got any cash?'

47

I heard her voice then. 'In my purse.'

I nudged the door open a bit wider with my foot so I could see into the hall. Done up like an old person's place, flowery carpet and suchlike. A dark-coloured sideboard. I could see him looking in the drawer.

'Where?' he called.

And then she came into the hall. She was in a pinkish tracksuit, or maybe it was pyjamas. She stayed back in the dimness but I could see her lean past him and pull the purse from the drawer.

'Right under your nose,' she said and kissed him on the cheek. So they were together. A fast worker then. I wondered where the old lady fitted in. He came to the door to pay me.

'Women, eh?' I said, thinking maybe to get something out of him, but he just smiled, took his change and milk and shut the door. Did he know what he was living with?

*

I had an appointment with Rose so I left work early. Stepping out on to the street, I looked around for Rupert but he wasn't there. No one followed me on the way to Rose's office, nor on the way home. I breathed out as I walked up Chestnut Avenue. Spring had really got a grip and though it was after five, the sun still glowed on the brick walls and the rows of tulips. I stopped to stroke a melting cat – and to look behind me once again.

Fay and her friend Maisie were in the front garden planting a bush. Fay was kneeling with a trowel, Maisie pulling the twiggy thing out of its pot. Fay was tiny, head the size of a coconut, and Maisie, with her trunk-shaped legs and slabby bosom, towered over her.

'What is it?' I said.

'Ceanothus.' Fay slipped me a glance.

'That'll just fill the gap nicely,' Maisie said. 'I'll tease out the roots.' She began to claw at the gnarly pot-shaped tangle. 'See these little blossoms?' She pointed out some blue flowers. 'Next year it'll be a picture.'

'Cup of tea or anything?' I said.

'We're quite all right, you get along,' Fay said and I went off into the house.

Despite the weather I wanted to draw the curtains, get into

49

my dressing gown and lie on the sofa till Charlie got back from Bradford. I like winter best when you can stay inside and no one thinks it's strange. I ran a deep bath, and wallowed, with the radio on quietly, not taking anything in but soothed by the sound of the voices. I lay there till the water was cold and scummy. Afterwards I fried myself an egg, listening to the sounds of Fay and Maisie below me. A meaty smell was floating up, chops maybe. I was glad Fay had company for tea. I sat in front of the telly and watched the egg yolk run and soak into the toast. There was a phlegmy skim of white left and I couldn't eat it.

Charlie rang to say he'd be back very late and not to wait up.

'I don't mind waiting up,' I said.

'I'll just want to crash out,' he said.

'We can crash together then. You'll only wake me when you come in – I might as well wait up.'

'How's Dave?'

'Haven't been yet.'

'Tell him I'll be round tomorrow.'

'OK.'

I could have lied and said I'd gone and not gone, but I got dressed again and caught the bus to Dave's. I thought I'd drag him out for a pint or two. The sky was dabbed with pink. I thought it might cheer him up. I rang and rang the front doorbell but no one answered. I walked round the block, then went back and tried again. Tripod, the three-legged cat who lived in the basement flat, wound round my legs, purring like an outboard motor. I stooped to stroke him, then stood back to look up. But it was no good, Dave's window was too high to see. And all it would have been was curtains, anyway.

I should have rung the other bells and got someone to let me in. I shouldn't have given up so easily but I did. I went home, got back into my dressing gown and spent the rest of the evening on the sofa watching telly. At about eleven o'clock, Fay's doorbell rang. I was in the kitchen making peppermint tea and I heard her moving about below me, the opening of the door, voices, a pause and then a cry.

I went upstairs to look out of the bedroom window. There was a police car parked in the road outside. It had gone cold like it does in spring and my veins were threaded through with ice. I stood without moving or even breathing for several minutes more until at last I saw two policewomen come out, walk up the path and get back into their car.

As soon as they'd gone I went down – there's a door in the hall that leads down to Fay's. She was standing in her kitchen with her hands over her mouth staring at a glass of brandy. She looked blankly at me.

'What's happened?' I said.

She didn't speak. Her fingers fenced but didn't hide the hole of her mouth.

'He's dead,' she said.

I went very still inside. 'Who?'

'Dead.'

'Who?' My voice came out harder and louder than I meant.

'David.'

The blood swarmed in my ears in hot relief and then in shame.

'No,' I said, 'no.'

'Yes.'

It took a few seconds for it to sink in. I pictured my fingers on the doorbell, the foggy little plastic labels with the residents' names, the bubbled green paint of the door.

'How?'

'Overdose they think.'

'When?'

'He's just been found.'

'I went round there earlier,' I said, 'I rang and rang the bell but no answer.'

'And what then?'

'I, well, I came home. I thought he must be out.'

'You came home?'

'I didn't . . . Oh Fay . . .' I tried to put my arms round her but she flinched away. She had cream on her face, not rubbed in yet and not a scrap of make-up, I'd never seen her like that before.

'Get out,' she said.

'You're in shock, Fay,' I said. 'Drink the brandy – or shall I make you a cup of tea . . . sugary tea . . .' I went towards her but she almost spat at me, her little body gone into a kind of cramp in the corner. 'Get out,' she said, 'get Charlie.'

It was the shock. Shock does strange things to people. It makes them rude. You should never take offence when someone is in a state of shock.

'I'll phone him now,' I said, but before anything else could happen Fay's phone rang from her sitting room. I answered. It was Charlie. The police had taken his number from Fay and got him on his mobile already.

'Christ,' he said. 'Is it real?'

'Do you want to speak to your mum?' I said. 'Oh Charlie . . .'

'Did you go round?'

'He didn't answer the door.'

'And?'

'I came home.'

'Did you try his phone?'

'Well he wouldn't have answered, would he? Sorry, Charlie. I'm sorry.'

'Give me Mum,' he said.

I stood in the kitchen shivering while they spoke. My feet were cold on the floor tiles, I hadn't even got my slippers on. I went to fill the kettle and her budgie cheeped at me and rattled his bell. Fay put the phone down and came back into the

52

kitchen. Her face was yellow, mauve shadows underneath her eyes.

'He'll be back in an hour,' she said, her voice gathered back into its usual shape.

'What can I do?' I said.

'You've done enough,' she said.

The kettle came to the boil and clicked off.

'I'd like to be alone, if you don't mind,' she said.

'But you shouldn't be alone.'

'All the same.'

She waited with stiff politeness till I left. I went back up the stairs. I made myself another cup of tea. I stirred sugar into it with a splash of brandy. My hand was actually shaking; I held it out in front of me and the shadow shivered on the kitchen table.

*T*he Merriams encouraged her closeness with Jeffrey. She didn't have any friends at school. Her accent was different; however hard she tried she was just different. She was a daygirl and most of them were boarders. She was common and they were posh. They tossed their silky hair at her and turned up their noses. She didn't care, she'd hardly ever had girl friends anyway. It was always the boys – who she knew, and they knew she knew, were only out for what they could get. She'd just been grateful to have something that they wanted.

But with Jeffrey she was a virgin again. Joan asked her if they were more than just friends.

'I do like him,' she confessed.

'You know he's off to university in September,' she said.

'I know.'

'Long as you don't get inseparable. We don't want you pining away.'

'Don't worry,' she said.

There was a spring concert at Jeffrey's school. They went as a party, the Sterns and the Merriams, all dressed up and keyed up with sherry and excitement. She wore a black skirt, a black sweater and a silver pendant, with her fair hair tied back with a velvet ribbon. She sat in the front row between his parents *and her foster parents, with her knees demurely together. And it was almost as if she really did belong.*

It was strange watching Jeffrey up there on the stage in front of everyone, quite cool about it too. She liked the music though she wasn't used to classical and with no words her mind kept drifting off. She forced her attention on to Jeffrey, the hunched back, the intense expression, the long fingers stretching across the keys. When he finished and took a bow, to rapturous applause, he directed a special smile at her and it struck her like a dart.

Afterwards there was tea and biscuits and mingling, and Jeffrey held her hand while he was congratulated on his brilliance, and some of the praise leaked down his arm and through his hand and into her. After all, she was his official girlfriend for all to see. He had chosen her out of all the other girls there were around.

She had never been as happy or as proud of anything.

^

S haved off the beard, made a trip to the barber and next stop John Lewis to get kitted out. Told the assistant I'd won the lottery and wanted to go for a new look. He was obviously a gay and in seventh heaven going round with me, getting me to stroke the fabrics and holding different colours of shirt up to my cheek.

Standing in front of the changing-room mirror in a soft black suit and creamy linen shirt I saw myself as I aimed she would. Narrowed my eyes and practised the Rupert expressions, the slow smile, the bashful grin. Remembering the hairy little C. Martin she lived with, I thought she wouldn't stand a chance. Spent over a grand in all once the leather jacket, the briefcase and the shoes were all totted up.

Once I'm in role I go to Green's Robotics at five-thirty. I wait round the corner – don't want her spotting me yet. I see Karen come out with a fat blonde and they stand there yacking for a minute before she goes off. I take the oblique approach and follow the blonde. She goes into a paper shop and I knock into her when she comes out. She drops her purse and goes scarlet grubbing about for the rolling coins and a Bounty bar. Taking a deep breath, seeing myself step out on to that stage, I tell her to stand up while I pick it up for her, and then insist on buying her a drink.

'You need to sit down a minute,' I say.

'I'm fine,' she says but I hardly have to twist her arm to get her sitting at a table with a glass of wine in front of her.

I take my time, small talk first then edging the conversation round to work. She natters away and is soon on her second glass of wine, with a bowl of peanuts to dip into, before at last the subject comes up.

'Ooops, I'm getting tipsy,' she says. I keep my eyes averted from the sticky lip-print on her glass.

'No harm in that.'

She frowns at me and then it all bursts out. 'I'm right pissed off actually,' she says. 'There's this new woman at work.'

'Who?'

'Why?'

Careful, careful. I shrug and sip my Kaliber.

'Well anyway, she's only been there five minutes, compared to me, I've been there since I left school, anyway, there's this course, right, and you get to go to Blackpool, stay in the Astoria which is four stars all expenses paid and all in work time, and who gets it?'

'She does?'

'Too right. Not fair, is it?'

I shake my head.

'I'll tell you why, she's thin, that's why, and pretty. It's discrimination. The worst thing is, she doesn't give a toss about going, at least she lets on she doesn't. I went up to Gary, our boss, and I was like, *What about me?* He was like, *It'll do her good.* But she hasn't been there five minutes!'

'What's her name?' I say.

'Nina, why? Oh my God, you don't know her! She's nice really, it's just . . .'

'It's OK. I know her boyfriend.'

'Charlie?'

'Yeah.'

'She wants it kept secret, her and Charlie, I reckon he's married but . . . ?' She looks let down when I shake my head. 'What then?'

'Not for me to say. When's the course?'

'Why?'

'I thought I'd look him up while she's away. She's the possessive type, never lets him out alone.'

'Is she?' She twiddles about with her hair. 'Week after next,' she says, 'the Monday to the Wednesday.'

'I'll give him a ring then,' I say.

She puts her hand up to her mouth. 'Here's me going on and on and you haven't said a word about you! You must think I'm a right motormouth.'

'Not at all.'

She edges her fat knee, shiny under the nylon, up against mine and her smile turns my stomach.

'Well, better get home,' I say, 'or my missus'll be on the warpath.'

She blushes and makes a little gulping sound.

The way she blushed right up into the roots of her hair proved she was a real blonde. At least she had that much going for her.

*

All I could think of to do was to help out in practical ways. After the cremation, I went to clear out Dave's bedsit. I did it to spare Charlie. The landlord wanted the room emptied as soon as possible so that he could re-let.

He rapped on the door as soon as he realised I was there. 'I'm very sorry and all that,' he said, when I opened it, 'but look at it from where I'm standing. Dead men don't pay rent.' He looked quite pleased with the ring of that and I slammed the door in his money-grubbing face.

It was weird to be alone in the bedsit. I'd only been there with both Charlie and Dave before and then it had always seemed hot and crowded. I would perch on the arm of Charlie's chair by the gas fire, while we listened to music and tried to bring Dave out of himself.

I drew the curtains that Dave always kept closed and looked at the sticky carpet and the tattered wallpaper patterned with race-horses plunging into nothing. It was worse than I'd thought. In the evenings, in the lamplight, it had never looked as bleak. I opened the window to let out the smell of stale smoke and in came the roar of traffic, the tough whiff of exhaust fumes. I know I should have done something more that night. But it wouldn't have made any difference. When I'd rung the doorbell he was probably already . . . well. I didn't make it happen.

I gathered up all the bicycle pumps and put them in a box for Oxfam. I flicked through Dave's books: *The Book of Changes*, a Bible I was surprised to see, some comic thing called the *Sandman* and a sketchbook of pornographic scribbles. I put the books and CDs in a box for Charlie to sort through. Dave would have wanted Charlie to have everything though of course he hadn't left a will, just a note that had been clutched in his hand when he'd been found.

Not worth the bother. No hard feelings. D.

He'd had very few clothes and they were too tatty for Oxfam so I put them into a bin bag. I held on to one thing for a moment: a T-shirt, black faded to grey, with an RSPB logo. It was identical to Charlie's – in fact it probably was Charlie's. I held it to my nose, soft, worn cotton, thin peppery smell of skin. The seam had come undone at the shoulder. I poked my finger through. An empty garment where Dave should be. Charlie could not have stood to do this.

In the bathroom there was a torn poster saying *Have Nothing in Your Home That You do Not Know to be Useful or Believe to be Beautiful* – a joke considering the heaps of squeezed-out toothpaste tubes, toilet-roll middles, rusty disposable razors and other rubbish. I stuffed it all, including the poster, in the bin bag with the clothes. I considered cleaning – but the grey ridges of scum round the sink and bath, the crusty scabs in the toilet defeated me. Leave it to the landlord, I thought. Dead men don't clean.

On the mantelpiece I found a stick of Blackpool rock. It had gone soft and my fingers squidged into the sticky pink coating as I picked it up. Charlie had bought that rock on the day we met.

I'd gone alone, on a whim, to Blackpool for a couple of days. Though when I arrived at the boarding house and saw the roomful of icy polyester flounces, the grey and freezing rectangle of sea, I wondered what on earth I'd been thinking.

The first evening I wandered about in the rain and bought chips with neon curry sauce and was under the covers by nine o'clock watching telly. But at breakfast the following morning I met Charlie.

He was eating scrambled eggs. Because it was off-season the landlady had opened up a small side-room for breakfast. The actual dining room was being decorated and there was a depressing smell of paint and white spirit. And the only guests were me and Charlie.

This is what I saw when I walked into that room. Curly hair, somewhere between brown and fair, blue eyes, a straight nose, golden stubble and a smile that took me in and gave me myself back, all bright and shiny new.

'Mind if I?' I said, just out of politeness, there was nowhere else to sit.

He had his mouth full, but he gestured and grinned while he chewed and swallowed. He was wearing a tweedy grey sweater, fraying at the cuffs.

We were quiet for a moment. I looked at the wisps of wool against the golden hairs on the back of his hands. The landlady came and took my order. I couldn't think straight so I copied him and asked for scrambled eggs.

She sniffed. 'If you'd have turned up ten minutes ago I could have scrambled them together,' she said.

'If it's too much trouble . . .' My voice came out sarcastic but I didn't mean it. I meant if it is too much trouble I'll have something else, I didn't care about the scrambled eggs, but she flounced off.

Charlie raised his eyebrows at me.

'I didn't mean it like that!' I said.

'She was in a huff with me for wanting filter coffee,' he said.

I said, 'You'd think she'd be grateful not to have to do sausages and stuff.'

And that is when it started, the feeling of complicity between

us, beginning with the landlady and growing to include everything. Charlie and me against the world.

'What are you doing here?' he asked.

'Just fancied blowing the cobwebs away,' I said. 'What
about you?'

He was working. He was an architect and was looking at
plans for a new municipal glasshouse and aviary. 'Perfect for
me,' he said. 'Birds and buildings. But we're getting nowhere
slowly. Red tape like you wouldn't believe. Public-health
issues, insurance issues, planning issues, etcetera etcetera.'

We chatted for a while and I blurted out my story, my lack
of family, the violent husband I'd fled to Sheffield to escape.
All my personal belongings were lost in a fire. I worked as a
clerical assistant at Green's. I lived alone in my own bedsit.

'Sorry,' he said, 'that you've had such a rough time, I mean.'
He gazed at me with calm blue eyes, eyes as blue as the sea
should be. 'Hey, what are you planning today?'

I shook my head. 'Dunno. A walk.'

'I've got a couple of hours free,' he said. 'How about we
walk together?'

It turned out that he lived in Sheffield too. He began to tell
me some of the architectural history of the city. I wasn't
bothered about that but I watched his mouth talking and I
watched myself eat the eggs and drink a cup of filter coffee and
even have another piece of toast with marmalade. The landlady came in again looking at her watch. 'I normally have the
pots done and the Hoover out by now,' she said and we took
the hint. I felt her eyes on me, wondering if he had picked me
up or I'd picked him up, but the picking up was mutual.

We'd walked in the wind and he'd pointed out birds to me
pecking in the fringes of the sea, their twiggy legs in the cold
water, long beaks piercing the sand. Birds have always given
me the creeps but I didn't mention that. Later we went in for a
coffee and wandered about afterwards holding hands. Our

hands reached out to each other almost of their own accord and it was a peculiar experience for me to be out with Charlie as if we were a pair of lovers, right there in the street for anyone to see.

And that is when he bought a stick of rock for Dave and one for me too and I sucked it as we walked along talking about this and that. And when he'd kissed me – our first kiss took place beside a pillar-box – the taste was of minty rock.

In Dave's bedsit I unpeeled a bit of the sticky Cellophane and put my tongue on the sweet mintiness, just to taste that kiss again. And then I threw it in the bin bag and hurried to finish the job.

I thought Charlie would be pleased I'd cleared the bedsit for him. I gave him the box of things I'd saved.

'Where's everything else?' he said.

'There wasn't much. It was only rubbish.'

'I wanted to look through myself,' he said. 'There may have been things.'

'There wasn't.'

'But I wanted to see for myself.'

'I've given the keys back now,' I said. 'I'm sorry.'

He took a deep breath in but instead of speaking he went out of the room and banged the door. I heard the jingle of keys, then the front door slam, the car start and roar off down the road. It was the first time we'd ever come anywhere near a row. I stood frozen for a moment and then I began to wash the floor. Cleaning can be soothing and it's never a waste of time. The grey suds squeezing from the mop showed how dirty it had been even though it had looked clean. I screwed the fronds of the mop into a tight grey topknot and put it outside to dry. I polished the taps until I could see wispy little me's reflected there.

While I was scrubbing the sink he came home, his arms full of files and papers from work. There was a peculiar, almost

63

exhilarated look on his face. Before he could speak I got in first. 'I'm sorry, Charlie,' I said, 'I was only trying to help.'

He shrugged. 'It's done now,' he said. 'But another time . . .'

'Walk on the newspaper,' I said. He stepped on to the sports section by the door. 'Another time I'll ask you first,' I promised. Though of course there could never be another time like that.

He went upstairs to his study and I went down to the basement to ask Fay to dinner. She usually has dinner with us on Sunday but this was a Friday. I was worried about her grieving away down there with only her budgie for company.

Photographs show that Fay was beautiful once, and there were still traces of it between the lines. She'd had her children late and seemed more the age of Charlie's granny than his mum. She'd always dress and get made up for dinner, her cheeks fierce pink, her eyelids silver, like metallic shutters when she blinked.

I knew she wasn't keen on 'foreign cuisine' and on Sundays I always did a traditional roast – but Friday night was curry night so I compromised. I ground cumin and mustard seeds, marinated chicken, mixed dough for fresh naan bread. I concocted a mild dish for Fay, cauliflower in a gentle coconut and coriander sauce, but I saw her nostrils twitch when she came up the stairs and surveyed the table.

Still, I hugged her. I always hugged her though she'd be stiff in my arms as a bunch of Coty-scented twigs.

'A nice mild curry especially for Fay,' I said. I lifted the lid of the casserole dish, 'And something hotter for us.'

'Curry, is it?' she said. 'When you and Nicky came back from India, Charlie, I remember her saying she'd had enough of that to last her a lifetime.'

'Yes, Mum.'

'You know Nicky sent a lovely card, Nina, when she heard about Dave? Those two were like this.' She twisted one finger round another.

'*Mum.*' Charlie gave her a warning look. 'This looks great, Nina.' Though he'd lost his appetite he tried to sound enthusiastic. I thought this meal would tempt him. All his favourite tastes and I'd even bought some Indian beer.

Fay took a teaspoonful of cauliflower and a few grains of rice and chased them round her plate. 'Very nice,' she said, 'though a simple cauliflower cheese would have sufficed.' She put down her fork and her eyes went far away. 'He loved that, didn't he?' A tiny vein fluttered in the silvery dampness beside her eye. 'Both of you did, a lovely milky cauliflower cheese. You used to fight to scrape out the dish.'

Charlie clattered down his fork. 'Today I was made redundant,' he announced.

Fay and I both stared at him. I thought I'd misheard or maybe it was a joke but it was no joke. 'It's been looming for a while,' he added. 'The firm's gone bust.'

I put down my fork.

He gave a strange bleat of laughter. 'Don't look like that! It's probably for the best,' he said, 'I was thinking of a change.'

To lose a brother, and then a job, all within the space of a week, I could not imagine how that felt. All I could think was that love might make him better and in bed that night I put my arms around him – but as my hand slid down his back I remembered Rupert. Maybe Charlie sensed or even smelt the sudden bolt of shock and guilt that went through me. He pulled away and got out of bed.

'It feels wrong,' he said. He was standing by the window and I could see his silhouette against the streetlight filtering through the curtains, the bunched shapes of his fists.

'What feels wrong?' I said.

'I don't know. Something's changed.'

'Something *has* changed,' I said. '*Dave* . . . it's just the shock of that. And what with losing your job . . . But it'll be all right. Come back to bed.'

But he continued to loom there against the curtains, petals of streetlight catching in his curls.

'Are we OK?' I held my breath till he said, 'Okey-dokey.' That's what we said when we were just checking. I did think then that it could still, somehow, be OK. After a moment he came back to bed. His skin was cold and I wrapped myself around him, tried to warm him up.

I was almost asleep when I heard him take a breath as if to speak.

'What?' I said.

He swallowed, but said nothing, turned on to his side. I spooned round him and my hand felt the scattered beating of his heart. I held my breath but he was quiet. A car passed and I watched its lights glide like oil across the ceiling, listened to its engine growl off down the street.

∧

G ot straight on to Directory Enquiries, found the Blackpool Astoria, got the last available room. I booked from
the Sunday so I could get there before her, get a proper lie of
the land. First time I'd stayed in a swanky hotel like that, en
suite bathroom, TV with round-the-clock porn if you were so
inclined. I had my scrapbook in the new briefcase. The
pictures and the clippings, the best one has their two faces
side by side, the blonde and the dark. Under one the caption:
'The Killer . . .' and under the other: 'The Victim'. They look
more like they should have been setting off on a picnic or
pyjama party or somesuch.

I didn't get more than a glimpse of her on the Monday. They
had their meal off a buffet in the Connaught Suite and they were
busy in the evening. I asked at reception for her room number
but the snotty cow said, 'We can't divulge that, sir, but you can
leave her a message,' which needless to say I did not do.

Monday night I watched the porn and I had to let go when
there were two girls, nothing like the two of them but still, long
hair, one dark, one fair, shaved whatnots and huge tits,
though, which is a turn-off, but it passed the time, listening
to them and looking at my scrapbook.

In the morning I got a good look. There she was at breakfast all
on her own. I watched her help herself from the buffet – grape-

fruit segments and a croissant, which she picked at and pushed away. She drank coffee which she refilled three times and kept her eyes down reading from a stapled handout. At one point she took out a mobile and tried a number, listened, frowned and put it back in her bag. When she got up I went towards her, hoping to catch her eye, but she walked straight past, unaware. She was so shut in to herself, you could see that. It seemed to me then that this might not be as straightforward as I'd thought.

Her course was taking place in the conference suite so I knew where she'd be all day and from five-thirty onwards I walked up and down the corridor waiting for them to finish. Then, after six, the door opened and out they came. Couldn't see her at first but then she followed, another woman trying to talk to her but her body language made it plain that she preferred to be alone, thank you very much. You could actually see the other woman get the hump and give up on her.

The lot of them got in the lift, going down, and I ran down the stairs but my mistake because she didn't come out. She must have gone back up to her room. The rest of them went into the bar. I waited in the lobby where I could see the lift door and the passage that led from the stairs to the bar where their buffet was going to be served, according to the sign, at seven-thirty. I thought it would be just like her, the little I knew of her, to stay in her room all night and nothing I could do. All that money on the hotel gone up in smoke for no result.

But then the luck changed. She came into the lobby at six fifty-five, hovered about outside the bar for a bit, then went in. I followed, thinking I'd intercept her before she joined her group, but she played right into my hands. She got herself a drink, then instead of sitting with the others went back out into the lobby and sat on a sofa, twiddling with a spoon. I watched someone come and clear the table in front of her. She swigged back her wine and looked as if she was about to go. I could see it was now or never so I made my move. I offered her a drink to which she said yes.

I fetched the drinks, sat down beside her, looked into her eyes, dark hazy blue. I couldn't come to terms with her grown-up face, still pretty but thin, with shadows under the eyes – what you might call haunted. She looked away and took a gulp of the wine, foot jiggling up and down fifteen to the dozen. I turned it on then, gave it to her full throttle, the voice, the looks, the 'Rupert, don't laugh'. I wondered if she'd get the significance but there was not a glimmer.

Isobel had loved Rupert Bear, had all the annuals lined up in her bedroom. And she wore a little enamel badge on her jacket that she'd sent for with jam labels. She'd been wearing it when she died, there was even a mention in the paper. I've got it now. Rupert with his famous scarf trailing out behind him, legs apart as if running.

It was hard for me to contain myself when she said her name was Nina. It was hard for me to look at her and I had to hold on to the part I was playing, relax back into Rupert's way of sitting, lounging back, legs crossed.

'Nice name, it suits you,' I said and then I asked her out to dinner. To do her credit she did hesitate for a moment, said she'd been thinking of having room service. I'd got her right then, not the sociable type. Enough socialising when she was inside to last a lifetime, I should think. But after consideration she said yes. She had a sweet smile though you could tell she didn't use it much. She got up, made a phone call and then we set off to a restaurant I'd checked out during the day.

It was not difficult to get her back and into bed. Her body when we got the suit off was a bit thin for my taste, small boobs, all right for some but nothing to write home about. Not your Page Three type. What was strange was that I couldn't think of her as Karen – after all the times I've pretended that it was. I had to shut my eyes and imagine she was a pro I was pretending was Karen in order to get it up. But she wasn't Karen to me then. If she had been all I'd have had to do was squeeze.

*

On Friday I went back to work. Christine was away. I looked at her desk. A picture of her parents and a dog; a Good Luck for your Driving Test card (she'd failed); and the white bear. His eyes peered at me, bright and blind. I moved him behind her computer out of my sight and went to my own desk. On my screen there was a sticky note saying 'Rupert, urgent' and a mobile number. I screwed it up and threw it in the bin.

I worked hard all day to try and catch up. Each time the phone rang – I had twice as many calls to deal with since Christine wasn't there – I answered, making the greeting come out friendly and interested as I had been taught. A smile in your voice is the key.

I worked straight through my lunch-hour and Gary called me to his office in the early afternoon. I sat down and he plaited his fingers together and looked at me for a minute without speaking. I saw his eyes rest on my flapping foot and forced it to stay still. He had one of those Newton's cradles that I thought went out with the ark. I longed for him to click it. He saw me looking, bent his mouth into a smile, pulled a silver ball up and we watched the matching click and swing for a moment till he stopped it.

'If object A exerts a force on object B then object B exerts the exact opposite force on object A,' I said.

'Quite,' he said. 'Now then, what's been the trouble?'

'Tummy.'

'Doctor's note?'

'Oh sorry!'

'That is the usual procedure.'

'I didn't go to the doctor's,' I said, 'it was just a horrid bug. Sickness and diarrhoea and that.'

'Spare me the details,' he said.

'Another time I'll get a doctor's note. Sorry.'

'How are you finding the job?' he asked. 'I'm aware you're working well below your capacity – but prove yourself reliable and who knows?'

'Thank you,' I said.

Almost as soon as I got back to my desk the phone rang. 'Good afternoon,' I said, 'Nina speaking, how may I help you?'

'It's me,' he said. 'What time do you get off?'

'Don't know.'

'Five? Six?'

'Not sure.'

'See you then.' He broke the connection.

I could have signed my flexi-form and walked out before he got there – but Gary was looking, his office door propped open, and I didn't dare. My heart was beating hard against my ribs. The columns on the screen turned to gibberish but I sat in front of it in imitation of someone working while I thought what I should do. I opened my drawer and looked at Charlie's calm blue eyes. I really mustn't let this happen. There was nothing I could do but wait till five o'clock, go outside and meet Rupert. Tell him that there was no chance. Eventually he'd have to get the message.

He seemed even taller than I remembered, his eyes a brighter brown. In my mind he'd become something like a fiend but face to face, still, he had the sort of looks girls pin up on their walls to moon at.

'Anyone would think you were avoiding me,' he said.

I looked round to see if anyone was watching. 'Look,' I said, 'let's get away from here.'

'I've got strawberries,' he said.

'Strawberries?'

He opened a Marks and Spencer's bag to show me a punnet of strawberries and a pot of cream. I almost laughed.

'Where shall we go?' he said.

'Come on.'

I walked fast with my head down till we got to the overgrown churchyard, which teetered with monuments to the steel magnates of the city. When I'd first come to Sheffield, before I'd started work at Green's or met Charlie, I'd spent ages there, making out the chipped and lichen-encrusted inscriptions, picking over the lumpy ground, between the brambles. I didn't know if the lumps were only root and broken stone or if they were bones, but I walked softly just in case. It was a peaceful place and, except for birds and dog-walkers, very quiet and private.

'You could nearly call this harassment,' I pointed out. 'Or stalking.'

He sat on the edge of a raised grave. *In Loving Memory of Isaiah Braithwaite* were the words beneath a wreath of stone. *1855–1949. The Lord Giveth and the Lord Taketh Away.*

'Sit down,' he said, 'have a strawberry.' He ripped the Cellophane off the fruit and opened the cream. He took a big berry between his finger and thumb and dunked it, then he held it out to me. I shrugged, took it and put it in my mouth. He licked the cream from his fingers as I licked it from my lips. The strawberry was too cold between my teeth and had a watery taste.

He dunked another but I shook my head. He put it in his own mouth and gazed at me, while he chewed.

'Look, this is ridiculous,' I said. 'Can't you get it into your head? I'm with Charlie.'

'Have you told him?'

'No.'

'That's not very honest.'

'What would be the point? Have you told your wife?'

'I'm willing to,' he said.

'Don't. Please.'

'She's a bitch.'

'Well, you're not exactly a model husband.'

He frowned at me, expressions moving like clouds beneath his skin.

'I hate her,' he said.

'Hate?' I said. 'What does that mean?' The corner of his mouth pulled up a fraction before he looked down. 'Leave her then,' I said.

He put the strawberries down and pressed his hands together. 'What kind of music do you like?'

'What?'

'Your favourite film? I don't know anything about you – I want to know. Your favourite food?'

'Soup,' I said.

'Soup?'

'Tomato from a can or home-made vegetable.'

'Do you support a team?'

I shook my head. 'There's no point in this, Rupert.'

'Just have dinner with me tonight. Whatever you like, wherever you want? What do you like?'

'No.'

'Come here . . .' He took my chin in his hand and tried to touch my mouth.

'No,' I said and jerked my head away.

'A bit of cream,' he said.

I scrubbed it off myself.

'Where were we?' he said.

'Sorry?'

'In the park the other day, where were we?'

'Don't know.'

'We were discussing the possibility of goodness.'

A woman was walking towards us. At first I thought it was Maisie. I flinched and, turning away from her, allowed myself to be pulled against Rupert's chest, so that she couldn't see my face. As soon as she'd gone past I saw it wasn't Maisie, but she could have been someone else that Fay knew. Fay had lived in Sheffield all her life. The woman had gone and Rupert held me tight.

'That's good,' he said into my hair. 'That's better.'

His arms were strong. My breath was muffled against him, my nose squashed against the crisp, new texture of his shirt. He smelt clean, biscuity. Just for a moment I let myself relax. His heart beat against my cheek. I felt a rush of tiredness. It reminded me of how I used to be with boys. I thought of Charlie and pulled away.

'Don't go yet,' he said.

'What do you want?'

'You.'

'Why?'

'When we're together you'll see.'

'We won't be.'

'You'll see what a connection there is between us.'

'Connection?' I said. 'Do you realise how creepy you sound?'

He didn't try and stop me going. We walked towards the gates of the cemetery. I watched our shadows precede us. They seemed to be holding hands.

'I'm sorry,' he said as we came out on to the road.

I looked at him.

'I don't mean to seem creepy. I'm just not very good at this.' His lashes shadowed his eyes.

'It's OK,' I said.

A gleam came through the shadow. 'It's just that you don't often feel this strong. I've been searching for you for years.'

I looked into his warm brown eyes for any sign of sarcasm or craziness but he just seemed sad.

'You've left the strawberries behind,' I said.

'They were for you.'

'Better in season,' I said. 'A few more weeks and the English ones'll be ready.'

'Sorry. I thought . . .'

'No, it was a nice thought.'

I wanted to put my arms round him. If it wasn't for Charlie, I thought, just at that moment, only because of the strawberries, only because of the hurt in his eyes.

'Goodbye,' I said.

He shrugged but didn't speak. I walked away. He didn't follow me but I could feel his eyes on my back, a light pressure between my shoulder blades. I held my head up and walked like a dancer. At the crossing I looked back at him, still there, still watching. I lifted my hand to wave and stepped out to cross the road. There was a shout, and a squeal of brakes that sounded miles away, and then I felt a slam before the road came up to hit me.

I opened my eyes to find Charlie's face hanging above me. A diamond came out of his eye winking through the blur. His hand squeezed mine. And next time I looked he wasn't there.

Charlie brought me in a bunch of creamy freesias. The blur had gone. His face was tanned and there were new lines on his forehead. He smelt of sunshine and cut grass. He kissed my brow but I couldn't feel it and only later realised it was because of the bandage.

Next time I woke Gita, a ward assistant, was arranging lilies in a vase. The smell was fatty and sweet.

'Who's popular then?' she said when she saw my eyes open.

'And look at all these.' There was a hellish jostle of carnations: red, pink, yellow and orange. 'Aren't they jolly?' She picked up the card. 'From all at Green's Robotics. Robotics, that sounds interesting.'

'It's not,' I said. 'Who are *they* from?' I was looking at the lilies, which dwarfed Charlie's freesias, smothering their delicate scent. It was hard for me to speak. Something had happened to my nose. I had to keep my mouth open to breathe and it was full of the waxy choke of the lilies.

Gita searched for a card. 'Don't know,' she said. 'It must have dropped off.'

'Can you take them away?' I asked.

'But they're beautiful!' She gave me a look, sighed and lifted up the vase.

'Give them to someone else,' I said.

'Some people don't know when they're lucky.' She picked up the freesias.

'Not those,' I said. 'Just the lilies.' She had a mustard streak of pollen on the breast of her pink uniform. She took the vase. The flowers almost hid her face. I could hear the soles of her shoes unpeeling right down the corridor and the sound of double doors swinging open and shut.

I lay back and stared at the slim white freesias. I was tired out with the effort of speaking. When Charlie came back he told me what the doctor had told him: my nose was fractured, my eye-socket traumatised and I was concussed. No other injuries. I was lucky. Lucky! If I could have laughed I would have.

For a few days I dipped in and out of sleep, surfacing from time to time, when Charlie was there and once Rose and once Christine who brought me a box of Black Magic, a Get Well balloon and a big card signed by everybody at Green's. I could just imagine it going from desk to desk with people saying 'Who?' then reaching for their pens.

Once I woke, startled to see Fay perched on the chair by the bed, feet dangling, handbag clamped to her lap. 'Well,' she said, 'that was remarkably silly. Didn't you get my lilies?'

'Lilies?'

'I'll have to chase them up,' she said. 'I really pushed the boat out with those.' She was all dressed up, with silver eye shadow and scarlet patches on her withered cheeks.

'They do sometimes go astray,' I said. 'Sorry.'

'Not your fault. But it's one thing after another,' she said. 'Whatever next?'

I was too woozy to say much as I listened to her wonder what Charlie was going to do and complain about her feet. It was like having a mother or a mother-in-law. I didn't care that she didn't fuss or pretend to be fonder of me than she was. You can't rush these things.

'Have you looked in a mirror yet?' she said.

I had been allowed up that morning to visit the bathroom and had caught sight of myself in the square of glass over the basin. I'd peered for a long time at the swollen lump of nose, the blackened ridge of eyebrow with its row of wiry insects' legs, the flat and dirty hair. How Charlie could still love me like that, I don't know, but yes I do know because I would love him whatever happened. If he were injured I would love him even more.

'Well you'll mend,' she said. 'Could have been worse. It's Charlie I'm worried about. He's really not himself, Nina, moping about, not eating.'

'I'll be home soon,' I said. 'I'll look after him.'

'It's you that needs looking after.'

'No, I'll be fine,' I said. And I meant it. 'I'll be fine. We'll all be fine.'

I'd been alone in a side-ward at first but now I was recovering they moved me into one with eight beds. In the mornings it was all business – doctors, cleaners, bed changes – but in the afternoons people visited and I got a jolt like an electric shock each time I saw a tall dark shape.

'Have you been keeping secrets?' Charlie said one afternoon. He took my hand but I didn't dare look at him.

'It doesn't matter, but you should have told me,' he said.

It doesn't matter, I thought. *It doesn't matter?* I bent my lips
into a smile. 'What?'

He shook his head. '*Women!*' he said and came quite close
to laughing. 'You're so vain. What was it like before?'

'What?'

'Honestly, Nina!' He did laugh then, for the first time since
Dave died. 'I was talking to the consultant – he mentioned –
assuming I knew – that you'd had a nose job.'

'Oh that.' The hot prickle of a blush crawled up my neck
and over my face. I wanted to say it was not vanity that made
me do it, but I couldn't tell him that.

'I was embarrassed,' I said.

'That's why you won't show me any pictures of you from
before!' he said.

'No. I told you. They went up in the fire.'

'What was it like then?'

'Huge,' I said, 'a huge great . . . hooter.'

'How huge?'

I held my finger a stupid distance from my face and he
grinned.

'I wouldn't do it now,' I said.

'When?' he asked. 'I mean how old were you?'

Gita came in. 'More flowers,' she said. 'Will you accept
these?' She was carrying a bouquet of rosebuds, red and white.

'Wow,' Charlie said. 'Who are they from?'

'I'll fetch a vase,' she said.

'What did she mean, will you accept *these*?' he asked,
burrowing through the buds looking for a card. I held my
breath as he opened the tiny envelope.

'Get Well Soon. R,' he read. 'Who?'

'I don't know,' I said, thinking furiously, then, looking at the pursed little mouths of the flowers, said, 'Rose. It will have been Rose.'

'Your friend?'

'Yes.'

'Seems a bit excessive.'

'She's like that.'

'Hmmm.' He frowned.

'She's an extravagant person,' I said.

'Why don't you ever bring her round?'

'I dunno.'

'What's she like?'

'All right. Nice.'

'Invite her round sometime. It's weird that I've never met any of your friends.' He got up and roamed around my bed, went to the window and looked out. All I could see was sky.

'Mum's still upset about her lilies,' he said.

'I sent them away. I'm sorry. I don't like the smell. I didn't like to say.'

We sat in silence for a moment, then he narrowed his eyes at me. 'So, what about the nose then? What was that all about?'

I swallowed. I was too tired. 'I was different then,' I said. 'Anyway, what's a person meant to say, "Hello, before we get to know each other any better, this is not my original nose?"'

'I don't like messing with nature,' he said. 'I would have talked you out of it – even if you'd looked like Pinocchio.'

Despite myself I felt the gurgle of a laugh in my throat.

'I don't know how you can bear to look at me now though,' I said.

'You'll heal,' he said.

'Yes.' I squeezed his hand. 'And we're going to be OK. We'll get through this. Are we OK?' I searched his face.

'Okey-dokey,' he said with hardly a pause at all.

~

O ne drowsy August afternoon when the sea slumped against the breakwaters and the tourists moved in a drift of treacle along the promenade Jeffrey had asked her if she'd wait for him. 'I'll write to you all the time,' he said, 'and in the holidays I'll be back.' He said he didn't want to go and leave her but he really had no choice.

'Of course I'll wait,' she said. 'I love you.'

It was the first time that word had been said. Perhaps the first time in her life. He breathed out as if he'd been punched in the stomach. 'I love you too,' he said. 'Come on . . .' They wound up steps through the Spa Gardens, past pensioners on benches, past scrubby shrubs and litter bins. Their hands were sticky with mingled sweat but still they held them. The word 'love' hovered round them like a bee.

'Where are we going?' she asked.

'Ah ha,' he said.

'Where?'

'Wait and see.'

They walked past a row of old ladies in wheelchairs, past an ice-cream van, round a corner and through a gate marked PRIVATE.

'Are we allowed in here?' she said and he said, 'Of course not, that's the point.'

They pushed between some overgrown bushes, the leathery green leaves spattered with white as if with paint, starting up a shock of little birds. They squeezed between more bushes, something thorny that snagged her sleeve, and emerged in a dank triangular space bordered on one side by the high wall of a building and on the other two by overgrown shrubs. There was no sunshine. The ground was blackish and litter-strewn and there was the sour reek of cat-pee.

'What?' she said.

'Will you really wait for me?' he said.

The corners of his mouth were chapped. There was a cluster of spots across his nose, but when he took his glasses off she saw herself reflected in the sweet brown of his eyes.

'Of course.'

He kissed her and there was more pressure in the kiss, his lips taking charge, forcing hers open for the first time. She could feel a tremble in him. She hoped that he wasn't going to want her to lie down in this gloomy place but he pulled away.

'Look.' He began kicking and scraping at the ground with the side of his shoe. He knelt down and swept with his hand and she thought he'd gone mad, brushing away grit and twigs and leaves – until she saw a circle appearing in the dirt, about three foot across, thick planks of wood painted with some-thing black and grainy.

'What is it?' She stood looking down at him, at the dull thickness of his side-parted hair, at his long dirty fingers fumbling about. Love? It struck her that he looked like his father, that he would be, one day, his father, a music professor, and she could be a professor too, or at least she could be his wife.

He might become a famous concert pianist and she could be there, beside him in all the praise and riches, just as if she belonged.

I went up to the hospital. There's no security, not like in the hotel, anyone can just turn up at reception and get the ward number, no questions asked. You'd think there'd be more suspicion. I peered at her through a glass door. Her face was all bandages. She could have been anyone.

I might have gone back next day but I had a call from Dad wanting me to go home. I tried to put it off but he said Mum was in a bad way and was asking for me so of course I said yes. She is my number-one priority and Karen was safe and sound. She wasn't going anywhere for a while.

Going home was like a trip back to the past. I'd never noticed the smell of the house before. Nothing I could name but it got up your nose, sad or defeated or somesuch. Everything was down at heel; no decoration or replacement for fifteen years. Stair-carpet a death-trap, frayed at the edges, paint chipped on the skirtings, dirt around the light-switches. They hadn't the heart, of course, and it was all down to Karen. But soon, I thought, when all this was over they could have a makeover like on the telly. Get an expert in, new anything they wanted and all on yours truly.

It was afternoon and they were watching racing on TV, curtains shut to keep the sun off the screen, room choked up with Dad's smoke.

He looked up at me from his armchair. 'Hello, son.'

'Hello, stranger,' Mum said, 'you're looking smart.' She held her head up so I could kiss her cheek. I'd forgotten how overweight she'd got, filling the armchair to overflowing.

Dad waited till his horse had lost. 'I'll put the kettle on,' he said.

'I'll do it.' I went into the kitchen. Minced meat thawing in a pan, a bag of spuds, so it would be shepherd's pie. The pattern of flowers had almost rubbed off the plastic tablecloth; the cruet set, two swans, had lost their beaks. Karen had done this. Any feeling of softening in me about her, if there'd been any, died off then. I wanted to rub her face on the frayed carpet, the worn cloth, the hole in the line in front of the sink; grind it into her what she'd done to this family. If not for her . . . I shut my eyes and tried to see it. The house bright and decorated. Mum cheerful and energetic and full of flair. Isobel paying a visit – maybe with kiddies even. I'd be Uncle Mark and there might be a wife. We might be thinking of starting a family. Not quite yet a while, but it would be in the pipeline.

'You all right?' Dad said and I opened my eyes. 'Good to see you,' he said. 'Too quiet about the place. Your mum's been missing you.'

'Has she?'

'You been keeping your nose clean?' He emptied the teapot into the sink and swilled it out. 'None of your nonsense?'

'How is she?' I said.

He filled the teapot and covered it in its stained and matted tea cosy. He looked somehow different, hair a bit darker, younger even.

'She's been down,' he said. 'Trouble with her legs though the doctors can't find anything wrong. As much as I can do to get her up the stairs. Vicious circle, she's so heavy now she gets out of puff at the slightest thing and all the sitting around just makes her heavier.' He took a Battenberg out of its packet and sliced it up.

'Reason I wanted you to come; I need a bit of a break, son. A night or two off. Since you've been gone I've hardly been out of the house.'

'I can stay a day or two,' I said.

'See if you can distract her a bit, get her up and about.'

'I'll do my best,' I promised, though I didn't hold out much hope.

Dad went out at lunchtime next day. He was wearing jeans and I'd not seen him in jeans before except when he was on the ground under the car but these were a different type, new and dark blue, embarrassing the way they hugged against his flat behind and drooping privates. I said nothing and spent all afternoon pestering Mum to sit out in the garden.

It was nice out there, smell of flowers, birds singing, I'd forgotten all about how a garden feels in May what with being stuck in the city with my mind on other things.

'How are you, Mum?' I said when I'd got her across the grass and on to the bench.

'Same as ever,' she said. I worked it out and she's only fifty-seven, not old, but the life she lives she might just as well be eighty. Hair all flat and grey and the rolls of fat, her little face perched on top of the mountain of her chest and neck.

'You ought to get yourself out and about a bit,' I said. 'Why don't I get you to the hairdresser's? Or out for a run some-where? We could go to Felixstowe—' and then I stopped like a punch in the gut, what was I thinking? It had been the promenade I'd been envisioning, imagining her down there in the fresh sea air, and I had forgotten, for the first time ever, about Isobel and Karen.

She said nothing for a minute, just turned her face away. If I could have thought of anything then to please her, I would have done it. It was almost unbearable keeping it all bottled up. I nearly told her then that I'd found Karen and that I was going to make everything right. But then she looked back at

84

me and said, in a meaningful voice, 'I hope you've been keeping out of mischief.' And the moment was gone.

I brought tea and biscuits out and we started a game of Uno but she was wheezing away what with the pollen and sweating in the sun so we soon got back inside in front of the telly and she had a tub of ice-cream in front of *Countdown* to help her cool off.

Dad came back in the early evening, flushed and rumpled. He wolfed down the chilli I'd made. We managed to get Mum up to the table, which was a bit of a victory; usually she stops in her armchair with a tray. He gave her a kiss when he came in and she looked up at him in a way that went right through me, so grateful he was back, beseeching you might term it.

Next morning at breakfast Dad was up with the lark and all spruced up again. Jeans and aftershave. 'Mind if I pop out for a couple of hours?' he said, all casual, looking at me over his piece of toast.

'Where?' I asked.

He looked down. 'Bits of this and that,' he said, 'errands.'

'Why don't we all go out?' I went. 'I think we could persuade Mum. How about Woodbridge? Fish and chips for lunch, a look at the boats.'

'That would be nice,' he said, though you could see the colour draining out of his face, 'but you see I've made plans.'

'Oh yes?' I said.

'Nothing much.'

'Can't you put it off then?'

'Dentist,' he said and I nearly laughed, thinking can't you do better than that?

'Not another woman, Dad?' I said, making it come out jocular.

He looked me straight in the eye and said, 'And what if it was?' I was struck dumb. 'Would you begrudge me a bit of pleasure?' he said so quietly I could hardly hear him.

He poured himself out some tea and I could see the tremble in his hand. 'A couple of hours,' he said. 'You take your mother to Woodbridge.'

'You know she won't come without you.'

'In that case we'll go when I get back,' he said. He pushed himself up from the table with the flats of his hands and went out, leaving his cup of tea steaming.

I took Mum up her magazines, a fresh pot of tea, the biscuit tin. A morning chat show on and she was happy as Larry. I told her I was going out for a bit and would she be all right and she hardly looked away from the box. I waited for him to go and followed him. His is not a car you could easily miss, an old Nissan sprayed turquoise for some reason. He drove out of town and left the dual carriageway after five miles or so. He could have seen me if he'd looked but he didn't. We went off down a lane, leafy trees almost blocking out the light at some points, and then out into the open and he pulled into the driveway of a redbrick semi, ugly little house in the middle of nowhere.

I had no choice but to drive straight past but half a mile or so up the road I stopped by a stand of trees and walked back past a cornfield. In front of the house were plastic toys, a football, a sandpit. I could see nothing of what was going on, of course, and I couldn't stand around outside without being conspicuous. I walked past, then a few minutes later walked back again. I was thinking of getting Mrs Chivers on to it but then it was taken out of my hands when the door opened and a woman stepped out. It took my breath away for a moment, because just for a split second I thought it was Isobel. She had her arm lifted to keep her long black hair away from her face. She was not teenage but more the age Isobel would be now, middling sort of height, slim, curvaceous. Dad came out behind her, holding the hand of a small kid. He was about to say something to her but then he looked across and met my eye. We stood there as if we'd got stuck, like on stage when the words go completely out of your head, and then he let go of the kid's hand.

'Jessica, this is my son Mark,' he said.

I went closer and saw that she was dark-skinned, Asian of some sort, but otherwise she looked so much like Isobel I couldn't believe it. Face a bit thinner, but the same dark eyes, a similar smile as she held out her hand, which I didn't take.

'He obviously thought it necessary to follow me,' Dad said. 'Well?'

But I was struck dumb again; it was too much to take in.

'Good to meet you, Mark,' she said. 'I've heard all about you.'

What had she heard? was what I wanted to know.

'Can I offer you a coffee?' she said. 'Or something cold?'

I walked off. I could sense the turmoil I'd thrown them into and I was glad of it. That I'd ruined their morning. I heard a kid's voice saying, 'Who's that, Mummy?' but I never heard the answer.

I went straight home to Mum who'd hardly noticed I'd gone. It was as if time had stood still in there, another chat show under way and her in the same position. I looked at her in bed, the bigness of her, her fat smooth hands on the duvet, and pictured the slim Isobel woman with her hair blowing in the wind. They were like creatures from two different planets. Dad came home soon after with his tail between his legs. We got Mum out to Woodbridge but a breeze had sprung up by then and we had to sit in the car to eat our chips, listening to the wind jostling the boats and rattling the rigging about and making a whining sound.

Mum heaved herself up to bed as soon as we got back and so it was just Dad and me. He was slumped in his armchair with a cup of tea. I looked down at his thinning hair and the shape of his skull underneath.

'I'm leaving first thing,' I said.

'It's not what you think,' he said.

'What do I think?'

He put his tea down and looked up at me. 'Sit down, son,' he said. I sat on the edge of the settee and waited.

'I'm fifty-nine. Not old. She showed an interest.'

'Are they your kids?' I said.

He looked amazed, then snorted and shook his head. 'I met her when I did my leg,' he said, 'my physio. She's divorced.'

'Are you leaving Mum for her?' I said.

'As if she'd have me!' he said but if he thought he was going to get me smiling he thought wrong.

'What then?'

'None of your business, son, is it?'

'It is if you get me here so you can . . .' I tailed off. 'She's the spitting image,' I said.

He picked his tea up again and took a sip. 'There's a superficial similarity, certainly. Perhaps that's why I felt well disposed towards her in the first place.'

'That's sick,' I said.

'Human kindness,' he said. 'She needed someone to talk to.'

'And what did you need someone for?'

He looked at the floor. I noticed the way his jaw had gone into pouches. An old man.

'How old is she?' I said.

'Mid thirties.'

'It might as well be incest,' I said. 'If Izzie was alive . . .'

He broke me off and his eyes bored into mine. 'If Isobel was alive everything would be different. *Everything*.'

Mum called from upstairs and he got up to go to her. Before he left the room he gave me a sort of look he'd not given me before, not father to son, more like man to man, a look with a warning in it.

*

I was in hospital for a week. When I got out, the weather was perfect and the chestnut tree wriggled its new green fingers to welcome me home. Fay had us down for a ham salad in the kitchen. Juice from the crinkled slices of pickled beetroot soaked into the ham, but I ate it, because she had made the lunch for me. She hurried us through it and while we were still eating our fruit cocktail and top-of-the-milk she went off to get herself ready for her bridge club. She came back freshly rouged and silvered and wearing a new hat. She looked like a little figure carved on a fairground organ.

When she'd gone, Charlie spread big towels out on the lawn and we sunbathed. I lay on my back, eyes shut and full of blurry sparkles. Charlie was reading a bird magazine; I could hear the flipping of the pages. After a long time, I took a breath and said what I'd been brimming up to say, ever since Dave died. 'Why don't we move?'

'Move?'

'Move house.'

'What about Mum?' he said.

'Of course she would come too,' I said. 'We could all move to the seaside or something, as a family. A fresh start.'

'She wouldn't.'

'She would if you wanted.'

He closed his magazine. 'I have seen a job,' he said.

'Yup?' I leant up on one elbow.

'Assistant bird warden,' he said.

I was surprised and then not surprised. Birds were his thing, after all.

'Where?' I said.

'Well that's the thing.' He was sitting up and I couldn't see his face but I could see the hairs on his forearms, golden in the sun.

'Where?' I said. 'Would it mean a move?'

'Orkney,' he said.

'Orkney?' My spirits rose like a happy loaf.

'But it's not a permanent job,' he said. 'Just six months or so. And it's not exactly paid – well the pay covers board. I'd be helping out in the bird observatory . . . temporary assistant warden. It would be perfect for me while I get my . . . get my bearings back.'

'Yes,' I said. 'Perfect.'

'You think so? Good.' He squeezed my hand. 'It might lead to something more permanent. I . . . I also think it would be good for us to have a break. And while I was away I'd have a rethink about my direction and then when I got back . . .'

I turned on to my front. My face was beginning to smart in the sun. The grass was dry and spiky. I watched an ant labouring up a green spear.

'You want a break?'

He swallowed. 'I thought—'

'Couldn't I come?'

'There's Mum,' he said, 'and it would be silly you giving up your job just for a few months' jaunt.'

'*Jaunt!*' I said.

'I didn't mean jaunt.'

'I wouldn't mind giving it up,' I said. I sat up and gripped his arm. 'I only do it for money.'

'I know but I don't think we should both leave Mum, not now.'

'She wouldn't like the idea of being left with me,' I said. 'She only tolerates me because of you.'

'Is that what you think?' He took my hand off his arm and examined my palm, ran his finger over the lines and the prickly imprint of the grass.

'Is it because of Dave?'

'No.'

'I've tried and tried but she doesn't like me,' I said.

'Maybe if you didn't try so hard,' he said. 'And be a bit more . . .'

'What?'

'Well she thinks you're a bit . . . not exactly an open book.' He cleared his throat. 'And you're not, are you?'

There were some children splashing and squealing in a paddling pool in another garden and the squealing bladed right through me. My vision blurred, a halo of light round everything, round Charlie's brown arm and his strong hand. I couldn't bear to look into his face, too much light there in his eyes.

He spoke in a low voice. 'Since you moved in here, I've never asked you for anything,' he said. 'I know you're vulnerable but . . .'

I didn't hear the rest. *Vulnerable?* Who said I was vulnerable? Vulnerable, the word was sandbag thudding in my skull. Light sizzled between the spikes of grass and my left eye-socket began to throb.

'Well I'm sorry about that,' I said and stood up too quickly. He scrambled up and put his arm round me. We went inside. The house seemed dark and to my left was a swarm of sparkly blotches.

'Migraine,' I said.

'You should have gone straight to bed after lunch,' he said.

He helped me up the stairs and I lay down on the bed. He drew the curtains but the light still stabbed through the gap. 'There's some pills in the bathroom cabinet,' I told him. I hadn't had a migraine for ages. The head injury must have brought it on. I lay waiting for him to come back and the word kept socking about in my head. Vulnerable? What made him think that? All right, I am not an open book, but what's so good about an open book?

I woke to feel the mattress tip as Charlie tried to sneak out of bed without waking me.

'Don't.' I reached out and caught him by the wrist.

'Want some tea?'

'Don't go,' I said and he knew what I meant. He lay down again. I buried my nose in the warm crook of his neck, breathing in the soapy animal scent of him. Pear drops and sawdust is his morning smell.

He sighed. 'Of course I won't.'

But it wasn't fair, I could feel his disappointment in my own stomach; hear it, not well enough disguised, in his voice.

I pulled myself away and looked at him. I felt small and detached, as I always do after a migraine, a husk.

'But you want to go?'

'Yes.' He sounded wistful and in the silence that followed I heard the scream of gulls. It was somewhere wild and desolate, away from everything. I saw us in a cottage perched on a cliff, white wings beating, wind rattling and, inside, a blazing fire.

'If only I could come,' I said. I knew what he would say; it would be yes. While I waited for him to say that my mind sped through my resignation, what I'd tell Rose and everyone, arrangements for Fay – she could follow us up once we were settled – even the clothes I'd have to buy. But he didn't say yes and the smell of his sweat took on a sour, anxious note.

'You don't think,' he hesitated. I could hear a click in his

92

throat as he adjusted his voice. 'You don't think it might do us good to have a little breather.'

'Breather?' I pressed my face into his skin. If it had been possible to get through it, to creep inside him, I would have done it then.

'It's been so intense. You moving in so quickly,' he said, 'and terrible with all that's happened.'

'You do think Dave's my fault, don't you?'

'I never said that.'

'Fay blames me.'

'No.'

My cheek peeled away from his skin. 'You want to break up with me?'

'Just a breathing space.'

'Do you still love me?' In the pause I noticed how grubby the sheets were. Today I would wash them. It was bright again, a good drying day. I could hear the glassy sound of a bird outside the window. I would feel strange today, hollowed out, but strange was normal in this case.

'It's nothing like that,' he said. 'I need time to take stock, that's all. After everything.'

'So everything's OK then? With us.'

'Okey-dokey.'

I breathed in, a good long breath. We kissed, hot dirty morning mouths, and made love and as I came I cried, tears mixing with the sweat. If I'd met Charlie when I was sixteen, if it had always been him, then the past would not have happened because he was faithful and true and the sex, the love, was such a way of letting go, a sparkling charge, such a soft explosion, it did sometimes make me cry.

I dozed off tangled wetly in his limbs until he moved and woke me.

'Dead leg,' he whispered, pulling it out from under mine. He stood up and hobbled about for a minute, stamping his foot,

93

then went downstairs, naked, to make tea. I wondered what he'd do if Fay came up into the kitchen, grab the tea cosy I supposed, that made me laugh but really I was laughing with relief. I lay in the damp sheets that certainly did need to be washed now, watching the dust shift and glitter in the light. I needed to get up and pee and shower but I could hardly bear to move.

In my softened-up state I saw that he was right. He had never asked me for anything. I had not thought of that before. I could see that it would do him so much good to get away, not from me, but from home, just for a while. From the situation.

He was obsessed with birds; the shelves packed with books about migratory passages, plumages, nesting habits. At weekends he often went off with his binoculars and his fellow twitchers. I never minded one bit. I liked to feel the house settle around me, peaceful and safe. I liked the gurgle of the pipes, the creak of the stairs, the feeling of the wires threaded through the walls that ran like veins.

When he came back, I hauled myself up and sat back against the pillow.

'Thank you,' I said, putting extra warmth and meaning in my voice.

He shrugged and handed me my tea. My favourite mug, the plain white one, so thin the sun shines through.

'I mean thank you for everything.'

'Nina, there's something I want to ask you about,' he said.

'I think you should go,' came out of my mouth, before I had a chance to stop it, and it swerved him away from whatever it was. I could hear interference in the air, the crackle of his disbelief. He took a sip of tea.

'You mean it?'

'I think so.'

'I have to let them know soon.'

He put his forefinger on my nose and stroked from the

bridge to the tip. 'It's healing well,' he said. 'I wish I could have seen your real nose though,' and then he paused before he said, 'The real you.'

'This is real,' I said, slapping my hand against my chest and making a sort of laughing choke.

'But . . . don't you even have a single photo?'

'They all went up in the fire. I told you.'

'How did the fire start?'

'Some sort of electrical fault. Look, Charlie, *this* is my life now. I can forget all the . . . sad mess.'

'I'd like to hear about the mess. I'm curious . . .'

'Why now all of a sudden?' I pulled the sheet up to cover me.

He narrowed his eyes. There were sharp little rocks of sleep in their corners. 'Are you serious? About me going?'

I picked up his hand, that still smelt of me, and kissed it.

'Sure?'

I nodded.

'Ta,' he said, 'that's ace.'

I went back to work on Friday. It seemed a good plan, one day at work and then the weekend to recover. The first thing I noticed was the bear on Christine's desk – and then the grin on her face.

'Lucky charm all right,' she said. 'Met a new fella and won a juicer since I got him.' She looked at my bruises. 'You should of kept him.'

'Ha ha,' I said.

'Come to the park with me, lunchtime,' she said. 'It's a lovely day.'

I looked at her. Her eyebrows were fine and pale, her lashes invisible. She blushed easily, the freckly skin filling up like a wine glass.

'That would be nice,' I said, 'only I'm having my hair done. Another time?'

'Yup,' she said and bent over her work. 'Oh by the way that guy rang again. I think it was that guy.'

'What guy?'

'Him that was going to take Charlie for a drink while you were on the course.'

My head was still cloudy with concussion. What did that mean?

'Tall, dark . . .'

'And fit. That's him.' She grinned.

'And *you* told him about the course?'

'Wasn't a secret, was it?'

I turned away and squinted at my computer screen.

'Was it?' she said.

'Sorry, Chris,' I said, 'I've got to get this done.'

'Sor*ree*,' she said and I heard the cross pattering of her keyboard.

At last it was lunchtime. I walked into town and had my hair dyed dark and shiny, cut to fit the shape of my head. I liked the light feeling as I ran my fingers through it, the cool sensation of air around my neck.

'That looks nice,' Christine said when I got back.

'Does it?'

'It suits you.' She lifted a wisp of hair to the light and examined it for split ends. 'I wish mine would suit me short but it's too thin. Mind you, Don likes it. He's my new fella.'

It got to five o'clock and I was about to divert my extension to the switchboard. I'd been watching the clock, willing it to speed round to this moment, and, just as I was ready to feel relieved, the phone rang.

'Glad you're OK,' he said. 'Thought you were a gonner there for a minute.'

'I'm fine.'

'Meet me.'

'No.'

'I'll be outside.'

'No.'

I held the receiver away from my face and looked at it. I could still hear his voice coming out of the pattern of holes: 'I'll stay here till you come out.'

I cut him off.

'You OK?' Christine said. 'Was that him?'

I closed my eyes.

'Want an Aspro?' she said. 'Shall I call you a cab? You've obviously come back too soon.'

She put her face close to mine and I could hear the rattle of a Tictac against her teeth, smell peppermint and smoke.

'I'm all right. Thanks, Chris,' I said.

'A cup of tea?' she said. 'Water then?'

I nodded and listened to the flap of her Dr Scholl's recede and return. She handed me a paper cup of chilled water from the cooler.

'Thanks,' I said. 'Why don't you go now? I'm fine.'

'I'll walk you out.'

'No, I'll just sit a minute,' I said.

She took her shoes out of her bottom drawer, high and red with ankle straps, and hesitated, half into her lacy cardigan.

'Sure?' she said. 'I'm seeing Don again tonight. Thank you, Snowy.' She picked up the bear and planted a kiss on his white head. I could see the peachy traces of previous kissings. 'Sure you're OK?'

'Fine.'

'Have a good weekend.'

'You too.'

I watched her sway away on her heels and then waited for twenty minutes. Almost everyone else had gone home. There was no flexi-time on Friday afternoons. I could hear the dim roar of vacuum cleaners on the floor below. I looked out of the window: sun on dusty roofs, a spindly rosebay willowherb

97

sprouting from a chimney. As I watched, some of its seeds were released in the breeze and floated upwards. Fairies, one of the foster mothers told me, and I'd believed her. But she was the same one who told not to lie. I can remember the conversation, remember her face, the little thread of spittle that stretched between the corners of her lips as she spoke.

'You must never lie,' she said.

'Why?'

She wrinkled her forehead. 'Well hardly ever.' And she told me that sometimes a little white lie did no harm.

'What makes it white?' I asked.

'If it's done out of kindness,' she said, 'or convenience.' She thought about this for a moment, pushing her lower lip out till the thread of spittle snapped and shrivelled back into her mouth. 'If there's no ulterior motive,' she said.

I peered out of the opening flap of the window but you couldn't see enough of the street to see who might be there.

Gary looked over on his way out. 'All right,' he said. 'Nice to see you back, Nina.'

'Thanks.'

'Can't tear yourself away?'

'I'm going.'

'Come on then . . .' I had no choice but to follow him out. He left a trail of harsh deodorant behind him. He must have had a squirt before leaving. I hoped it wasn't in aid of anything underhand. It made me sad to think of him betraying that square of happy sunshine on his desk. He paused to chat with one of the cleaners and I left him behind.

Rupert was outside, leaning against the wall, legs crossed, giving me a quirky smile. Linen suit, pale and baggy. I was startled by how good-looking he was. I kept forgetting. Brown eyes like velvet flowers. I hardened myself and began to walk. Last thing I needed was for Gary to see us. Rupert walked along beside me.

'How are you?' he said.

'OK.'

'Did you get the roses?'

I didn't answer.

'Didn't you like them?'

I kept my eyes down, watching my feet taking two steps for every one of his.

'I wanted to see for myself that you're all right,' he said.

'I'm all right. The roses were lovely. Thanks. You shouldn't have.'

'You had me scared,' he said.

We parted round a gaggle of little kids holding Pizza Hut balloons and when we came back together I said, 'Rupert, I'm with Charlie. And we're happy, whatever you might think.'

'You've got a new hairdo. It's nearly black.'

We'd passed the cemetery and reached the crossing where I'd been knocked down. I pressed the button this time, to wait for the Green Man. He tried to take my arm but I pushed his hand away.

'Are you honestly saying you don't feel any connection?' he said.

I stepped out in front of the stopped cars with a shudder of memory.

'Even if I did . . . I'm with Charlie.'

I wondered at that moment if Charlie would have pursued me like this, whether he had ever felt as strongly about me as Rupert seemed to.

'Come and have a drink.'

'No thanks.'

'A quick one.'

'No.'

'A peace offering.'

'There's no need.'

'Just a glass of wine,' he said, 'as an apology. If it wasn't for me you wouldn't have walked out under a car.'

'It was my own fault.'

'Couldn't take your eyes off me?' He laughed.

'It wasn't like that!' My mouth dragged unwillingly into a smile. 'You did freak me out though. All that rubbish about goodness.'

'Sorry,' he said. 'You can't imagine how I felt . . . I rang the ambulance, you know.'

'Did you? Thanks.'

'A large glass of cold white wine.' His words made me picture a glass, straw-coloured wine, beaded with condensation. It was exactly what I needed. It was a hot dusty afternoon, the air tired and used up. My mouth ached for the taste of cold white wine. Maybe it wouldn't hurt, I was thinking, just one quick drink and over it I could explain to him properly the impossibility of this.

'Maybe a spot of dinner?' he said. 'Ring Charlie and say you'll be late.'

But hearing Charlie's name spill so familiarly from his mouth changed my mind. Better to buy some wine and take it home. Charlie and I could laze on the grass and catch the last of the afternoon sun.

'Look,' I put my hand on Rupert's wrist, 'nothing's changed.'

'Does he know about us?' he asked.

'There isn't an "us".'

'Did you tell him? Maybe it'd be easier if I did?'

I froze. 'I'm going straight home now,' I said, my eyes skidding away from the shine of his, 'and I'm going to tell him and ask him to forgive me.'

'What are the chances of that?'

'I think he will.'

He pressed a card into my hand. 'Ring and let me know how you get on.'

I took a deep breath and turned away – but then was

overcome with a sudden surge of curiosity. 'I don't understand what it is you want.'

'*You*,' he said, as if that was obvious. 'But it'll wait.' He walked away. I looked at the card – his name, his mobile number, that's all. I watched the back of his dark head, taller than anyone else on the pavement. I made a detour to the off-licence and chose a bottle from the chiller. And then I sat on the bus, cooling my wrists on the glass and gazing out at the stale rind of the afternoon. To have someone who looks into your eyes and says '*You*' like that. That doesn't happen every day.

~

'Here we are,' Jeffrey said. Black dirt fell from between the rusty links. The chain was looped under an iron ring that was obscured by one of the sprawling bushes and fastened with a padlock, big as a man's heart. He snapped it back and open.

'No key?' she said.

'Hey presto,' he said, grinning up at her, 'watch.'

Grunting with the effort, he stuck his fingers under the edge of the wooden circle, lifted and opened a gaping slice of darkness in the ground. Grit and leaves pattered off the lid. 'This hasn't been opened for ages . . .' he muttered, 'maybe since . . .' He slid the lid halfway across the hole.

'Jeffrey?' She stepped back from the edge.

He knelt and peered down into the hole. 'When I was a kid we discovered this,' he said, 'Steve and me. It was like our secret hideout.'

'You went down there!' She knelt to look. He took a torch from his pocket. The wavery beam barely reached the bottom. The sides were slimy with a dripping, blackish weed. It was about twelve feet deep. An old, cold smell floated out and she shuddered.

'Coming down?' He flickered the torch about.

'No way,' she said.

'Come on. Chicken.'

'I'm not chicken but . . .' She shivered. 'How would you ever get out?'

'Climb. It's not hard.'

'But why?'

'Why not?'

'What is it anyway?'

'A well, I think,' he said.

'But there's no water.'

'No, I don't understand that either,' he said. 'I haven't been here for years. I thought you'd like to see . . .'

'I'm scared of the dark,' she said.

'I'll look after you. There's nothing to it, watch. You hold the torch.'

He put it into her hand, took hold of the chain and let himself down over the edge. 'You get this far and . . .' she could hear his feet scrabbling about, 'there are steps. Ah, here, a kind of ladder.'

She shone the beam down and saw a rusty ladder bolted to the wet black brick. The torch lit up the comb marks in his hair before he hit the bottom with a squelching crunch.

'All right?'

'Fine!' His face was a pale balloon floating in the darkness, the torchlight glinting on his specs. 'Come on, I'll help you.'

'No,' she said, 'honestly, Jeff, I can't.'

'Come on . . .'

'I'll mess up my clothes,' she said, looking down at her summery skirt. 'My sandals will slip.'

His tut was amplified. She shone the torch and watched him haul himself back up the ladder and grab the chain, pull his head up into the daylight. He scrambled out and stood for a moment before heaving the lid back into place, a huge black eye, winking shut.

'Come in jeans next time and proper shoes,' he said, breathlessly. He held her hand as they walked home and the smell of rust rubbed off on her, setting her teeth on edge, making her queasy, uneasy, reminding her of blood.

∧

Dad and I said nothing more than 'More tea?' or 'Pass the butter' over breakfast, then it was time for goodbyes. I leant over Mum in bed and kissed her cheek, smelt the staleness of her pillows, grease from her hair.

'Don't be a stranger,' she said and flicked me a look that went right through me. 'And none of your nonsense now.'

'I'll take care of everything,' I said and her mouth opened in a question but I was out of there.

As I went through the front door, Dad handed me an envelope. 'Have a read of that, son,' he said, 'and a bit of a think, will you?' I put it in my pocket and got in the car. He stood on the doorstep to wave me off but he went back inside before I'd even gone round the corner.

I drove not straight back to Sheffield but the way I'd followed Dad the day before. I drove by her house and stopped the car under the same stand of trees. Before I got out I looked to see what Dad had given me. It was an old cutting from a magazine and the first thing that caught my eye was a photo of Isobel, not one I'd seen before, it was Isobel with the boyfriend and the caption said, *'Steven Spencer and Isobel Curtis pictured shortly before the tragedy.'* There was a larger picture of the Spencers standing in front of a mantelpiece full of trophies. The caption said, *Mr and Mrs Spencer pictured with a collection of Steven's cricket cups.*

There was a throbbing in my head as I read the article, which was about how the Spencers had forgiven Karen Wild and had channelled their grief into setting up a charity to counsel the families of murdered children. I looked at the date on the top of the page. About five years after the event. *Forgiven*. Forgive and forget is how it goes but how can I forget? And the idea of *forgiving*! To think of Karen free in the world, all educated up at the taxpayer's expense, some of Dad's earnings will have gone into that, and some of what I've paid in tax, and the Spencers channelling their grief – well it was plain they'd gone off their heads and you couldn't blame them for that but if Dad's thoughts were going along the same lines . . . I screwed up the cutting and threw it out of the window, then I got out and ground it into the grit with my shoe. *Forgiven!*

I went and knocked on Jessica's door. She opened it, surprise written all over her face. She was pulling a dressing gown together over her chest, silky white material. 'I thought you were going to be your dad for a moment there,' she said. 'Do come in.'

We walked through a room full of toys, the smell of sweet cereal. Two kiddies were on the settee in their pyjamas, thumbs in their mouths, goggling at the box.

'Excuse the mess,' she said, 'bit of a late start this morning.'

I said nothing. I wasn't here to put her at her ease. She turned the volume down and the children moaned and squirmed and then settled back. You could see the cartoon colours flickering in their eyes. 'Shouldn't let them really,' she said, 'but it keeps them quiet. What did mums do before TV, eh?'

Her accent was local. As she spoke some of the Isobelness fell away but when she turned, I could see it in her profile, the way her hair fell forward as she stooped to pick up the plastic cereal bowls.

'What can I do for you, Mark?' she said.

'I want a word,' I said.

'Sure.' She went through into the kitchen and I followed. She switched on the kettle. 'I'm having a cuppa, you?'

She put the bowls in the sink and ran a tap over them. It was a tiny kitchen but immaculate. A clean J-cloth hung over the sink, rubber gloves on a special hand-shaped stand by the window.

She turned and waited for the kettle to boil but nothing came to me to say. 'Well, I reckon I know why you're here,' she said in the end. She waved a mug at me but I shook my head. She went ahead and made herself a cup, teabag straight in a Tellytubby mug.

'Go on then,' I said.

'I know all about what happened.' She looked me in the eye. There was a strand of hair caught in the corner of her mouth and the way she pulled it out made my heart turn over because that was something Isobel did and I'd forgotten. It makes you wonder how many of the little things you do forget, the gestures and inflections, the funny little ways.

My heart was going like a drum. 'What do you mean?' I said.

'Your sister . . . your dad's poured his heart out to me. I know you're . . .' she stopped.

'What?'

She coloured up a bit then, even with her dark skin. 'Er . . . troubled.'

'Troubled.' I said it quietly. So he had been confiding in her, this stranger, this impostor, raking over our private family business with her.

'Sure you don't want a cuppa?'

It was too much for me. I shouldn't have been there. I couldn't be Mark and stand for this, I didn't know who the hell I was, I reached for Rupert and tried the smile but I'd started off on the wrong foot and it was too late. I should not have done this, should not have come.

'He's a wonderful man, your father,' she said and I could hear it as a line from a play, or a soap, it all started to seem like that, as if everything you could possibly come up with was some stale old line that had already been trotted out to kingdom come. One of the kids came in then and she bent to talk to him and there was the flick of the hair again, the dark crease where the silk fell apart and you could see the start of her breasts. She sent him off with a couple of chocolate biscuits, closed the door and then faced up to me.

'Have you come to warn me off then?' she said and then she laughed and it was Isobel's laugh. I hadn't forgotten that. It was so much like her laugh, the giggly sound, the way she lifted her chin and looked into your eye, that he couldn't possibly have missed it. She used to laugh at me like that, tease me, till it drove me mad.

Sick, it was all sick, if he had to screw around why couldn't he have picked someone his own age, or someone different? The more I looked at this one the more I saw Isobel, or the more she mutated into Isobel, blurred my memory, and that was even worse.

I looked away from her at the magnets on the fridge. 'You Have to Kiss a Lot of Frogs Before you Find a Prince!' one said. Was Dad supposed to be the prince?

'He must be nearly thirty years older than you,' I said.

'I can do the maths,' she said, tightening up the dressing gown.

'What about my mum then?' I said, thinking I'd appeal to her better nature.

She raised her chin. 'What about her?' And then she sighed. 'He said you'd be upset.'

'Upset?'

'I'm sorry about your mum but that's his problem, isn't it? His business, I mean. He's an adult. He . . . I mean I wouldn't have dreamt of chasing after him. I'm not a home wrecker.

Anyway, we hardly see each other, don't get much of a chance. It's more a friendship.'

'If he leaves Mum . . .'

'Whoa,' she said, 'hold your horses.'

'But if he does.'

'You're afraid you'd be dumped on, is that it?'

Her neck was slender, her hair was long. Something smug about her in that way of pretty girls, like they think they've got one over on you just by existing. It brought back a feeling I'd had from Isobel when she was always right, her big-sister smugness and goody-goodyness and the frustration that would boil up in me though never any comeback because she was older and always right. It's possible that maybe once or twice I wished her dead but only in the middle of the frustration.

What happened next wasn't in my plan and I can't quite remember straight. I think I only wanted a feel of her hair, which was so much like Isobel's, but she moved and my hand somehow got her tit, I felt the slide of it against the silk and the gown fell open as she jerked away and there was her dark bush on display. She seemed to be coming on to me then – her eyes close up and wide open, huge, so dark, darker than Isobel's and with more of a slant to them and this sweet smell to her – but when I touched her she froze up and said in this gritted voice to back off or she'd call the police.

What was she doing inviting me in when she was hardly dressed? I backed off like she said and she wrapped the dressing gown round her tight and huddled back against the sink. The kids didn't even look up from the box when I went. The screwed-up article was still there in the dirt and I thought of the picture of Isobel which I should have given more respect and put it in my pocket, then I sat in the car to get my head straight before I drove away.

*

On Sunday, as usual, Fay came to supper. Though she'd painted her face and sprayed her thin hair rigid, she looked pinched and rickety. She and Charlie hugged and the tears stood in their eyes, but did not fall. When Fay sat in the armchair waiting for the meal, her little feet did not quite touch the floor.

She lifted and lowered her metallic shutters. 'You've got a new style,' she said.

'Yes,' I said. 'Sherry?'

'You should try it long,' Fay said. 'Remember Nicky's hair, Charlie? Like a cornfield.'

He grimaced at me. I went through into the kitchen to fetch the drinks. Harvey's Bristol Cream for Fay, vodka and tonic for us, and a bowl of cashew nuts. I stood listening to the rain against the window and the faint crackle of roasting potatoes. Condensation ran down the windows. It was cosy. Charlie hadn't mentioned the bird-warden job all weekend. I thought it was forgotten.

I carried the tray of drinks through. Charlie was poring over something. 'Dave's friend Barry came to see me this morning,' Fay explained. 'He found Dave's wallet in his flat.'

'What was it doing there?' I said, handing her the gold-rimmed sherry glass we kept especially for her.

'He was always losing things,' Charlie said. He was empty-ing the wallet and lining the contents up on the coffee table. It was just what you'd expect: bankcard; bus ticket; a tenner; a packet of Rizlas with phone numbers scribbled on the flap; a voucher for a free pizza. He lay each item down with a special kind of reverence as if they were about to add up to some new meaning.

'Gave him quite a turn, he told me, finding it,' Fay said. 'It had got into an old *Radio Times*. He thought we might want it.'

I handed Charlie his drink. 'Cheers.' I chinked my glass against his and Fay's.

'Nuts?' I offered Fay the bowl.

'Not with my teeth.'

'Anything else?'

She gave a tight little shake of her head.

I crunched a cashew nut. 'I love rainfall,' I said.

Charlie gave me an odd look. I don't know what was wrong with that.

'On the windows, I mean, the smell and the sound of it and everything.'

Fay picked up the wallet and held it to her cheek. There was a long silence.

'Let's eat,' I said. I had set the table carefully with a white rose from the garden in a narrow vase and one thick green candle I'd found in the cupboard, which I lit as we sat down.

Fay examined each forkful of roast chicken and sighed. Charlie kept looking at me nervously.

'What?' I said, in the end.

'Nothing. This is great, thanks.' But it was an effort for him to eat. I shouldn't have bothered. I'd thought a roast would be good on a rainy day. I'd thought we'd draw together as families do, comforted by each other and the food. But the chicken was comforting no one, congealing greasily on the plates. And there was a horrible oily whiff, faint at first but getting stronger.

'What's that smell?' I said.

'The candle,' Charlie said. 'It's meant for outdoors – to keep bugs away.'

'You could have said!' I blew it out but the snuffed odour was even worse. We sat in silence. I wished I'd thought of music to help the mood. It was too late now.

'Finished?' I asked Fay and she put her knife and fork together gratefully. There seemed to be more on her plate than when she'd started.

I fetched the thawed-out cheesecake from the fridge and put it on the table. The squashed rosettes of cream were tinged pink from the scarlet of the berries and colour had also run into the cheesy middle.

Fay tilted her little nose and sniffed. 'I, for one, am quite replete,' she said.

'Maybe some fruit, or cheese . . .'

'Nina. She's had enough,' Charlie said.

I forced a smile and hefted a slice of the soggy cheesecake on to Charlie's plate and on to mine. I took a mouthful. It was heavy, damp and over-sweet, the berries still frozen in their centres.

Charlie cleared his throat. 'Mum,' he said, 'I'm thinking of going away for a bit.'

I swallowed and put down my fork.

'Where?' Fay said.

'Orkney.'

'Orkney!' she said, as if it was the moon.

'Just for a few months. Relief bird warden. Nina and I've discussed it.'

Fay darted me a look and I nodded.

He said, 'It's just what I need in my . . . career break.'

'So it's all decided?'

'No,' I said, 'I mean, no . . . nothing's definite.'

She looked from Charlie to me and picked up her glass. She had lasted her sherry right through supper and now she finished it.

'More?' I said and was amazed when she said yes.

'So you and Nina can look after each other.' Charlie began with an attempt at bravado that fell away before he'd finished.

'*If* you go,' I said.

Fay and I glanced at each other and quickly away.

I took Fay's glass and went to pour her sherry.

'It wouldn't be so bad, would it?' I said, handing her the glass. 'Girls together.'

I tried to read her eyes but they were just old eyes, the blue running into the white in a way that reminded me of the cheesecake. But when it was time for her to go downstairs, something happened to give me hope. I bent down to give her my usual hug and instead of a stiff armful of twigs I felt something give, a slight return of pressure.

On Monday there was no call from Rupert. When I left work he was not there. Rain plaited itself in the gutters and I was grateful to hide under my umbrella, though I felt a thread of disappointment. I'd imagined how it would have been if I'd told Charlie. My story was ready and rehearsed: a night of tears, a long walk pouring out our hearts. On impulse, I'd say, we'd booked into a country hotel with a roaring log fire and made love in a four-poster before dinner with champagne, no not champagne . . . red wine . . . and roast beef maybe, a lavish pudding trolley . . . It was almost a shame not to be able to tell him all of that.

By Friday, I'd stopped jumping whenever the phone rang. The sun came out again and steamed the rain away. I was enjoying the daily updates on the progress of Christine's romance.

'Don's a right laugh,' she said, 'and that's more important than looks, don't you think? We've been out eight times now if you count the first time. You could count that as steady, couldn't you? We went to that new Thai place last night, been?'

I shook my head.

'You should, it's brilliant, if you like it hot.'

'Yes, maybe we will,' I said.

Christine and I left work together. She was telling me what she was planning to wear when she met Don's parents for the first time on Sunday. We stepped out into the gluey afternoon heat, smiling, and then I saw the tall figure leaning against the wall.

'There's that guy,' she said.

'I'm going this way,' I said. I walked fast to the corner and when I turned back to look, I saw that they were talking. My instinct was to bolt but then they saw me, and he came towards me.

'What did you say to her?' I said.

'This and that,' he said. 'You shot off in a very suspicious manner. You'll have people talking.'

He smiled and the beginnings of lines crinkled round his eyes. He was wearing linen trousers and a black T-shirt; the pale jacket slung over one shoulder.

'Well?' I said.

Christine walked past. 'Fancy a coffee?'

'Got to get home,' I said. 'Good luck on Sunday.'

'Sure?' Her pale eyes quizzed mine. 'OK then. Ta.' She smiled uncertainly and wobbled away on her heels.

'Come and have a drink,' Rupert said.

'There's no point in this,' I said. 'I did tell Charlie.'

'Oh yes?'

I opened my mouth but my story, the roaring fire, the trolley of desserts, seemed ridiculous in the hot street. All I could smell was exhaust.

'Come on.' He got hold of my arm and steered me round the corner. We went into the Tavern, a dark, smoky place full of flashing, squealing games machines and a gigantic screen showing cricket. A girl eyed him up as we went in and gave me a dirty look. I felt a despicable flicker of pride.

He ordered a couple of beers and we sat down. I watched the lights of a machine, the numbers 54321 spiralling downwards again and again.

'Where do you live?' I said. 'I mean, doesn't your wife wonder where you are?'

'She's not bothered. I've moved here.'

'What?'

'To be near you.'

I tried to stand but he drew me back down.

'That's mad, Rupert.'

'I told her about you.'

'No.'

'I've left her.'

'No!' My voice came out loud enough for the barman to look up, eyebrows raised till I nodded my head at him.

'Do you think I should have lied?' Rupert said.

'I don't know.' I tasted the beer but the thin yeasty edge of it puckered my mouth. 'I hope you haven't really done anything so drastic because of me,' I said. 'Charlie was upset but he's forgiven me. We're not splitting up. I can't see you again. This is it. Finito.' I sliced my hand through the air.

He licked a trace of beer-froth from his lips and looked into my eyes. I could see slivers of moving light in his, red, white, yellow, green and small reflections of myself. It's the pigmentation in dark eyes, you rarely see yourself like that in blue. I sat back and away from him.

'Test your nerve,' said a computerised voice and there was a volley of machine-gunfire. It made me laugh.

'That's it,' he said, 'lighten up.'

'You didn't really leave her for me?' I said.

'Among other reasons.'

'I'm glad there are other reasons because I'm not one.'

He swilled the beer round in his glass and took another sip.

'You'll meet someone else,' I said, gentling my voice. 'You're so gorgeous.'

'You think so?'

'You know that.'

He held my gaze for a minute and I had to tear my eyes away. 'Why *me*? Look at that girl over there . . . look at that woman . . .'

'Don't put yourself down,' he said. 'I like the hair, actually. A bit Audrey Hepburn.'

I puffed out a laugh. What rubbish! I picked up a beer-mat and rotated it in my hands. He took it from me and kept hold of my hand. You can have chemistry with someone even if you don't like them. I could feel the chemicals fizzing in my blood.

'Have you really told him?' he asked and the question caught me all wrong. I said yes, but he knew I was lying even though I looked him straight in the eye. 'Yes,' I said again. 'And promised never to see you again.'

'You've already broken that promise.'

'That's your fault.'

'I know someone he knows,' he said. 'It'd be child's play for me to find out.'

All the fizziness drained away and I withdrew my hand. 'Who?' I said.

'John.'

I didn't know a John – or was there someone at work he used to mention? It was such a common name, everyone knows a John, and if I were bluffing I would have said John too.

'John what?'

'Smith,' he said.

'Come *on*.' Someone won the jackpot on a fruit machine and shouted *Yes!* and there was the steady chunter of pumping coins.

'It is a common name,' he said, 'because there are a lot of them. I have a drink with him now and then. And so does Charlie, as you'll know.'

'Of course,' I said.

'*Of course*,' he mimicked and there was a change in the way he looked at me, a hardening edge to his smile. 'You need to brush up on your lying, Nina Todd.' He stood up. 'I'll ask John to talk to Charlie about it,' he said. 'Be seeing you.' He strode out of the pub. I watched the door swing open and shut again. I waited a moment, pushed the horrible beer away, went out and hailed a passing cab. I would go straight home and confess. It was only a stupid little fling. He'd surely forgive me that.

But when I got home, the car wasn't in the drive. The kitchen had the air of a room rushed out of: a half-eaten slice of cheese on toast; a book open; the bird-warden's letter on the table beside the phone. I took a bite of the rubbery toasted cheese. My stomach was a knot of snakes. I chucked the rest in the bin. And then I saw a note scrawled on the top of the RSPB letter.

Ring me on mob. Urgent. Cxxxx

My teeth were greasy from the cheese. I sat down. Maybe John Smith had already rung him . . . but that was stupid. There was no John Smith. I made a cup of strong coffee and braced myself – but when I rang his phone was switched off. Why ask me to phone and then switch it off? The coffee buzzed through me and I couldn't sit still. There were crumbs on the table and flecks of grated cheese. I got a cloth and wiped it, sprayed it, wiped it; decided to clean the kitchen window and then the phone rang and it was Charlie.

'Mum's had a fall. We're in Casualty.' He rang off. A fall, I thought, that doesn't sound too bad. She'd tripped over a kerb; or slipped in the kitchen. She'd be all right. I was more worried for Charlie.

We met at the entrance to the ward and I put my arms round him. 'She's broken her hip,' he said into my hair. 'She's badly shocked, I've never seen her so . . . small.'

'Poor Fay,' I said. 'Poor you.'

'She's sedated. She's got to have an operation to pin it.'

I hugged him tighter. Past his shoulder I saw a sign with a mobile phone crossed out. SWITCH OFF it said. They could have added PLEASE, I thought. You should be gentle with people in shock.

We went in to take a peep at Fay. She did look tinier than ever and older too; her unpainted eyelids stretched yellow in their cavernous sockets; her little coconut head balanced on a fat white pillow. Charlie took one of her hands and raised it to his lips.

'It's OK, Mum,' he said and her eyes opened, liquid slits of blue, and looked straight at me.

'Hello, Fay,' I said. She closed her eyes again. 'Whatever happened?' I asked.

'Stairs,' Charlie said. 'I heard the crash.'

'Good job you were there,' I said. 'What a shock though.'

We sat hand in hand for an hour or so while Fay slept. I stroked her thin puff of hair and felt the warmth of her skull, the strong beat of her life. The food trolley came round.

'She can't eat, she's sedated,' Charlie said, but the woman shrugged and dumped a tray down anyway. On the tray were a defeated salad and a dish of tinned peaches. I went to the window and looked down at roofs and the tops of cars queuing at the lights. Charlie came and gazed out with me. 'Funny,' he said, 'all those people out there going about their lives. Makes you realise, doesn't it?' He turned to me. 'You look shattered. Let's go home.'

'You stay,' I said. 'What if she wakes and wants you?'

'I need to collect her nightie and things.'

'I'll bring those,' I said.

'Sure?'

'Of course!'

He walked me to the lift and we stood together waiting. 'Well, that decides that,' he said.

'What?'

'Orkney. Would you ring and explain?'

'Wait and see how she is,' I said. 'We don't have to let them know tonight, do we?'

'I couldn't leave her now,' he said. 'She'll need me – and the car.'

'I can look after her.'

'But you don't drive.'

'Why don't you see about the relatives' room?' I said. 'I'll bring your stuff in later. And we'll worry about the job tomorrow.' I hugged him. 'You need a clean T-shirt,' I said, sniffing. 'It'll be all right. Don't worry. She's not going to give up that easily!'

The lift pinged open and I stepped in.

'Still, you could ring them.'

'I'll bring your stuff,' I said as the lift doors closed.

But he would have to go to Orkney. Once he was out of the way I could get things sorted out with Rupert and be free just to be with Charlie again, to get back to where we were before I ever set eyes on Rupert.

I wandered about the house: strange to be entirely alone in it, not even Fay downstairs. I'd always been aware of her creaking around down there. I'd hear the faint sound of her TV, the cheep of her budgie, or a gurgle in the pipes when she turned on her hot tap.

I packed a bag for Charlie – T-shirt, wash-stuff and *Migratory Patterns in Common European Species* – and then

I went down to Fay's. The budgie flew at me and I ducked, hands over my hair. He perched on the table till I straightened up and then fluttered up and landed on my shoulder. I had to force my arms to stay by my sides and not to bat him away. I walked slowly over to the cage. 'Good boy, Charlie Two,' I said through gritted teeth. She'd taken him over when a friend had died and he'd already been called Charlie. She had added the Two to avoid confusion, she said, though I don't know what kind of confusion there could have been.

I waited and eventually he went into his cage. I shut the door quick, and he shrieked and clung to the sides with his beak and claws. He was blue with black and white stripes on his head and little flashes of purple on his cheeks, pretty when he kept still. Fay had taught him to speak a few words and he hopped back on to his perch, puffed up his feathers and demonstrated in good imitation of Fay: 'Davy-boy,' he said. I thought it must have been torture for her when he said that. Or maybe it was a comfort.

I found a nightie for Fay, a bar of soap, a pair of slippers – though she wouldn't be doing much walking. The slippers were red brocade, doll-sized, moulded into bony angles by her toes. I sat at her dressing table, looked at myself in the three mirrors. The darkness of my hair made my face seem pale as milk. Before I put them in her wash bag, I picked up her silver eye shadow and did my own lids like hers and smoothed pink circles on my cheeks. Her perfume was in an atomiser with a silky tasselled bulb. I squirted some on my wrists and neck.

I picked up the book – something by Colin Dexter – that lay beside her bed. She was using a photograph as a bookmark: Charlie and Dave in their Boy Scouts uniforms, hair parted beside their ears. I stared at the two small shining faces. Our phone rang upstairs and made me jump. I hadn't realised how loud it sounded down here. She must hear it every time and hear our feet walking across to answer it, hear our muffled voices through the ceiling.

Before I returned to the hospital I heated up a bowl of soup and ate it watching the red light winking on the answerphone. I washed up my pan and bowl and spoon before I listened: there were three messages from Bruno James, the bird warden from North Ronaldsay, who sounded not Scottish, as I'd imagined, but posh English. He needed to know Charlie's decision this evening and if he heard nothing would assume it was no go. He said he'd be sorry not to meet him and continue their discussion about redpolls.

I phoned him back. Knowing that the call was travelling right out to the Northern Isles, I expected a faint and crackly line but I was answered by the loud clear voice of a child. 'What?' it said.

'Can I speak to Bruno James please?'

'Da-ad,' the child shouted into the receiver.

'I'm ringing on behalf of Charlie Martin,' I said, when Bruno had come on. 'I'm his girlfriend.'

'I'd almost given up on him,' Bruno said.

'He asked me to ring you back; he's tied up at the moment. He asked me to say yes.'

'Yes?'

'He'll come.'

'Oh.' There was a pause. 'Hold on,' he said.

I could hear a conversation taking place through the muffling of his palm.

'Well that's great,' he said, 'Charlie does sound like our man. How soon could he get up here, do you think?'

'Pretty soon.'

'By mid-week?'

'*That* soon?'

'We've been left in the lurch.'

'I'll get him to ring you tomorrow,' I said.

I found Charlie in the waiting room. He'd picked up a wildlife magazine and was reading about mallards. He looked startled to see me. 'You're all made up,' he said. My hand flew to my face. I'd forgotten all about it. I went straight into the toilet. I looked like a Dutch doll with the red circles on my cheeks. In the dim light of Fay's bedroom it hadn't looked like that. It must be why Fay always looked so gaudy. I'd have to find a subtle way of telling her when she came out. I scrubbed off all the pink and silver with a rough green paper towel.

I didn't tell Charlie about his job that evening. He had enough to worry him. I was tired and went home for an early night. Even without him, I slept soundly. I'm good at sleeping, whatever's happening, however bad; I can usually get to sleep. I have learnt to sleep through almost anything.

∧

Don't remember much of the drive till I was turning off the A1. I stopped in a Little Chef for a cuppa and a full English breakfast. They do bottomless coffee and I was on my third before I felt I could face straightening out the screwed-up paper and looking at Isobel again. She was wearing a beret, which I'd forgotten she sometimes did, in a way that made her seem French. She was staring straight at the camera and it was like she was looking at me with a plea like don't listen to this forgiveness bollocks and of course I wouldn't.

Soon as I got back to my digs I showered off and changed. When I switched on my mobile it rang straight away. No surprise that it was Dad.

'Come back here now,' he said. 'I've stalled her from calling the police but—' and he went on and on.

'She came on to me,' I said when I could get a word in. I could hear the way he was breathing, laboured I think you'd call it, coming to terms with what I'd said.

'Don't give me that,' he said. 'If you weren't my son . . . You're damned lucky she didn't call the police. Now get back here or I will.'

'She came on to me,' I said again.

'What were you doing there?'

There was such a silence I thought he'd gone, then he sighed like he had the weight of the world on his shoulders. 'Why don't you find a nice girl of your own, Mark?' he said. 'Settle down and forget this nonsense.'

'I have,' I said and that took him aback.

'What? You never said.'

'You never asked.'

'What's her name?'

'Nina.'

It was like another script unfolding in front of me, the words waiting in the wings. The more I go on the more I realise how it's all planned out, words and all. We really don't have a choice. That's a dangerous way to think because it leads to the conclusion that Karen didn't have a choice in what she did, but if that is so then nor do I.

'Come home, son,' Dad said, 'you need the stability.'

'Soon,' I said.

'Stay away from girls, Mark. Promise me.'

'Promise me *you* will,' I went.

The sigh again. 'You frightened the life out of Jessica. If she so much as sees your face again . . . You're lucky she called me first and not the police.'

'If she does I'll tell Mum,' I said and cut him off. I pictured Mum in her chair, her little world of TV and magazines, Dad waiting on her hand and foot. I didn't mean it, I wouldn't upset her for anything, and the way I had it planned out, she'd never need to know.

Five-thirty on the nail Karen and the blonde came out of Green's. She was looking bright and breezy till she saw me – then she bolted off so fast it was nearly comical. I thought she should take to wearing trainers if she was going to keep on like that. The blonde stood there giving me a funny look.

'Hello,' she said. 'Did you get to see Charlie?'

'We had a pint. What's up with *her*?' I said.

'She was OK till she clapped eyes on you,' she said.

'She's a bit on the nervy side, isn't she?' I said. 'I'd better catch her up.'

I took her into the nearest pub. She'd had her hair cut like a boy's and darker than ever and though it's not a look I could go for I could see it suited her – what you might term chic. She was hot in her suit, wriggling about, jigging her foot as per usual, gnawing at her thumbnail.

I ditched the wife, a complication too far. 'Not because of me,' she said, all flushed, pretending that she wasn't flattered. And then she said, looking up through her eyelashes, that I was gorgeous. That's the word she uttered, straight out, gorgeous and then started fishing for a compliment in return. It was sickeningly easy to turn her head.

'Told Charlie?' I asked, then went out on a limb, saying I had ways of knowing things and she should watch her back. Like, despite her lies, I knew she hadn't said a word to Charlie.

'How could *you* possibly know that?' She sounded just like Isobel at her most superior.

'John Smith,' I said, catching sight of the name on the beer-mat she was fiddling with. It was hard to keep a straight face at that point. 'Friend of Charlie's,' I explained, 'though of course you'd know that.'

'Oh yes,' Karen said. You can see right through her. You'd think she'd be a better liar what with her pedigree. Charlie must be, well, a right Charlie to be taken in by her.

I was tired out what with the day I'd had and all the driving. My phone vibrated in my pocket. Of course it would be Dad. I switched it off. It made me sick thinking about Jessica and sick looking at Karen who despite what she said was soaking up the attention like a sponge. I was sick and tired of women, sick and tired of their wiles and ways. I got up and walked out and, to tell the truth, at that moment I'd have been happy to give up on the whole sick business.

*

We went in to see Fay before the operation. She was deeply sedated, with a drip threaded into the thin mottled skin on the back of her hand. Under the skin blood had leaked and flattened out into an oval bruise. Her face had caved in because she didn't have her dentures. I'd never seen her without them; she had that kind of pride in herself. She wouldn't want me to see her like that, I knew her that well.

We went and stood by the coffee machine beside the lifts. I pushed 20p's in to get Charlie a coffee, but the stuff that came out was tainted with soup and undrinkable. He hadn't slept all night he said and I believed him; the smell of hospital had soaked into his hair and clothes.

'I had a call last night,' I said. 'It was Bruno.'

'You told him?'

'I said you'd take the job.'

'Are you off your trolley?' he said. 'I *can't* leave Mum now.'

I tried to hold his hand, but he pulled his away. In the waiting area there were two long sofas and a pile of magazines on a table. We could have sat down but there was a young Indian man on one of the sofas and he was crying. He had his elbows on his knees and his face in his hands and each sob was a soft jab in the ribs.

'Why don't we go out?' I said. 'Get some fresh air, or breakfast or something.'

'I'm waiting to hear,' he said.

'Think about it,' I said. 'Fay'll be fine in a few weeks and you'll have given up this chance for nothing.'

'There'll be other chances.'

'There might not.' I traced the shape of his heart on his white T-shirt. I could feel the texture of the hairs on his chest through the cotton.

'Don't.' He pushed my hand away. 'Sorry, that tickles.'

The man blew his nose loudly and then groaned as if his heart was breaking.

'It'll give me and Fay a chance to bond,' I said. 'Isn't that what you want?'

'That was before.'

'Before what?'

He didn't answer.

'She'd want you to go.' We looked away from each other with a slight wince. 'I think you should take *this* chance.'

'Anyone would think you were trying to get rid of me!' he said.

'That's not fair!'

'Joke,' he said, flatly.

A sort of laugh hacked out of me. 'You could always come back,' I said, 'if anything did go wrong. It's not as if you'd be leaving the planet.'

'No.' He rubbed his hand against his stubbly chin. It made an almost inaudible scrunching sound.

'She'll be fine,' I said, 'I can feel it in my bones.' Then I pictured Fay's thin shattered bones. 'I mean I just have this feeling she'll be right as rain.'

'I don't know,' he said.

I could see how torn he was. He wanted to go; of course he really wanted to go and for me to make it all right for him to go.

'You'll be letting them down if you pull out now,' I said. 'And you could fly back in a few hours if necessary.'

There was one rogue hair in his left eyebrow, white and thick as fuse wire. Sometimes he let me pluck it out but not lately. It curled down over his eye. I thought it must have driven him mad but he didn't seem to notice.

'I'm going to the bog,' he said. 'You wait here in case . . .'

'Of course.'

I went and sat down on the sofa opposite the man. He'd stopped crying and sat looking dazed, his hands dangling between his knees. I gave him a sympathetic smile but he didn't notice. I picked up a magazine and flicked through. It had the soft weary texture of waiting-room magazines, saturated with boredom and stress. I read how good tomatoes are for you, especially cooked. A woman in a sari with a long white plait over her shoulder came and sat beside the man and took his hand. That set him off again.

When Charlie came back his face was damp and there was a little fleck of paper towel caught in his bristles. I picked it off.

The lift opened and a bride stepped out in a wide cream puff of a dress. She carried a bouquet and was followed by a small woman clutching a can of hairspray.

'Granny wants a glimpse of the big day,' she explained, squirting it at the bride's head as she swanned off towards the ward.

'That's nice,' I said, watching the dress crush as the bride passed through the swing doors. The man and woman stared after them and blinked. We were all left in a reeking cloud of lacquer.

Charlie and I went over to the window and gazed out at the city. The day was overcast, the sky a strange pinky-buff like a pigeon's breast and the street-lamps, still on for some reason, prickled orange amongst the trees and buildings.

'I wish you'd let me make my own decisions,' he said.

127

'But you would have made the wrong one.'

He gave me a look.

'I'm sorry,' I said, 'but I couldn't ring you, could I? And it had to be yes or no then and there. I thought it would be for the best.'

He swallowed and buried his face in his hands for a moment, then looked up. 'Assuming Mum gets through the op OK, I might go.'

I spooled out my breath, slow and steady, and wiped my hand on my skirt.

I went with him to find a nurse. She phoned down to the theatre. 'It went fine,' she said, 'like clockwork. She's in recovery now, why not come back and see her this afternoon?'

'You see,' I said. 'Told you she'd be all right.' In the lift going down we hugged and this time his arms tightened around me too. 'I guess that means you're going?' I said.

'Maybe.'

'I'll miss you.'

The lift stopped, the door opened and a whey-faced woman wheeled her own drip inside and leant against the wall, clutching a pack of fags and a lighter to her chest. I pressed the button and we went on down.

'And it'll do you good,' I said as we stepped out at ground level and made our way through the cluster of flower-clutching visitors.

'Yeah.' He gave me a slidy look.

'What?'

He shook his head. 'I'm shagged out, that's all.' Too tired to lift, his lips tilted down at the corners. Under his eyes the scoops of shadow were almost black.

When we got home I said that he should catch up on some sleep but the first thing he did was to ring Bruno and confirm. Hearing the suppressed excitement in his voice was hard. It was hard seeing him empty his drawers, seeing all the jumpers and jeans flung on the bed.

'You don't have to pack yet,' I said, but he was too jittery to rest.

While he was packing, I stayed near the phone so that I could answer first just in case there was something bad but there was nothing. No call at all. I hovered about listening to him booking his flight: Manchester to Kirkwall via Aberdeen; Kirkwall to North Ronaldsay. I opened our atlas and looked at the north where Scotland dissolves into rags, the merest snippet of which was his destination.

On the evening before he left, I cooked mushroom risotto and opened a bottle of Chablis, though he would only have one glass. While I washed up he made calls: to Bruno, I know, finalising arrangements; and he talked to someone else, I didn't know the name but it was not John Smith.

'Come to bed,' I said, though it was only about eight-thirty when he'd finished on the phone.

'No.' He bit the corner of his thumbnail. 'I know it's my last night and all but I don't feel like . . . you know. I don't feel like getting all stirred up.'

'Stirred up?' I looked at him. 'Well OK.'

'Sure?' He held me and I rubbed my face on the shoulder of his jumper, a scratchy green thing that made me itch. 'Ta. I ought to go and see Mum again.' He felt light and twitchy in my arms as if he was already on his way.

'We could stop at the garage for chocolates,' I said.

'Nina, she doesn't eat chocolate,' he said and I knew that, of course I did, it was just that I was nervous. 'I'll go on my own,' he said, 'if you don't mind.'

I made a stupid swallowing sound as if an egg was stuck in my gullet.

'I'd just like a bit of time alone with her,' he said, 'but come along for the ride if you want.'

'We could go for a drink on the way back,' I said.

'I'm setting the clock for five-thirty,' he said. 'I need a clear head.'

He held me at arm's length for a moment and studied my face, which I kept a smile on though it nearly killed me. Then we hugged and the moment stretched. I could hear the clock ticking and then Charlie was swallowing and swallowing as if he had something to say. The budgie was cheeping downstairs. Charlie spoke into my hair. 'Anything you want to tell me?' he said.

I started to pull away from him and then pushed my face back into his shoulder. My heart scrabbled up my ribs as if it was trying to get out. I arched back so that he would not feel it. We held still, as if frozen.

'I love you,' I said at last, 'is that it?'

'No,' he said, 'that isn't it.'

'We haven't been saying that much lately, have we?'

'No.'

'Is it still true?'

'*Nina.*' He said it in that exasperated way that means, yes, of *course.*

I went to the window and stared at the hard glass but saw nothing beyond it. I took a deep breath. 'What *did* you mean then?'

He didn't answer. I went to him and held the top of his arms. I could feel the muscles of his biceps through the woolliness. 'What?' I said. I was ready then, I could have handled it then. I would have simply said it was all a lie, that Rupert was a troublemaker, a stalker, a lunatic, anything.

He stared at me, his eyes the same blue as Fay's, so liquid they seemed about to spill.

'Nothing,' he said, and turned away. And the moment went off the boil, like milk snatched from the heat.

The tap was dripping. I turned it off and noticed how smeary it was. I scrubbed at it with a J-cloth until it shone.

I heard Charlie take his car-keys off the key-rack in the hall. Just a small silver chink of a sound but it was the sort of thing I wouldn't be hearing any more. Not for a while. But that was all right. The car would be on the drive and he'd shown me how to turn the engine over every week or so, just so it didn't seize up. I would be in charge of the house and his mother and the car and everything would be safe and fine.

'Tell Fay I'll see her tomorrow,' I said.

'I will.'

'And send her my love.'

'OK.'

'We are all right then?' I asked.

'Okey-dokey.' He looked at his watch, awkwardly like a man in a play. 'Better get going or they won't let me in.'

I listened to the car start and drive away. Another sound I wouldn't be hearing for a while. When it had faded to nothing, I listened to the house, for the throb of its heart. A curtain stirred though the window wasn't open; a floor creaked. Downstairs the budgie shrieked. I went and fetched him. He clung to the bars and watched me with the bright dots of his eyes. I put his cage on the kitchen windowsill. He fluttered about and little feathers and wisps of down floated out. A blue curl of feather on the breadboard. He would be all right there. He would be company.

I watched the sun rise, a sickly yellow line soon squashed under a bundle of clouds. I hardly ever look out at the street so early. Curtains still drawn, an upstairs light on here and there. How obedient everyone is. It's not prison, there are no banging-up times, yet everyone conforms. And so do I.

He'd brought me up a cup of tea before he'd gone. The favourite white mug.

'Thanks,' I'd said. 'I love you.'

He'd kissed the top of my head. 'You take care now.'

'Ring me when you get there.'

'If I can.'

'It'll only be a couple of weeks. I'll book a flight.'

'Better wait and see how Mum is.' He went to the window and twitched about with the curtains. 'And what the scene is there.'

'Scene?'

The urge to cling to him was overwhelming. I once saw a man with a baby orang-utan, in a zoo. He was trying to make it stay in its enclosure but it clung to his leg like a furry boot. That is how I felt and yet I looked up at him and even cracked a smile.

'Bon voyage,' I said.

He made a kind of salute and went downstairs. I listened to the clump of his feet, heard him say something to Charlie Two in the kitchen and the opening and closing of the door.

I got out of bed, moved the curtain aside and watched him walk away, a little man with wild hair, rucksack as high as his head. At the corner he turned to look back. My face was pressed against the glass; I raised my hand but I don't think he could have seen me.

Back in bed, I lay on his side, breathing in the smell of his hair on the pillow and listening to the sounds of a street waking up: a dog barking; the grey scrape of a car's engine; the lime squeal of a bird. I shut my eyes and plummeted back to sleep.

I was late to work, stretching the very limits of the flexi-time. Gary raised his eyebrows as I walked past but said nothing. When I sat down Christine pulled a face. 'He's on the warpath,' she whispered. 'He had a complaint – you cocked something up.'

'Oh?' I sat down and looked at the mess on my desk. My in-tray was overflowing and I knew that there were hundreds of emails too. It was coming in faster and faster, the work, and just when I couldn't think straight.

I stared at the columns of things on my screen and clicked the mouse on something. *Are you sure you want to delete file?* came up and I did delete it, and then something else and something else. It was lovely the way they simply vanished. My finger just kept on clicking.

Christine craned her neck to see my screen. 'Nina! What the hell are you doing?'

I said, 'Nothing.' But I stopped deleting.

'You're gonna be in deep doodoo. What's up with you?'

I shrugged and started typing rubbish. I was supposed to be processing orders for components. I don't even know what for.

'Coffee?' She burst into my thoughts.

'Not yet.' I squinted at the screen, trying to work out what I was doing.

'You look like you need one.'

'Go on then.'

'I'll put an extra spoon in, to perk you up,' she said and smiled with a kind of complicity. 'And then we'll see if we can retrieve those files, shall we?'

My extension rang and it was Rupert. I was almost glad. I was ready for him. Before he could say a word I said, 'Charlie's gone off to think things over.'

I heard him suck in a breath. 'Where?'

'Away.'

'Has he left you?'

'Why don't you ask John Smith?'

'Did you tell him the rest?'

There was a long silence. I could hear him breathing and picture his face, the narrowed eyes, the half-smile.

'I'll be round tonight.' And then he rang off.

'You're white as a flipping sheet.' Christine put a mug of coffee on my desk. 'I'll get you a couple of Jammie Dodgers.'

The phone rang again and I jumped.

'Blimey,' Christine said, 'hang on.' She leant over my desk and I caught a breezy whiff of her deodorant. 'Nina Todd's phone,' she said. 'She's away from her desk at the moment,' she winked at me, 'can I help?'

I could hear that it was a woman's voice and my hands relaxed. I hadn't realised how tight my fists had been. I opened my palms and looked down; each line was bright with sweat. Christine scribbled on my jotter, her big breast jiggling a few inches from my eyes. I could see the stretched white lace of her bra-cup through her pink blouse.

'OK, have a nice day,' she said and put the phone down.

'Ta,' I said.

'No probs. Just bung her a blue form and a grovelling letter. Why don't you go home?'

'No,' I said, 'but thanks.'

I didn't go out of the building for lunch. I did ring Rupert, though, while Christine was out, dialling the mobile number on his card. His phone was switched off. I left a message saying, 'Don't come round, people will be there. Ring me again and I'll meet you.'

It seemed best, better. How did he know where I lived – unless there was a John Smith.

All afternoon I tried to concentrate on the orders, but I was tensed up for Rupert's call and waiting for Charlie's. Whenever I went to the window there was another plane trail scrawled across the sky, I'm sure there are not usually that many.

Rupert didn't ring but Charlie did, at last, towards the end of the afternoon. He was full of skies and skuas and how in another universe he felt.

'You were right about getting away,' he said. 'I've hardly arrived and already I'm starting to feel . . .' he paused and I heard the miles between us rushing down the line, 'renewed or refreshed or something. Better anyway. Thanks, Nina. Sorry

I've been a bit . . .' His voice sounded more loving than for ages.

'Don't be sorry,' I said. A big warm gush of relief welled around my heart. 'After all you've been through.'

'And I rang the hospital and got to speak to Mum,' he continued. 'She was back to normal, complaining away! They're discharging her at the weekend if she continues like this.'

'Told you so.'

'Bruno drove me right round the island,' Charlie said. 'You wouldn't believe it, Nina, so tiny yet so much sky. Makes me feel free.'

'Can't wait to see for myself,' I said. I could hear voices in the background. 'By the way,' I said. 'Do you know anyone called John Smith?'

'Smithy? Why?' Someone called his name. 'OK,' he said, 'coming. Sorry, Nina, got to go. Speak later.'

When he'd put his receiver down, my ear was filled with bees.

After work, I went to visit Fay. I took her some fruit jellies. She was in the last bed in the ward, propped up with enormous pillows.

'Has something happened between you and Charlie?' she said, as if she had been waiting all day to ask.

'No.' I handed her the sweets, but she scarcely glanced at them. 'Except that he's gone away. That's something. Why?'

'I don't know,' she said, 'just his demeanour last night.' She plucked at the sheet.

'What about it?'

'Do sit down,' she said, 'don't loom over me like that.' She looked at the jellies. 'Thank you.' I pulled a chair over and sat down. The bed was high so that, for the first time ever, her head was above my own. She'd painted herself up ready for visiting time. For me? But her hair was greasy and stuck thinly to her scalp.

'What?' I said.

'He seemed uncharacteristically evasive.'

'About what?'

'Oh . . .' she raised her hand, 'I don't know, can't put my finger on it, call it a mother's intuition.'

'Well, everything's fine,' I said. 'Soon as you're up and about I'm going to visit him.'

'Are you sure that's wise?' she said. 'It's true, you know, that absence makes the heart grow fonder.'

'The heart is fond,' I said. 'I told you.'

She looked at me from under her heavy silver lids. 'Good,' she said. 'I haven't the stamina to get used to anyone else.' And she gave the faintest smile.

It was the nicest thing she had ever said to me. I sat and treasured it for a moment while she complained away about standards of hygiene and the decline of the National Health Service.

'I'm being discharged on Saturday,' she said.

'I hope you'll stay upstairs with me,' I said.

'Do you?' Birdlike she cocked her head.

'Of course I do. I can take time off to look after you.'

'No need. Maisie's already offered.'

'Well anyway I'll cook for you. Cauliflower cheese, chops, whatever you fancy. No curry!'

'It'll be an improvement on hospital food, anyway.'

We were quiet for a moment. The theme tune to *EastEnders* drifted through the ward.

'I've brought Charlie Two upstairs,' I said.

'Is he all right?'

'Right as rain.'

'Perhaps you'd like to take those.' She jerked her chin at a box of Quality Street. 'I know you're partial to a chocolate.'

'Thank you,' I said. As I left, I bent over to kiss her cheek. The hospital smell was overlaid with her perfume and I felt a tug of true fondness for her crabby old bones. She accepted the kiss, and, looking away, grasped my hand and let it go.

When I got home I drew the curtains and locked the door. I would have to see Rupert soon and sort things out, but not that night. Not then. The budgie gave me a critical look. I sat all evening in the darkness eating Quality Street, even the orange creams that I can't stand, until I felt sick. I couldn't play music or put the TV on. I needed to listen for the sound of the gate. People who know us come to the back door, strangers to the front. The doorbell did ring once but I didn't answer or even look to see who was there. Whoever it was gave up easily and went away.

~

The following afternoon they returned to the well. She wore blue jeans and her black school plimsolls. Jeffrey called for her and Joan chatted with him in the kitchen – he'd got his A level grades that day – good enough to get into Birmingham. She kept her face in order, expression open and pleasant, while she listened.

As they went out, Joan patted her on the arm and gave her an approving smile, approving of her with this nice, clever boy, this good influence. He had a little rucksack on his back.

'What's in there?' she asked.

'Rope,' he said, 'to make it easier.'

Her heart sank. She had hoped he'd forgotten. A sea mist was clinging to the coast, everything damp and faded, moisture visibly suspended in the air. From the top of the Spa Gardens you couldn't see the sea but you could hear the grate of shingle rolling in the waves. There was no one about though the ice-cream van sat there, the man inside turning the pages of a newspaper.

They went through the PRIVATE *gate and the shrubs. A blackbird defied them, stood a moment cocking its head before giving up and jerking back into the shelter of a bush. Jeffrey heaved up the lid and the gap opened into a black smile. He took a coil of blue nylon rope out of his rucksack.*

'Right,' he said. 'I'll go first and then I'll help you. He swung easily down, found the ladder and dropped to the bottom. It did seem easier this time, she told herself, it didn't seem so deep. You can get used to anything, she did know that much.

'Chuck me down the torch,' he said, 'and I'll shine it for you.' She looked around, half hoping for a man in council overalls to come and shout at them for trespassing, but there was no one.

'Come on,' Jeffrey called. She dropped the torch.

'Ouch!'

'Sorry.'

'Come on.' The light flickered up at her, watery on the slimy brick. She sat on the edge and dangled her feet inside.

'Turn round and let yourself down over the edge,' he said, 'just lower yourself a bit, your feet will touch the ladder, then I can help you.'

The smell of the walls was cold mushrooms. Her hands slid on the rope, her foot flailed for the ladder, found nothing and she let go, didn't mean to, it was just too much, too black all in her nose and eyes and mouth and she gave up. She fell on Jeffrey. The torch was knocked from his hand and went off.

'Jeff?' she said, terrified for a moment that she had knocked him out, but he laughed.

'God, you weigh a ton,' he said. 'You all right?'

They stood up; underfoot was crunchy and moist; all sorts of rotting things, she supposed, maybe even rats. She couldn't see him or even herself. The light reached as far as the top of the ladder. It looked bright up there in the white crescent of daylight, much brighter than it really was.

'Well done,' he said.

'Now what?' Her eyes were beginning to accustom themselves to the dark so that she could see the outline of his head.

'This,' he said and began kissing her – tastes of toothpaste, smell of Clearasil – with the new hard kiss. He pushed his body against hers, moving his hips.

'We didn't have to come down here for that,' she said, pulling her face away.

'Can I touch you?' he said.

'But how are we going to get out?'

He put his chilly hand up her jumper and clamped it on her breast outside her bra, and breathed out a long juddery sigh. 'Lovely,' he said.

'Let's go up,' she pleaded. 'Jeffrey, we can do this up there. Somewhere nice.'

'Don't you think it's sexy down here?' He twisted his hand so that he could wangle a couple of fingers inside her bra, wriggle them against her nipple.

'No.'

'When we go up, I'll buy you a ninety-nine,' he said and kissed her again. 'When I was a kid I always had a funny feeling down here in my . . . well you know. I always thought when I had a girlfriend I'll bring her down here.'

Girlfriend. How she loved that word.

'Have you been here with other girls?' she asked.

'You're the first.' He twiddled the end of her nipple between his fingers intently, as if he was tuning a radio. 'Have you, I mean are you, I mean have you, you know, done it before?'

'No.' She looked up at the light. Something crunched under her feet as she shifted; like the splintering of a tiny bone.

'Can I?' He slid his hand down her tummy. She sighed and pulled it in to make more room. His hand reached the edge of her knickers – and stopped.

'Go on then.' She smiled into the blackness. A hot tear rose in her eye and trickled down her invisible face. She undid her zip to make it easier for him and then his cold fingers were feeling about, a finger jabbing trying to find a way in. His breathing was hard and concentrated as if he was playing his music. *'It's complicated down there, isn't it?'* he breathed. *'Lovely. Just lovely. Will you . . .'* He took her hand and pressed it over the ridge of erection under his cords. He shuddered. His dabbling finger was beginning, despite everything, to interest her but just as she thought that, he sobbed and moaned, grabbed himself and pulled away.

'God, you've made me ejaculate,' he said.

Her laugh flapped like a bat up the sides of the well and out into the bright.

*

I went into work early next morning, and sat alone staring out across the rooftops. At eight-thirty, the moment the switchboard became operative, my extension rang. It was someone from the hospital to tell me that Fay had died.

A pigeon was hopping on the ledge outside the window, nudging its dirty feathers against the glass.

'No,' I said, 'that can't be right. She was fine yesterday.' The pigeon opened its crusty beak but I heard no sound and then it flapped away.

'Sometimes happens, I'm afraid. Post-operative complication.'

'But it was only her hip.'

'She suffered a cardiac arrest during her sleep. She won't have known a thing.'

'Fay *Martin*?' I said.

'Mrs Martin, yes. I'm very sorry, dear. I've been trying to contact her son – your husband, is it? On his mobile but to no avail.'

'Oh.' An old bloke was limping round depositing the post on people's desks. He looked surprised. We'd never seen each other before; I'd never been in so early. He handed me a pile of papers.

'Do you have a landline number for him?' the woman said.

'I'll tell him.'

'Yes, dear. It would come better from you.'

She began to talk about arrangements but I couldn't take anything in. 'I'll get back to you later,' I said and put the receiver down.

I went across to Christine's desk and picked up the bear, all pink now with kissy smudges. I took it to the window and stared out across the city at the tall hospital building where Fay was. Or where her body was.

'Good morning,' Gary said and I turned. 'What's this?' He looked at the bear clutched in my hand.

'It's Christine's,' I said, 'her good-luck mascot.'

'Do you believe in luck?' he said. 'I wouldn't have put you down as the superstitious type.'

'I don't think luck is something you can believe in or not,' I said. 'It either happens or it doesn't. Like rain.'

He blinked at me. There was a little slice of unshaved skin under his bottom lip. I wondered if it was accidental or meant to be a style statement. His suit was navy blue, the sort that would crackle if you brushed against it.

'Well, nice to see you in so bright and early,' he said. 'Work hard this week and let's see if we can get back up to speed, shall we?' He cocked his head encouragingly. 'And you're looking well. So much better.' He patted my arm and went off, leaving a prickly smell of aftershave behind him.

I sat down, legs suddenly weak with the shock. Fay dead. Fay gone. I couldn't take it in. I sat blankly staring at my screensaver. Christine came wobbling in. 'Good God!' she said when she saw me. She sat down, and sighed with relief as she freed her feet from her pink stilettos and shoved them into Dr Scholl's. 'What are you doing in so early?'

'Why do you wear them?' I nodded at the stilettos.

She gave me a quizzical look. 'Want a coffee? I'm having one to kick off with.' She took a chocolate muffin, wrapped in a paper napkin, out of her handbag. 'Breakfast,' she said and slopped off to get the drinks.

And then it came crashing in on me that Fay was dead. I saw the puppet head on the pillow, the bony hands that would never clutch at anything again. My hand still remembered the feeling of hers last night. I pictured the box of jellies on her locker. She had been pleased with them, I think.

Christine came back and put a mug of coffee on my desk. She was talking about the film she'd seen with Don last night. 'And then in the pub after, you'll never guess what he . . .' She tailed off. 'You OK?'

I took a sip of coffee, too weak and milky, and then my vision clouded. I lowered my head on to the desk and closed my eyes.

'Oh my God,' she said, 'are you blacking out?'

'No.' My voice was squashed. I sat up. It was running up through me like light, like the sun rising, what this meant. I could leave here now, leave all this and go to Charlie. A hurting sort of smile broke on my face.

'Nina?' Christine said. She sounded nervous.

'It's all right,' I said, 'but something's happened.'

'What?' She eyed her muffin, then gave in and took a bite.

'Charlie's mum's died.'

Her pale eyes opened wide. 'Oh my God,' she said, through a mouthful of black crumbs, 'when?'

'Just now.'

'*Just now?*'

'Shhh,' I said. 'I mean last night. The hospital just rang.'

'Oh my God.'

'I need to go to the hospital . . . Tell Gary that . . . I don't know, tell him I've gone down with something,' I said.

'Why don't you just tell him the truth?' she said.

She watched me gather together my things, slide my arms into my jacket. I opened my drawer and took out the picture of

Charlie, such a smile; I hadn't seen him smile like that for weeks. I put it in my bag, heart vaulting against my ribs.

'Please, Chris,' I said, 'I can't face him.'

'What about tomorrow?'

'I'll ring in or something, don't worry.'

'Tell Charlie, I mean I know I don't know him or anything, but tell him sorry from me, will you?'

'I will,' I said. One of her bra-straps had escaped from her sleeveless top. I realised I might never see her again. I paused. 'So, everything all right with Don?'

'We're thinking about holidays,' she said. 'He asked me if I fancied it. Malaga or Tenerife.'

'Have a great time then,' I said.

'It's not till August!' She picked a chocolate chip out of her muffin. 'But it goes to show he's thinking long-term.'

'That's great,' I said. Gary's door was closed. 'I'll nip out now. Thanks, Chris.' I hesitated for a moment. 'You're a good mate.'

'Don't be daft,' she said, blushing.

At home I banged the door shut and it seemed stiller and emptier than ever before. The budgie was silent and hunched as if he knew he was bereaved. I imagined taking the cage outside and opening it, and him soaring away, higher than he'd ever flown, a vivid scrap of blue amongst the sensible English birds. And what would happen then? He might be eaten by a cat or a magpie or a hawk. Or maybe not, maybe he'd adapt, pass himself off as a sparrow, join a flock.

I had the number ready to phone Charlie, and was preparing my words. It's not an easy thing to say to someone. I couldn't think how to put it. Should I come straight out with it, or try and soften it? But how can you soften news like that? While I considered I wandered down into Fay's flat.

On her mantelpiece was an array of framed photos but none of me. One of the frames, which was in the shape of a heart, held Charlie and a girl. A girl with pale green, wavy hair. They were holding hands in the shadow of a leafy arch. He looked unbelievably young which proved that it was long ago. It must have been Nicky. I did what I'd been itching to do for four whole months and turned that photo to face the wall.

I looked at all Fay's things, not hers any more: the special high-seated armchair; a tube of handcream; a crossword snipped from a magazine; the TV guide with her choices circled in red.

I walked into the bathroom, where peachy satin underwear hung on a line over the bath. I looked inside the bathroom cabinet at the denture cream, the Vaseline, the Alka-Seltzer, the brown jars of prescription pills with her name, *Mrs F.J. Martin*. I didn't even know what the J. stood for.

As I went back into her sitting room the torn-out crossword fluttered to the floor though there was no breeze and I got the sudden strong uneasy sensation that she was there.

'I'm sorry, Fay,' I said and my own voice scared me. I don't know what I was sorry for.

I went quickly upstairs to phone Charlie. I would put it simply: 'Sorry, Charlie, Fay passed away in the night.' Passed away was better than died, I thought. Or passed on, or passed over. 'She won't have known a thing,' I'd say, while he took it in.

I actually had my hand on the phone when it rang. I thought it would be him, but, 'Nina,' the suede voice said, 'shouldn't you be at work?'

'How did you get this number?' I said.

'Ways and means.'

'John Smith?'

He didn't answer.

'Look, this is really not a good time,' I said.

'I'm just outside now.' As he spoke, I saw, or felt, the shadow of him through the kitchen window. I opened the door and he stepped in. He looked so tall in the kitchen, far taller than Charlie. He had an Oddbins carrier bag with him and he took out of it a bottle of champagne.

'I didn't take you for a pet person,' he said, clicking his fingers at the budgie.

'It belongs to Charlie's mother,' I said. 'Look, I've got a family crisis. Can we meet later?'

'Family, eh?' he said.

'I've got to make a call. An important call.'

'Don't mind me.' He smiled as he popped the cork off the champagne. The sound made Charlie Two jerk on his perch. I watched the little ghost rise from the bottle and disappear. It was ten-thirty in the morning.

'Glasses?' he said but I just stood there thinking how to get rid of him. He found glasses in a cupboard. 'No flutes?' he said. 'Ah well, we can make do.'

He poured the champagne into the glasses and the faint hissy sizzle of it made my mouth water, gave me a sudden desperate thirst. And a drink probably was what I needed to steady my nerves.

He raised his glass to me and took a sip. 'Mmmm not bad.'

'What then?' I said. He sat down on one of the kitchen chairs and stretched out his long legs. Moleskin jeans, I noticed, olive green, brand new. He was quite comfortable in his skin in this kitchen, more comfortable than I ever was.

'I really do have to make an urgent call,' I said. 'I'll go upstairs.'

'Something secret?' he said.

I put my glass down. Should not drink more. There must be lots of things to do, as well as phoning Charlie. What do you do when someone dies? First you tell the next of kin.

'Private.'

'Is there any difference?' he said. 'I know all your little secrets.'

The glass broke in my hand. Curved shards of glass,

champagne, blood welling up and mixing to a rosy fizz like pink champagne. The alcohol stung, the blood dripped on to my skirt. It was linen; it would be ruined. I don't know what would have happened next but then the back door opened and Maisie came in.

'Hope you don't mind . . . just wanted to drop this in for . . .' She stopped and stood looking between my bleeding hand, the bottle and Rupert. 'Oh my giddy aunt,' she said. She put a parcel down on the table.

I reached for a tea towel to stop the blood.

'I'll give it to her,' I said.

'You've been in the wars,' she said, her eyes fixed on the champagne. 'Celebrating?'

'Would you like a glass?' Rupert asked.

'Goodness me, no!'

I should have thought of something, introduced Rupert, he could have been anything, a champagne salesman maybe, but I couldn't think straight. My hand was stinging and my eyes smarted.

'Will you be seeing her today?' Maisie said. 'You look like you could do with a trip to Casualty yourself.'

'No, I'm OK,' I said.

'It's a bed-jacket,' Maisie said. 'I'd take it up myself if I didn't have this blasted leg.'

'She'll be out on Saturday,' I said.

'Well, I'll be off.' Rupert took Maisie's hand. 'Nice to meet you.' He slid me a smile. 'I'll be in touch.' I heard his footsteps going down the side of the house, the jounce of the gate on its hinges, the clang as it shut.

'What's been happening then?' Maisie said.

'It's nothing.'

'Doesn't look like nothing to me.'

'It's superficial.' I made a ghastly sound, meant to be a laugh. 'It's just . . .' but somehow nothing would come.

'What you want is a cup of tea.' She headed towards the kettle.

'No,' I said, more sharply than I meant. 'I mean, thanks but I've got stuff to do.'

'Well at least let me help you with that.'

'It's OK. Really.'

She looked from the champagne to the blood to me and tutted. 'I don't know. Well, anyway, send her my love,' she said, 'tell her we missed her at Spanish.'

Spanish?

She hovered for a moment. 'Are you sure I can't . . .' but I shook my head and shut my eyes against her, willing her to go. I could hear her mind whirring as she planned what to tell Fay, and eventually the back door clicked shut. I took my hand to the sink, peeled off the tea towel, and held it under the cold tap. As the blood rinsed away the wound gaped open like the mouth of a fish.

I turned off the tap and watched the blood ooze across my palm. I thought then that it would be easier than anything just to let the rest of my blood flow neatly down the drain, to wipe up behind me and be gone.

But I wrapped my hand tightly in a clean tea towel. It was one brought back by Fay from a holiday in Wales. It was printed with a recipe for barmbrack held by a woman in a tall Welsh hat. The word Welsh was squashy and sickening. I heard a loud buzzing and my knees went soft. I think I fainted, at least I opened my eyes to blood, and the words two hundred and fifty grams, two hundred and fifty grams, and felt a jab of sharpness in my side where my ribs had fallen on the glass, a tear in my blouse and more blood. The table loomed above me and I could see the undersides of chairs and something that looked like a woolly chip under the cooker. When did we last have chips? I could hear Charlie Two cheeping and I don't know what next, everything soft and leaky and warm, quite comfortable, until the phone sent sparks jangling through me.

I crawled across the floor and reached up to get it. Charlie's voice came out. 'Your mobile's off,' he said. 'What's up?'

I looked down at myself. There was actually still a curved piece of glass sticking out of my side and I choked out a laugh, I couldn't help it, and then felt the gorge rise in my throat.

'Come back,' I said.

'What's going on?'

I breathed out. 'Sorry, Charlie. Your mum. I was about to ring you.'

There was a silence then he said, 'No.'

'Heart attack,' I said. 'A post-operative complication. I'm so sorry.'

It seemed ages before he spoke again. I could hear his breath. I plucked the glass out of my side. It had only been dangling there. My blouse was ruined, and my skirt, but it didn't matter.

'I can't believe you laughed,' he said at last.

'I wasn't . . . it was just nerves. Shock.'

There was a pause, then he said, 'When?'

'Early hours.'

'Oh God. Mum.'

'Charlie.' I tried to make my love stream down the wire and over the miles to him. 'She won't have known anything. It was in her sleep,' I said.

'Last night?' he asked.

'She was her usual self. I took her some jellies.'

'I'd better ring the hospital.'

'Then get back to me,' I said.

'I'll get the first flight.'

'Yes,' I said, 'yes, of course you must.'

When I put the receiver down it was sticky with blood. Of course he would have to come straight back. Funeral, funeral.

I rang the hospital and asked them what to do. I called her my mother. She could have been my mother. They gave me the number of a funeral director. When Charlie rang I could say it was all in hand, all he had to do was get here.

I drank another glass of champagne while I gathered my thoughts; it was just as good as brandy for the shock. The budgie was cocking his head at me. I opened the cage and he came straight out, almost brushing my hair with his wings, and circled the room in a blue blur, claws scrabbling for something to clutch. He finally clung to the lampshade. Cheep, cheep, cheep. I was drinking from Rupert's glass because mine was in pieces but not me. I had pulled myself together and even when the bird, from the lampshade, said, 'Charlie-boy, Charlie-boy,' I was all right.

I phoned the funeral director's and it was easy, it was easier than booking a train trip: a few questions, the first available date, cremation I chose, that's what we did with Dave and it seems the best solution. I thought I should invite people. Do you call it 'invite' for a funeral? Maisie was her friend. I should have told her. That would have been the normal thing to do.

I took off the bloody blouse. It was only a scratch. I took off my skirt and stuffed it with the blouse into the bin. I swept up the bits of glass, the tea towel making me clumsy. I peeled it off; it was heavy with blood but I could still read the recipe: *steep fruit overnight in tea*. I wondered if barmbrack would be suitable for a funeral.

I rang Rupert's mobile and to my relief he answered. 'Listen,' I said, 'Charlie's mum's just died.'

There was a pause. 'Just now?'

'Early this morning.'

'Why are you telling me now? I mean, why didn't you say?'

'Don't know,' I said and it was the truth. 'I hadn't even told Charlie . . .'

'Have you now?'

'Just did. He's coming back, there's going to be the funeral and everything. Rupert, look, I'll meet you when it's over. We'll talk. Please just leave me alone till it's over.'

There was a silence. I could hear voices in the background of wherever he was. It sounded like a pub. 'Promise?' he said.

'Yes,' I said. 'I absolutely do.'

'Why should I believe you?'

'I'm just . . . asking. Begging. *Please*.'

'My mum isn't too well,' he said and I was so surprised I had to hold the receiver away from my ear and look at it.

'No?'

'She's had a bad life. Shocks. My sister was killed.'

'How awful,' I said, 'how dreadful.'

'It was years ago,' he said, 'but something like that – it never goes away.'

'No,' I said. 'I'm sorry.'

'Sorry!'

'Yes, I can imagine . . .'

'Can you?'

'I think so.'

I could hear a fruit machine. I wondered if it was the same pub. 'All right,' he said. 'I know how I'd feel if it was Mum. A week. Might visit Mum. She lives in Suffolk.'

'Thank you,' I said.

'A week,' he said and rang off.

I tried to bandage my hand but couldn't do it. I decided to go to Maisie's and tell her the truth about Fay and ask her to the funeral. Also ask her to tie the bandage. But I didn't know where she lived.

I got dressed and then went down to Fay's. I kept my eyes straight ahead because I didn't want to see her. She was definitely there. Having a last linger. A shudder at the edges of my vision. I was scared at first but then almost comforted. Perhaps she hadn't left me after all. 'Fay?' I said and held my breath, waiting for I don't know what. But nothing happened except the dripping of the kitchen tap. I turned it off, made sure the windows were secure.

Beside the phone was an address book. I didn't know Maisie's surname so I had to go through it all. Many people crossed out in there with a date written in Fay's precise handwriting beside each. I puzzled for a moment, then I got it: they were people who had died. Except for Dave. She hadn't crossed him off.

I found Maisie under the S's. She was a Smith. I knew that her husband was dead, and wondered if he had been a John. Or maybe they'd had a son? I walked round the corner and found her bungalow. It was squat and out of scale, the only bungalow in a street of bigger houses. There was a buddleia bush in the front garden, a loud bee hum coming from its nosy purple spikes.

I rang the doorbell and she opened the door with such a startled look that I glanced behind me to see if someone else was there.

'Come in,' she said. I saw myself in her hall mirror as she led me through and I did still look a sight, hair sticking up, bruises showing through my smudged make-up. I was no oil painting, as Fay would have said, or if I was it was a bad one.

We went into her sitting room. It smelt of toast and eucalyptus. There was a gaudy painting of a desert landscape above the gas fire and the phallic stump of a cactus on the windowsill, sporting a waxy pink bloom.

'You've hit lucky,' she said, seeing me looking. 'It only blooms once in a blue moon and then only for a day.'

'Lovely,' I said. 'Maisie, I've got some bad news. Just after you left I had a call from the hospital, I'm afraid Fay's passed away.'

'Oh my giddy aunt.' She bumped down into an armchair.

I didn't know what to do next. She put her hand up her sleeve and brought out a balled-up hankie. A tear ran down her cheek. 'But I only phoned her yesterday,' she said. 'She was full of beans.'

'I know,' I said, 'I saw her last night.'

'So she'll never get the bed-jacket?'

'No.'

She held the handkerchief to her nose and then looked up, wet eyed. 'It was fifty per cent angora,' she said and then, 'That poor, poor boy. What hasn't he been through?'

'He's coming back,' I said and told her about the cremation. She offered to help with the food.

'Yes please,' I said, 'and maybe you could tell me who else I should ask?'

'Leave it to me.' She spread out her fingers and stared at them for a moment, then shook her head. 'I need a good strong cuppa. You'll stay for a cup of tea?'

'*Would* you help me with this?' I held my hand out to her. 'I'm sorry about . . .'

'First things first.' She went off into the kitchen. The radiator was on although it was warm outside. I put my nose close to the pink cactus bloom but there was no smell at all. It might as well have been plastic.

'It just won't sink in,' she said, coming back with a tea tray and a first-aid box. 'Do sit down, dear.'

'I know. I'm the same.'

'She was so full of life.'

I was startled. That was not my picture of Fay at all. I sat down on the mock-leather sofa.

'Full of fun,' she said.

Fun?

'I'll miss her terribly.'

'Me too.'

'Of course you will.'

'We were getting very close,' I said.

She looked sharply at me. The tears glistened in the crumples on her cheeks. She opened her mouth as if to contradict me, then thought better of it. She had that milkiness in her eyes that old people get but Fay hadn't, her eyes had remained bright and clear. We were quiet, contemplating how much we would miss Fay, and then she reached for my hand.

'Let's see what we've got here then.' She unwrapped the clumsy bandage and dabbed the cut with TCP. It stung like hell but I kept my mouth shut.

'It could do with a stitch,' she said, but I shook my head. She took a clean bandage from her kit, folded a piece of lint over the cut and wound the bandage round and round, firm and tight, and pinned it with a silver safety pin. She poured the tea and offered me a piece of cake. It was a spicy sponge with slivers of crystallised ginger.

She took a noisy slurp of tea and sighed. 'It just won't sink in,' she said again, 'it just *won't*. I thought Fay would outlast us all.'

'What was your husband's name?' I asked.

She blinked. 'What? Oh . . . it was Jack. John really, but always known as Jack. Why?'

'Did Charlie know him?'

'In passing.'

'Do you have a son?'

She shook her head. 'Why? No. Oh I just can't take it in.' Fresh tears were standing in her eyes.

I looked away from her and at the picture above the mantelpiece. 'That's a nice picture,' I said.

'It's painting by numbers,' she said and then sniffed. 'Do you know, if I won the lottery, I'd be there in a jiff.' She gazed at the painting as if it was a window into a better world. 'Arkansas. They have retirement places in the desert – whole villages, not *homes*, all that sunshine and dry air, a miracle cure for arthritis. We often talked about it, Fay and me.' She put her cup down and pulled her hankie out again.

'*Really?*'

'I can tell from looking at you, Nina, that what you want is a good cry. Let yourself go.' She reached forward and patted my hand. We sat and stared at the switched-off television while we finished our cake. There we were reflected like ordinary people having afternoon tea, the cactus bloom outlined against the window behind us. The only movement was the waggling of my foot. I pressed it to the floor.

'Did she really want to go to the desert?' I said.

'It was a daydream we shared.'

'God,' I said.

'More cake?' she offered.

'No thanks. It's nice though.'

'I'll make some for the wake.'

'Thank you.'

'It's a good keeper,' she said, 'I'll do it this afternoon. At least it's something I can be getting on with.'

'Well.' I stood up to go.

'Do pop round if you want me to do your hand again,' she said. She followed me to the door and as I went out she said, 'By the way, Nina, who was that handsome chap this morning? I didn't catch the name.'

'Just someone from work. He might look handsome but . . .'

'Handsome is as handsome does?'

'You've got it.'

'I know the type. You want to watch them.' She looked at me, expecting more. 'Was that champagne?' she said.

'Oh yes, he's been promoted,' I said. 'Bit of a show-off, going round drinking a toast with everyone – even me when I was off!'

Of course she didn't believe me, it was the weakest lie in the world, but what could she do? I walked away and the bandage was as firm round my hand as if Charlie was holding it.

~

T *he night before Jeffrey went to Birmingham they made love in his parents' garden shed. They had made a nest in there, with a sleeping bag, old cushions and sandalwood joss-sticks to mask the oily lawn-mower smell. It was cosy and private and it was theirs. She loved, after they had finished, to lie back, sharing a cigarette, and to gaze up through the cobwebbed window into the night sky. The tips of the branches of the tree behind the shed touched the roof and when it was in the least windy would make a scraping swish. A cosy sound when you are safe in the circle of someone's arms.*

'I love you,' he said, on their last night, 'I love you, Karen.'

'I love you too,' she said, 'but tomorrow you'll be gone.'

He laughed, a damp snuffle against her neck that made her shiver. 'I'll still exist, I'll just be a bit further away, that's all.' He put his face against her front where her shirt was un-buttoned, her bra unfastened and all askew, and kissed her nipple so gently she felt nothing at all. She closed her eyes against the moonlight stinging through the glass.

'You'll meet someone else,' she said.

'I'll meet loads of other people,' he lifted his head and looked at her, 'and none of them will be half as beautiful,' he kissed her collar bone, 'half as sexy,' he kissed her chin, 'as you.' He kissed her on the mouth but she was tired of his kisses

that night, she only half believed them, knew that really he was excited about going away and that Birmingham would be full of posh, beautiful and brainy girls beside whom she would seem like nothing.

He wrote to her every day at first and they talked for hours on the phone. She was miserable and lonely and though she tried to cover it up, the doctors could see. 'He's a nice boy,' Joan said, 'but you're only fifteen. Don't pine away. Plenty more fish in the sea.'

Roger suggested that she bury herself in her work; this was her important GCSE year and she could see the sense in that. If she wanted to be like the doctors or the professors with all that they had, then she had to work at it. And work she did, trying not to notice how the letters became fewer and had a dutiful feel about them, always ending, 'well better get back to . . .' whatever it was that was more important. And just before he was due to return for the Christmas break she received a note that went like this:

Dear Karen,

I'm really sorry but I think we should cool off a bit. I've got so much work to do I can't concentrate on having a girlfriend as well and it's not fair on you. Though you're very mature for your age you are only fifteen. I'll see you over Christmas when our folks get together, but I think we should just be friends.

Yours,
Jeffrey.

The letter was written on a sheet of paper from a shorthand pad with a frill of papery curls where it had been ripped from the spirals. 'Yours, Jeffrey.' Yours. Why did he say 'yours' when he meant the opposite?

But after all, it was only what she expected. She screwed up the note and tossed it into the bin, opened her history book and got on with revising the causes of the First World War. After Christmas came her mock exams and she would not let him ruin her chances. And she knew that, whatever he thought, when she was with him again she could win him round. She remembered his kisses and the way they had grown so bold, the way she had let him use her body to learn on. There was still much more to teach.

∧

M y digs had not the privacy I'd need for stage two. It had to be the right setting. It took a bit of finding but you only have to persevere. I began wandering non-residential streets and in a high-up, filthy window I saw a FOR LET sign above a disused factory. Peerless View was the name of the street. When I rang the agent he sounded incredulous. 'Is that still on the books?' he said. He told me the place was scheduled for demolition next year but I made out I was only interested in a short let and asked to view it. He came down like a shot to show me round.

It was a big dark flat: 'ripe for improvement' would be the terminology. In the kitchen was a deep sink, the wreck of a cooker and a Sheila Maid up near the ceiling all draped with cobwebs. There were two bedrooms at the back looking out over a yard full of old machinery and suchlike, all overgrown with weeds and a straggly tree pushing out of a crack in the concrete. But it had a high and lockable gate, perfect for pulling the car in out of sight. The street was empty at night and in the day a rat-run for traffic heading from the city centre to the north.

You could see the surprise on the agent's face when I said I'd take it, no quibble about the price. He was bursting to ask what on earth for. What came out was that I wanted it to practise on my drums and it was hard not to laugh when I said that. I do have to be careful of the laugh. Unfortunately it turned out he was in a band and we had a sticky conversation about music and so on till I said I was on a deadline.

'Well you won't have trouble with the neighbours, that's for sure,' he said as he locked us out.

Now was the time to have a store of readies. I went to the building society and emptied my Instant Access account. It was ten thousand and fifty-five pounds. You could see the woman on the desk didn't want me to have it.

'But it's mine!' I said.

She had a mouth like a little purse all snapped up tight. I had the passbook and my driving licence for ID but she had to go and have a word with her supervisor all the same. The supervisor must have put her straight because she came back looking like she'd sucked a lemon.

'Are you closing the account, sir?' she said and when I said yes took pleasure in snipping the passbook in half. She counted out the money twice in twenties (much fidgeting in the queue behind me), secured it with rubber bands and handed it over in a plain brown envelope.

I went back and told my landlady I was leaving straight away, giving her a bit extra in lieu of notice, and went round John Lewis to get a new mattress (which didn't come cheap). I put the old one out to rot. It turned your stomach, the stains there were on it. I got a couple of new sleeping bags to save worrying about sheets. It would be more like indoor camping than gracious living was my plan. I went looking for a long blonde wig too, which I thought would be a nice touch. The woman at the wig shop said it was two-for-one-day and threw another one in for free. A plastic bag of hair is a strange thing to walk through town with. I bought a hammer, nails and plywood.

While I was doing the shopping I somehow wandered into a

sex shop and had a bit of a turn seeing the stuff in there, like handcuffs, gags and whips. And women browsing, looking like respectable types yet feeling up the vibrators and suchlike. Strange world we live in where a woman can buy what they term a butt plug (of which I for one had never heard) without so much as a blush. Since I was there I took advantage of a special offer and bought some items of restraint.

I chose the room at the back for her. What with the new mattress and sleeping bag and the lino swept there was nothing she could complain about. It wasn't the lap of luxury but after being inside for fifteen years it wouldn't come as strange. I hammered plywood over the window so there was no need for curtains. I tried out music in there at top volume and went out into the street and you couldn't hear a peep, nor could you see the light through the boards if you were standing in the yard at night, although who in their right mind would be?

There was a lot of argy-bargy from her on the phone at work. Attempts to put me off and to call my bluff. It was no more than you'd expect and in any case I was happy to bide my time. At last I was ready. The flat, her room, all sorted, food in the cupboard and I was only waiting for a sign that it was all systems go.

And it came out of the blue. One day when I rang her at work she said she'd told Charlie and he'd gone away to think it over. Told him about us, I took her to mean. For once I believed her, she sounded so choked up. I said I'd go round. I was keeping my mobile off because of Dad but when I switched it on to look, among all the expected messages was one from her saying, 'Don't come round, I'll meet you.' It was working like clockwork. It was such progress I allowed myself a celebration, bringing the wig and the item of restraint into play and varying it, which added an extra bit of spice. But it was that bitch Jessica who kept popping up, trying to eclipse Isobel in my mind.

I woke up late and hungover on the bed that will be Karen's. I had a shave and coffee and did some finishing touches like putting out a brand-new toothbrush and a box of Kleenex. When I was ready I rang her at work, only to be told she'd gone off sick. I bet you have, I thought. It couldn't have been better. She was playing right into my hands.

I bought a bottle of the trademark champagne and drove to Chestnut Avenue, parking under the tree. I went and stood on the front doorstep. Last time I'd stood there I'd been a milkman called Mark but all that was faint now, way back in the past, proving what progress had been made. I didn't ring the doorbell but phoned instead. She tried to put me off, as per usual, and I went round the back to see what I could see. There was a budgie sitting in a cage on the kitchen windowsill. That took me aback. I thought for a moment I'd got it wrong but I peered through the bars of the cage and sure enough there she was.

She opened the door but didn't smile or meet my eye or ask me in. Her face was white but her voice cold and business-like. You could see the emotion bottled up inside.

'What do you want?' she said.

I pushed past her. It was a big moment, entering the house at last. I waited for the words to come.

'Didn't you get my message? I said I'd meet you later,' she said.

I took the bull by the horns and opened the champagne. I knew her well enough to know she wouldn't resist and I was proved right. I did a toast, 'to us' or somesuch. She shrugged as if this was no big deal to her, as if she quaffed down champagne every morning of the week, and knocked half of it back. Now, if she'd been serious about getting rid of me would she have done that? I could see right through her like she was made of glass.

I remembered how Isobel would always get her way – 'She's

got you wrapped round her little finger' (Mum to Dad) – and look at how Charlie has been taken in by Karen! It makes you wonder why we bother, except for the sex of course and the cooking, and a certain tenderness or what you might call togetherness that you do sometimes see between couples. It's one of life's big mysteries to me.

It made me want to laugh or spew the way she gulped down the champagne, snooty as they come, nose up in the air, and then, 'I really must make a call.' She looked at me like I was nothing more than a piece of dog-do and it boiled up in me then behind the Rupert face, the fifteen years of waiting, the cold-blooded murder, ruination of my family – and there she was guzzling my champagne without a word of thanks, Miss High and Mighty Common Criminal, expecting me to exit off stage at her convenience. It just burst up out of me and I wanted to bite my tongue off but too late it was out there. I said, 'I know who you are.'

You could have cut the atmosphere with a knife and then there was a crack and her glass was broken and there was blood and one thing I cannot stand is the sight of blood. She stood there looking at it with her mouth open and then the door opened and an old lady came barging in. She was carrying a parcel and about to say something but she was brought up short. You could see her eyes darting about from Karen to the blood to me and ending up on the bottle of champagne.

'Oh my giddy aunt,' she said and that nearly took my breath away because last time I heard that expression it was out of Izzie's mouth. I had to get a grip. 'Would you like a glass?' I said. You could see she was lost for words. I was at a loss too then, this not being part of my calculations, so I took my leave.

I sat in the car under the tree until the old lady came out. I waited till she was past me, then got out and followed at a snail's pace until she went into a bungalow, the odd one in a street of terraces and semis and easy to remember in case I ever had the need.

I went to a pro that day and she was more like Karen than Karen was and I asked her if she minded if I called her Karen and she had no objection. She was one of the street ones and about the age Karen would have been, or maybe less, though that's her business and no fault of mine. I held her hair while she did the mouth thing on me in the back of my car and her hair was silky in my hand but she yelled when I pulled it hard and so I stopped. I am not an animal nor out of control. I tried to give her extra money but she shot out of the car like a bullet.

'You should have a care,' I said, leaning out of the window, 'I could have been a nutter and you dead.'

'You are a fucking nutter,' she said as she went off and then turned round, her voice shaking. 'Don't try round here again, I'll tell the girls.' And all because I gave a little tug on her hair! If you can't stand the heat stay out of the kitchen, miss, I thought as I drove off and would have given my eye-teeth to have said it. No skin off my nose. Not as if I'd need prostitutes much longer anyway. I would have the real thing.

*

After the cremation we had sherry in the sitting room. Maisie arrived with a stack of Tupperware boxes filled with several kinds of sandwich as well as her ginger cake. I put squares of cheese on cream crackers and pickled onions on a saucer, though I wasn't sure about the onions – whether they showed respect. Maisie had invited everyone Fay knew and that was a lot. There weren't enough chairs and people had to loom about with their glasses of sherry and their plates.

Charlie was pale in his badly fitted suit and a new, brutal haircut. He looked young and ill. Of course when he'd walked through the door, he had come straight into my arms and I had held him tight. He hadn't cried, though, it was more as if he was stunned.

As the sherry got into everyone's blood, the babble rose, people full of memories about Fay and the joie de vivre that I had never seen. Then there was a lull in the conversation; a moment of reflection into which the budgie said, 'Davy-boy, Davy-boy,' and a shudder ran round the room.

'However must she have felt, hearing that day in day out?' a woman said.

'Salt in a wound,' agreed somebody.

'Would anyone like to take him?' I said.

Charlie scowled across the room at me.

'I thought somebody might like to take him, that's all.'

'She would want *me* to keep him,' he said. There was something like grit in his throat.

'But *you're* not going to be here,' I said. All other conversation in the room had stopped though there was the sound of teeth munching an onion, lips slurping a drink. We never quarrelled. We could not quarrel now in front of all these people.

'Only for a few months,' he said, 'surely you can look after him for a few months? He's only a little bird, for God's sake.'

'Shall I put the kettle on?' Maisie said into the silence. 'What we all want is a nice cup of tea.'

'Is there anything else that anyone wants then,' I said, 'a souvenir?'

Charlie looked at me blankly. 'Before we have a clear-out,' I explained, 'Fay's friends might like something to remember her by, rather than sending it all to Oxfam.'

Someone gave a snarl of a laugh. 'Memento, rather than souvenir, is what you mean, dear, I think.'

It went quiet again; you could hear Maisie turning on the tap in the kitchen.

'Why don't we take a look?'

'Fine.' Charlie shrugged his shoulders and averted his eyes from mine.

We all, except Charlie, trooped down. I had already taken the things we wanted – a carriage clock, a tea set, an almost brand-new kettle – and Charlie had brought some books and all her photo albums upstairs.

Her little flat was overcrowded with these sherry-flushed people and nobody wanted to be the first to claim something; but eventually Maisie picked up her crossword-solver's handbook. And then there was a rush on the portable items: a jug; a shoehorn; a Spanish Linguaphone set; the bathroom scales. A man with a nose like scaffolding went up to fetch his car so that he could load the television into it. Her clothes and shoes were too small for anyone, but someone did make off with her furry winter hat.

Most of the guests left then, just a few gathered round sipping tea and eating slices of Maisie's ginger cake. 'Fay loved this,' she said and I saw Fay lifting a piece to her fastidious little nose and sniffing before she nibbled, the picture so vivid it stopped me mid-chew. The budgie cheeped and cheeped. There was a fuzzy halo round my cup. I put it down.

The man with the nose embarked on an anecdote about Fay and a stray dog she'd met on a coach trip to Torquay. She'd bought it some fish and chips and it had tagged around behind her all day. 'She had a heart of gold,' he said, finishing on a sob. Maisie, sitting beside him, patted his knee.

'She was one in a million,' she said and then looked across at me. 'How's your hand, Nina?' she asked. 'Want me to have a look before I go?'

'It's OK, thanks,' I said. 'I must have the recipe for this cake. Isn't it nice, Charlie?' But Charlie was staring at his knees.

'He was a handsome chap you had here the other morning,' Maisie said, 'reminded me of him in that film, you know the one . . .'

I'd thought there'd been sympathy between us, what with the bandage and the sandwiches and the cake. Her cheeks were hot with the sherry and there was a hectic look in her eyes.

Charlie raised his head. 'Who's that?' he said.

'Tall, dark, handsome . . . something French or Italian,' she said. 'You know that film, with the aeroplane, with her that's dead now.'

I handed the cake round. The pattern on the carpet was jumping so that I could not look down.

'Blood everywhere,' Maisie was saying, 'gave me quite a turn.'

I put the plate of cake slices carefully down on the coffee table. 'Excuse me,' I said. I went upstairs to the bathroom. My face was throbbing. I looked in the mirror. The traces of bruising were like dirt. I fumbled in the cupboard for my migraine pills. The tastes of sherry and ginger cake crawled up my throat. I swallowed a pill and drank water from the tap. I pressed my face against the mirror till it clouded with my breath, then I went back downstairs.

'All right, dear?' Maisie said. 'She does look pale, doesn't she? The two of you need looking after. They're like the babes in the wood, aren't they?'

I sat still and said not very much more and soon everyone took the hint and left. As soon as the last one had gone, I lay down on the sofa and closed my eyes.

I could feel Charlie looking at me and I heard him sigh. 'Must you keep making these unilateral decisions?'

I opened my eyes a slit, light sizzled round him against the window.

'I thought that was what people did. It would have only gone to Oxfam.'

'What was the hurry? She's only just . . . And what about Charlie Two!'

'She wouldn't have minded,' I said.

'The *point is* you should have asked me.'

Inside my head fuzzy human shapes swelled and shrunk in a throbbing rhythm. Images of Fay, her eyelids flashing as they clicked open and shut. I squeezed my eyes tighter shut but the images were burned inside. I could feel the shadow of him looking down.

I nearly told him about Rupert then. Maybe if I told him in a small flat voice with my eyes closed it would be OK. It would be over. Like breaking a spell. It seemed almost like nothing now, a one-night stand. But today?

'Who did Maisie mean? That was here?'

'Gary.'

'From work? What did he want?'

'When I cut my hand, he drove me back.'

'Why not to Casualty?'

'I didn't want to go to the hospital again.' I was meting out the words quietly and levelly so that they did not make me sick. I could hear activity in his brain like feathers rustling.

'Funny how I've never met anyone from your work,' he said. 'Or any friends. Even Rose.'

The clock ticked and Charlie Two snickered quietly to himself.

'Who's John Smith?' I said.

'Smithy? Why?'

Nothing would come.

'Why?'

'I'm getting a migraine,' I said. He sat down on the edge of the sofa and put his hand on my forehead. I felt myself flow into him. He took my hands and pulled me up to my feet. Lights spat and sparked and I retched. He helped me up the stairs and I lay down carefully, you can't move too fast or you are sick. I used to get migraine all the time. I thought that love had cured it. It was the accident that set it off again. Now it was as bad as ever.

He drew the curtains against the light. The glass was stained red, I suppose the sun was setting. An inflamed pinkness reflected on the wall. He slipped my shoes off and put a blanket over me.

He brought me a bowl in case I was sick and went downstairs. I lay and listened to the budgie noise, a clinking as he washed the dishes and put them away, the phone drilling out its sound and Charlie speaking for a long time, but not the words he said.

When the light had gone and I was cocooned in the dark and the drug that softened everything, he came upstairs with a glass of water. He made me undress and get between the sheets. I asked him who'd been on the phone and he said it was Tony ringing from the bird observatory to see if he was OK.

'Sounds a nice bloke,' I said and he grunted. I felt him slide into bed, and though I wanted to put my arms round him it was as much as I could do to stretch out a finger and touch his skin.

The morning Charlie went back, I switched on my mobile and there was a message from Rose.

'I'm very concerned, Nina,' she said. 'What's happened with work? I've called round once or twice and you're always out. You know the terms . . . well anyway if you're not at work tomorrow I'll be round at eleven.'

A fork of lightning zipped through me. It was ten past ten. I'd have to go straight there. I hadn't been to the other place for ages. My 'official' address. I had to make believe I still lived there because I hadn't told her about Charlie. I hadn't told her about Charlie because she would have had to meet him and make sure he knew everything and I hadn't filled him in on all my background. I always meant to but *now*? How could I *now*? But how could I ever? A plan was forming. I would leave. I would stop it. I would change it. But now, now I had to hold Rose off, even if just this one last time.

I pulled on my clothes and rushed round snatching things to take: a couple of Get Well cards left from my accident, a handful of carnations someone brought for Charlie; I took the end of a loaf, a tub of margarine and half a bottle of old wine from the fridge.

It was a hot day and the patch of garden at the front was parched and yellow. I took a deep breath before I let myself in to a stale fusty smell. It was like stepping back into an old life or discarded skin. The staircase always stank of other people's dirty minds, their dinners and their breath. It was even worse than Dave's place had been. There was a pile of junk mail, bank-statements, bills, lots of them addressed to me. There were other letters too and I took them up and opened them, pinned a couple with recent dates up on the board; switched

171

on the radio; opened the windows; flung a dead geranium in the bin. I fried an onion though I wanted nothing to eat, searched for a vase but there wasn't one. That is something I forgot, stupid, stupid, the easiest thing to get in a charity shop would be a vase. The onion slid apart in greasy white strands and I switched off the gas sickened.

I rumpled the bed and wet the soap and toothbrush in the bathroom – just in case she went in there. There was a monstrous spider's web stretched between the bath and toilet. I stamped it down and the spider scurried away into the dank space behind the basin. I tipped the wine in a glass, tasted it – OK – squeezed the carnation stems into the bottle just in time.

I heard her clumping up the stairs. And then I remembered milk, no milk; she would expect a cup of coffee. Stupid, stupid. I could not afford to make mistakes like that.

I opened the fridge: a sour smell hit me. There was a bottle of milk, half full, gone green and solid. I gagged at the smell of it, too late to tip it away so I chucked it out of the window. Just as she knocked, I heard a smash, from out there, and a yell.

I opened the door to her, my face dented with a dolly's plastic smile.

She came in, eyes darting round, and sat down at the kitchen table. 'At last,' she said. 'I was beginning to worry that you'd done a bunk.'

'As if,' I said.

'Why have you been off work? Gary seems confused about the reason. You're lucky to have this chance, you know.'

'I think it's concussion,' I said, 'I keep getting headaches.'

'Been to the doctor?'

'I will.'

'You're not . . . I mean, you are going to stick with it?'

'Of course. Tea?' I said. Forgetting, I opened the fridge and then shut it as fast as possible to stop the smell coming out. 'No milk – I've been drinking it black since hospital.'

'That's OK,' she said. 'It's hot, isn't it? A glass of juice would be nice.'

'Sorry.'

'Water?' She saw the wine glass and raised her eyebrows.

'From last night,' I said. 'I'd had enough.' I was pleased with that, a good encouraging detail. I filled a glass for her from the tap.

'Nice flowers,' she said approvingly. 'Good value carnations, aren't they? I'll just spend a penny if that's OK?'

She went to the bathroom and I knew it was to check up on me. I was so glad I'd got rid of the cobweb and then I heard feet on the stairs and a hammering on my door. I had to answer it, Rose being there, or it would have seemed suspicious.

A woman with a face the colour of ham stood there, sweating and puffing from the stairs. She had a pierced eyebrow. 'You stupid fucking cow,' she shrieked.

'What?' I said.

Rose came out of the bathroom. 'Is there a problem?'

'Someone threw a fucking milk-bottle out of the window and nearly fucking brained my Brian.'

'I don't know what you're on about,' I said. 'I don't even drink milk.'

'It came out of your fucking window.' She glared at Rose.

'It didn't,' I said. 'Did it?' I looked at Rose. 'It must have come from someone else's window.'

'Is your son all right?' Rose said.

'He's not my son he's my husband,' she said.

'Well let's just be thankful that he's not hurt.' Rose's sensible voice seemed to soothe the woman but I started to shake. I wasn't up to this kind of stress. Rose noticed. Sweat crawled in the roots of my hair; something fizzed in my ears and eyes. I stared at the glass of wine, but I couldn't drink it, not in the morning with Rose there to see.

'Go and sit down,' she said. She talked to the woman for a minute or two more until she went away. 'I'll make you some tea,' she said.

'No,' I said.

'You seem shaken up.'

'I'm OK.'

She stared at me for a moment, hands on hips. She was wearing a sleeveless dress and I could see the wet wisps of her armpit hair and white rings of dried sweat or deodorant on the armholes. Her toenails were painted red but they were chipped. Surely she shouldn't have been so scruffy? It made me like her more though. I'd never noticed that before, only her stern glasses and the dry puckering of her lips.

'Was it you?' she said.

'What?'

'The bottle?'

'Of course not! Why would I want to do a thing like that?'

She shrugged. 'That woman, Lorraine, lives two doors down. Do you know her?'

I shook my head.

'She says she's never seen you about either.'

'Well I've never seen her about,' I said. 'We probably keep different hours or something.'

She gave me a weighing-up look, then nodded and said, 'Probably, yes.' She asked me questions about everything: work, why I had left the self-esteem course early? Anyone special in my life? Because of course I knew she'd need details of a significant other. She had a bad feeling about me, she said, and maybe we should up the supervisions again. OK, I said, anything, just to make her go. And then, at last, she did. I gave her half an hour in case she popped back, or was watching, and I washed out the fridge, gagging at the cheesy reek of solidified milk spills, swallowed the wine and rinsed the glass, shut the window, locked up and went out, picking my way

174

over the shards of broken glass and sour green slime to the dustbins with my old bread and flowers.

When I got home there was a message on the phone. It was someone from the crematorium inviting me to collect Fay's remains. The other option was that they would scatter them in the Garden of Remembrance but I said no, of course I wanted them. I took a taxi and picked up the blue urn-shaped plastic jar. It came to me clear as a chiming bell that this was my reason for going north. Charlie would want to have the ashes as soon as possible. I could go north, I could simply disappear. But Rose and the authorities . . . I didn't know, I couldn't think, too many things, one thing at a time. To go north. The urn sat on my lap in the taxi on the way home from the crematorium and I swear it felt warm.

I packed a bag and ordered a taxi for first thing in the morning. It was a week and Rupert had given me the week. But he would never trace me. Not to Orkney. I was too excited to be hungry but, still, opened a tin of pea and ham soup. I sat Fay on the table in her usual place. I may have talked to her a bit. It was cosy, the three of us, Fay, Charlie Two and me. All in harmony. Charlie Two quiet in his cage, ruffling through his feathers with his beak. It felt like family. And then I had an idea. It started with curiosity. I unscrewed the urn and looked inside. Pale speckled gritty powder. I poured a little on to my bandaged hand and ran my finger through it. Incredible to think that this was actually *Fay*. I'm not mad, I knew this wasn't *her*: this was just the remains of her body. *She* was crouching on the table, watching.

The beautiful and simple idea came to me then. How I could actually become part of the family, become Charlie's flesh and blood. Because you are what you eat. I sprinkled some of the powder on to my soup like a seasoning and stirred it in. There was no taste, just a grittiness against my teeth, a slight scrape in my throat, and then she was inside me.

~

O n the twelfth of December, the day Jeffrey came home,
she stayed away from his house, didn't even let herself
walk past, though was painfully aware of the phone, jumping
and straining her ears whenever it rang, which it frequently did
in a house of doctors.

Next day, after school, she walked past his house a few
times and then, suddenly resolved to confront him, went back
and rang the doorbell. He opened the door, but didn't ask her
in, instead he stepped out into the porch in his socks and
pulled the door to behind him. His hair was longer now,
parted in the centre, and his chin was covered in curly fluff.
From inside the house she could hear music and smell the
warmth of a baking cake.

'Aren't you going to ask me in?' she said.

'Got a friend here,' he said, 'they've come to stay for the
weekend.'

'One or more?' she said.

'What?'

'You said they.'

He blushed. 'All right. She.'

'Can't I meet her?' Behind the lenses of his glasses his eyes
darted about in a panic, his mouth opened and closed. 'Oh I
get it,' she said. 'I'm too common?'

'No!'

'Too *thick* then? Too *young*?'

He shifted from one sock to the other looking so desperately uncomfortable that she almost laughed.

'Your new girlfriend?' she said.

He smiled sheepishly.

'Oh.' She looked at the brass numbers on a plaque beside the door. Fifty-three. They were smeared and dull. With the corner of her scarf she began to polish the five.

'What are you doing?' he said. 'Karen, I'm freezing my bollocks off here.'

'Jeffrey . . .' a high voice drifted out. 'I think it's ready.'

'Go in then,' she said.

'I'm sorry.'

'Don't be.' She started on the three.

'See you then.' He hesitated, half through the door, letting out the warmth and music and cake smell – it smelt like chocolate – then stepped inside and closed the door. She polished the three until it shone, breathing on it and scrubbing at it with the thick wool of her school scarf. She could sense him standing behind the door waiting for her to leave. When she was ready, when the numbers were shiny enough, she walked away.

She walked back home and took out her physics books. The three laws of motion was her topic of the day: balanced force; resultant force; reaction force. If object A exerts a force on object B then object B exerts the exact opposite force on object A, she read. And that seemed fair enough.

∧

I went back to Peerless View. High ceilings, gloom, smell of engine oil or somesuch that comes up through the floor however much Haze you squirt about. It's a very private street considering the amount of lorries and cars that thunder past. No one would ever look up and see you. Even if someone did happen to look up, the windows were so thick with muck they wouldn't know a thing. I stood with my face against the dirty glass for a whole morning and no one walked past or stopped. It was more private than the middle of the countryside. It was like an island in the city and not a place anyone would ever think to look if a person was to go missing.

This was when I made a big mistake. It was out of being soft. I don't know what came over me except it was the aftermath of the blood and then the silly little pro. I had to get out of there and I went to the pub for my lunch. I was eating a Tex-Mex when my phone went and I knew before looking who it would be. She was getting predictable. But what she came out with caught me unawares.

'Charlie's mum has just died,' she said and her voice had that ring of truth to it. I put myself in Charlie's shoes for a minute, how I'd feel if it was Mum. And it came to me stronger than ever how vital it was to get this sorted out, how I'd never forgive myself if Mum were to go to her grave before Karen was dealt with. I gave her the week.

I checked with the hospital and confirmed that the death was true. I got details of the cremation and went along, sitting in the back. Charlie stood up and said a few sincere words and I got quite choked up. It was him I felt sorry for. She had the wool pulled over his eyes so far he was tripping up on it.

I left before she saw me. Keeping to my part of the bargain but I might have known she would not keep to hers. I got a drum of paint from Wickes and started to do the kitchen. The walls were done in a thick paper textured with something like medallions but it was all greased up what with the generations of cooking that must have gone on in there and the paint wouldn't stay on. I went over and over one patch and then gave it up as a bad job. I was sleeping in the lounge, the other bedroom being so damp there was fungus on the walls like orange sponges. The lounge had a high ornate ceiling and a boarded-up fireplace with a mirror over it. Under the settee I found a mousetrap and under the toothed wire was pinned the skeleton of a mouse. You could see the breakage in the ribs and back.

I stuck to my part of the bargain re contact but that wasn't to say I couldn't keep an eye open. I sat in the car under the tree and saw the comings and goings. Him white as a sheet and with those shadows under his eyes that show he hadn't slept going out for a paper and a pint of milk. Every night the downstairs lights went out at ten-thirty and the upstairs about thirty minutes later. And then, after a bit, the downstairs light would come on and go off again and there would be the flickering of light from the box. I went close to the window, just once, careful not to scrape the gate. Through the gap in the curtains I could see him sitting there, a glass in his hand, the TV light moving on his face.

She wouldn't have had the chance to get away if I hadn't let my guard up. I'd popped into the pub for an early-evening pint. Usually I keep myself to myself but this night, as I was looking at my brochures, a man came up.

'Mexico, eh?' he said. 'It's the dog's bollocks if you ask me.' He happened to have been to his sister's wedding there which coincidence I took as a good omen. He went on about the girls and the beaches and the food. He'd stayed on after the wedding to make a holiday of it and been there for a festival to mark Independence Day, music and coloured lights, girls dancing (though he was with his wife and it was on a strictly look-don't-touch basis), beer and tequila.

We started knocking it back as he fired me up on all cylinders and I forgot the time and when I went to speak to him again he'd gone and I was the last one in the pub and the landlord was pushing me out of the door and all I was fit for was getting back to Peerless View best I could and if it hadn't been for that I'd have seen her go.

*

As I stepped off the tiny plane, the wind lifted my scarf and whipped it against my face. It was a sweet cool wind, salty and grassy. The airport was nothing but a shed on the edge of a field, a small strip of tarmac with sheep grazing on either side. As soon as my foot hit solid ground, I saw Charlie standing at the gate. He had one leg bent up on the bottom rung, talking to a man in overalls. He squinted across at me, shading his eyes with his hand – the light was stinging bright. I walked towards him and couldn't stop a big grin from splitting my face. It was just a few metres but they seemed to stretch for ever.

'Nina,' he said flatly, then to the other two visitors in a heartier voice: 'Hello, welcome. Here we are. Good flight?' He walked off towards a Land Rover and threw open the back door. The others climbed in and then he came round to the front. 'Get in then,' he said to me, indicating the passenger seat.

He jumped in beside me and turned round to the couple. 'Been here before?' he asked and when they said not, 'Welcome to North Ronaldsay. Mind a detour before we go to the observatory? Got to fetch someone from the top of the island.'

'Super,' the woman said from the back. They pumped him for information on what was about – meaning which birds – as we drove up the narrow road that is like the spine of the island. I stared out of the window adjusting my expectations to the actuality: I had thought there would be cliffs and trees but the island was as flat and sprawled open as a naked body. There were cows in fields and ruined buildings, a church, and a clear and vivid scudding of clouds.

We drove to the tip of the island where there are two lighthouses, a working one – the tallest in Britain, Charlie said as proudly as if he'd built it himself – and the stumpy original at the end of a stony spit.

We sat there for a moment while the person we were picking up, a female in a knee-length cagoule and wellies, loped across the shore towards us.

'Isn't it beautiful?' Charlie said quietly.

'Super,' the couple agreed, in unison. They were both peering through binoculars at something or other.

'Beautiful,' I said, though really it looked like the end of the world to me.

The woman shouted, 'Hey Charlie,' quirked her head at him and hopped into the back. We drove to the bird observatory at the other end of the island – maybe ten minutes away. It was a modern, wooden, solar-heated building with big rooms, glass everywhere and through each window more and more of the same – sky and sea and fizzing salty light.

'If I ever go back to architecture,' Charlie said, 'this is the sort of thing I'll do.'

'*If?*' I said.

He shrugged and led me through into the kitchen. I tripped on a plastic doll – toys were scattered everywhere as if this was a nursery school. Charlie introduced me to Ruth and Bruno and their two small children, both of whom looked at me unsmilingly with the same bright incisive eyes.

Ruth was plump and blonde with a squinty glance. 'Welcome,' she said, ' 'scuse the mess.'

'Welcome,' said Bruno and crushed my hand in his huge one. His name suited him. He was dark, squat and as hairy as a bear. Springy curls spilled out over the neck of his T-shirt and climbed up to merge with his beard.

'Bruno's the GP and lifeguard,' Charlie said, 'Ruth's the bird warden and runs this place too – B&B and evening meals – there's nowhere else for the poor buggers to go.'

'God!' I said.

'I run it after a fashion,' she said, gesticulating at the mess. 'So, you're Charlie's . . .'

'Girlfriend,' I said.

'We didn't know you were coming.'

'It was a surprise.' I smiled. 'A sort of impulse.'

'And what do you think so far?' Bruno said.

'It's very . . .' I hesitated and he boomed out a laugh.

'It certainly is very . . .' he said. 'Extreme is the word I'd use. But watch out, people do fall in love with it. They could have one of the guest rooms for a night or two, couldn't they, Ru? There's a double empty.'

'Tonight there is,' she said.

'Don't go to any trouble,' I said.

She laughed and her breasts shoogled under the RSPB logo on her T-shirt. 'Not much danger of that,' she said, 'you'll have to make the bed up yourself. Sheets on the line. Charlie, maybe you could get them in?'

She went off then to greet the other guests and Charlie and I went out to get the sheets. They were blowing horizontally, flapping and snapping, straining at the clothes pegs. We bundled them in, cold dry cotton scented with the fresh air, and Charlie took me up to our room. The window looked out over the sea towards the white ridge and tiny stub of lighthouse – the visible signs of the neighbouring island, a flat and sandy place I'd seen from the plane, white beaches and bays, sea as turquoise and azure as any in a Caribbean brochure.

He stood behind me, not touching. 'I've been in the bunkhouse up to now,' he said. 'This is luxury.'

'Glad I came then?'

He gave me a look. The sky was silver along its rim, long streaks of cloud racing. I willed him to put his arms round me but he moved away and began to make the bed, tipping the pillows into their clean cases and thumping them into place.

'I know but . . .' I said, 'Charlie, I was lonely. I was scared.'

'Scared?'

It was true. Last night I'd woken with a jerk to hear a regular clicking like the sound of a doll's eyelids sliding up and down and it may only have been an airlock in a radiator, something like that, something with a tidy everyday explanation, but with every click I'd seen Fay's eyes opening at me and blinking shut. I was wet with sweat. She was angry that I'd eaten her. Though it was only the tiniest bit. I couldn't stop wondering which bit, which one of her ground-up bones. I shouldn't have done it. I couldn't get it out of my head.

Charlie huffed and sank down on the bed. 'How long have you got off work?' he said.

'A few days.'

'You'll get the sack if you don't watch it. And what about Charlie Two?'

'Taken care of.'

I had left him on his own, cage open, lots of seed in his feeder and in a saucer on the windowsill in case he needed more. He'd been quiet when I left, huddled on his perch in a feathery huff. I wondered what was happening in his pea-sized brain. I hadn't liked to leave him alone but there hadn't been the time to organise anything. If I stayed on I'd send a card to Maisie, I thought, get her to go and see to him.

He was facing away from me and I could see the tender hollow at the back of his neck, exposed by the funeral haircut. I went and sat beside him. He lifted my hand. It had almost healed and I'd replaced the bandage with a sticking plaster. '*How* did you do this again?' he said.

'Told you.'

He looked into my eyes and his pupils were flared hugely and I know that means emotion; it means love. He seemed about to say something and then he changed his mind.

'I need a drink,' he said and stood up.

'I really came to bring you this.' I knelt down and opened my bag. Carefully snuggled in a cardigan was the plastic urn. 'Your mum,' I said. 'I thought you'd like to have her with you. It didn't seem right to put her in the post.'

He took the canister and tipped it from side to side. You could hear the slight shifting movement of the gritty ash.

'You might want to scatter her. Or bury her and plant a tree.'

He swallowed and put the canister down. 'Let's get that drink then,' he said.

'How far's the pub?'

He almost laughed at that. 'This is the pub.'

'I'm sorry. I shouldn't have come.' I put my arms round him. 'We haven't even kissed.'

He kissed me then, first just a brushing of lips and then a real deep angry kiss, the edges of his teeth against my lip. He looked hard into my eyes. 'You drive me mad, you know,' he said, 'you never listen, you never wait . . .'

'Sorry,' I said again but this time I was smiling inside.

I didn't want to go downstairs but he insisted and led me down into the big central room of the observatory. In one corner was a little bar, which he went straight behind. He poured himself a beer, me a glass of red wine from a box and we went over and sat by one of the windows. He seemed so much at home, walking about in his woolly socks, helping himself to drinks.

'Did you get my letter?' he said.

'No. Why did you send me a letter? I must have missed it.'

He sighed. I didn't want to know about any letter. I don't trust letters.

'Anyway, I'm here now,' I said, 'you can speak to me in person.'

He took a swallow of his beer and shrugged. 'Yeah. Well.'

He got up to serve cider to some twitchers, then he came back.

'Don't,' he said and I saw my foot was going. I pressed it to the floor.

'What do you think of the place then?'

'Not what I imagined,' I said.

'No.'

'I thought it would be more . . . that there would be more *things*.'

We gazed out at a long sweep of pale beach lipped with frilly waves. The sun was still high, and glinting on the wet sand.

'Doesn't get dark till late here,' he said. 'We get amazing sunsets.'

'Do we?'

'You wait. This is good beer, try it.' He pushed his glass towards me.

'I'll stick to wine.' I peered through the window. I could make out a huddle of sluglike lumps just at the edge of the waves. 'Seals?' I asked.

'Grey seals,' he said, 'there's a colony of common a bit further along. Tomorrow, when I've done my stuff, I'll take you to see. You can get up really close if you're quiet and slow.'

'Done your stuff?'

'I'm on breakfasts.' He looked past me. 'Hi Tony,' he said and I turned to see this Tony, but there was only a scruffy woman there, the same one that had jumped into the back of the Land Rover. 'This is Nina,' Charlie said. 'Nina, Toni.'

She was tall and thin, bare-footed with a tatty sweater that reached her knees over frayed jeans. Her hair was long and toffee-coloured, wild as if she never brushed it.

'Nina,' she said. She gave me a long look, then shrugged,

grinned and held out her hand. 'I've been hearing all about you,' she said in a lilting Scottish accent – the first I'd heard since I'd been here – and with a kind of mischief.

'Hi,' I said, thinking I've heard nothing about you.

'I'll get a beer. You two all right?' she asked. She walked like a duck, her bottom sticking out, and I was glad of that. I watched Charlie but he didn't follow her with his eyes.

'Short for Antonia,' he said.

'Was it her that rang you?'

'Yup.' He swigged back his beer. 'Want another?'

I shook my head. I'd hardly taken more than a sip. People were coming in the bar, the couple from the plane wearing identical hand-knitted sweaters with robins on the front, and a family with two children of about nine or ten. Charlie stayed at the bar serving them and Toni sat down opposite me.

'Half an hour off before we eat.' She opened a bag of peanuts and put it between us. 'Help yourself.' She took a long swallow of her beer and wiped her mouth on her sleeve. 'Needed that. Charlie didn't say you were coming.'

'No, it was sort of a surprise.'

She gazed at me as she chewed a mouthful of peanuts. Her eyes were slanting, green-flecked blue. 'Good trip?' she asked.

'Bumpy,' I said. 'But the views—'

'Awesome eh?' She stretched her arms back and I heard her vertebrae click. 'You're lucky it was clear, you see fuck all when it's cloudy.'

'You work here?' I said.

'Six months voluntary,' she said, 'same as Charlie.' I noticed the way she said his name, her accent caressing the R sound. 'Only I'm more than half done,' she added, 'I'll be away at the end of August. Hi,' she smiled over at the family, settled down on the table beside ours, the parents sharing a bottle of beer, the children bickering over Pringles.

'What do you normally do?' I asked.

'Teach.' She screwed up her nose. 'Wee ones. Supply up to now but after this I'll find something permanent. I dunno. I'd rather run away and join the circus.' She grinned again. It was a huge grin that stretched her dry and flaky lips and showed far too many uneven teeth.

'What about you?'

'Office work,' I said. 'Don't like it but—'

'It pays the bills.' She took another handful of peanuts. 'Tell me about it!'

We ate dinner at a long table, guests, family and workers all together. I sat down, expecting Charlie to join me, but he went off into the kitchen to help. I was next to one of the twitchers.

'See the godwits?' she said. I could only shake my head. Ruth, Charlie and Toni served the food, a chicken casserole with beans; ice-cream and pears.

'No, you stay put,' Ruth said when I tried to get up and help.

'We do all muck in,' Charlie explained, 'but you're a guest.' He didn't say 'just' a guest but that's how it sounded. I didn't want to be just a guest. I was tired. I wanted Charlie to myself. I'd pictured the two of us alone in a cottage on the edge of a cliff, a tiny room with a fireplace, a bed under the eaves, not this bright endless chatter and clatter.

At last we were able to go upstairs. We undressed and lay together between the crisp wind-scented sheets. We started to touch. I ran my hand along his side, his cool fuzzy thigh, curve of his hip, round to the warm small of his back. I moved in to kiss him and felt wetness on his face.

'Sorry.' He rolled away.

'OK, OK,' I said. I put my arms round him and felt him shudder and gulp trying to get back in control. 'I'm here,' I said soothingly, 'I'm here now.' We had not drawn the curtains and the last traces of orange sunset glinted on the varnished ceiling, maybe reflected from the sea.

∧

I rang Green's next day, which was a week to the dot from when we'd spoken, and was told she was off sick again. Sick my foot. I drove to Chestnut Avenue and sat in the car under the tree but hours went past and dark came and there was still no sign of anyone. She didn't know what thin ice she was skating on. It got to midnight, the lights out in all the other houses in the street. Rain was coming down on the car window and it was hard to see. I got out and went to the front door. The key was under a stone by the doorstep – you'd think a criminal would have a better idea of home security.

I put the light on in the kitchen and it made the budgie jump. I took a look in his cage – the water had all spilled out of his feeder. I topped it up for him and gave him a bit of Trill. He got stuck into that water like there was no tomorrow.

I drew the curtains so that nobody would think it amiss as I went from room to room. I used the bathroom, then started my search for clues as to her whereabouts. The house was all done up in an old lady's way, and I twigged that it was really Mrs Martin's but she'd been relegated to the cellar. I'd like to have put it to Charlie then, man to man, how could he treat his mother like that? Where was his respect?

In the bedroom was a wooden bed, a duvet with a design of clouds, not my taste and more modern than anything else in there. You could tell which was her side from the nightie under the pillow – a baggy pink T-shirt, not the sexy type. I got in the bed and pulled the duvet over my head to get the smell of her. There were bits of dyed hair on the pillow and lower down some of the fair and curly ones.

I took my time then, going through her things. On her bedside table was a white china lamp; a couple of paperback novels (unread by the look of it); an alarm clock set for seven-fifteen; a box of tissues, soft peach. On his side were a bird book and a couple of wildlife magazines. There was anti-wrinkle cream by the mirror and a photo of Charlie on a bridge.

The wardrobe was an old dark job with carving on the door. I went through her clothes: size ten and a few twelve. I picked some out to take for her: the nightie, a warm jumper and some undies; white with lace; navy with red dots; silky beige. Two bras, 34B, one white, one black. I took all the personal items out of her undies drawer. Underneath was flowery lining paper that gave off a bit of a scent, which I thought a nice touch, and underneath that an envelope.

Inside the envelope was a piece of paper entitled *Licence. Crime Sentences Act 1997.* And it went on to say: *The Secretary of State authorises the release on licence within fifteen days of the date hereof of Karen Mary Wild who shall on release and during the period of this licence comply with the following conditions . . .* and so on and then a list of the conditions including supervision by a probation officer which I already knew, but still, it felt like treasure. It was my first piece of written proof. I put it in my pocket.

There was Tampax in the bathroom and I took it in case she had the need. Isobel used Tampax. It seemed to me one of the special and secret things about girls. Once I took one from the box hidden in her room. I opened the papery casing round it and it was a white telescope with a cotton tail. I thought it a beautiful thing, so white and innocent, but that was before I knew about the blood.

All the time I was in her house a voice was nagging at me, saying, *What if you've lost her? What if she's gone?* I searched for clues but there was nothing – then I remembered the old lady who'd come right into the kitchen without knocking – which I took to mean she was a family friend.

That is why I'd followed her the week before. There always is a meaning for these things though sometimes you have to wait to find it out. I switched off the alarm clock, got into bed and slept for the rest of the night. It was not a bad mattress and I was woken by the rattle of the milk float. Funny that she must have been woken in the mornings by that sound when I was the milkman and had no idea she was here. I walked about till it was a decent time, went round to the bungalow and rang the bell. She was aware of security and kept the chain across at first, talked to me through a gap.

'Didn't I see you round at Fay's? Charlie and Nina's rather?'

'I'm a friend. Very sad about Fay.'

I could see half her face round the door. 'Didn't I see you at the crematorium?'

'Paying my respects.'

'But not back at the house?'

'Didn't want to intrude.'

It was the right thing to say and she stepped back to let the chain off.

'Come in.'

When I got into her lounge I could have laughed out loud when I saw the cactus and the picture on the wall, a desert scene, maybe actual Mexico, and, despite the sun outside, the gas fire blasting out a desert heat. As if her décor was telling me I was on the right track here. She saw me looking.

'You a fan of cacti?' she said and she gave me a spiel about

191

the different types before offering me a cup of tea which I turned down.

'I was just wondering if you knew where K . . .' I turned it into a cough. 'Beg pardon, where Nina's got to?'

'I expect she'll have gone away with Charlie,' she said, then looked up at me in a way that you might have termed flirtatious from a younger woman. 'You're a tall chap, aren't you? Would you mind changing the landing bulb?'

She flicked the light on and off to check it was working and then we were back in the lounge again. 'Sure you won't have a cuppa? Do sit down.' She lowered herself on to a chair and waited for me to do the same. We sat there for a minute, her dabbing her eyes in a spot of reminiscence, me waiting for the lines to come.

'How well do you know Nina?' she said.

'A bit.'

'She's rather . . .' she tailed off. A cunning look came across her face and you could see she was fishing. 'Well, it takes all sorts.'

'She *is* rather . . .' I began and she leant forward but I was stuck.

'To tell you the truth,' she said at last, 'between you and me, I wonder if Charlie didn't rather go up there to get away from her. Fay always said it had gone too fast, her moving in almost the moment they met. She never really took to her, you know. She thought her a bit of a closed book.'

'That's right,' I said. 'That's her to a tee.'

'What do you know about her?' she said.

'She's had a troubled past.'

'Ah yes . . . that makes sense. Why don't I put the kettle on?'

'I can't stop. I know she had an unhappy childhood,' I said, 'foster homes and suchlike. What you'd term insecure.'

'Ah yes.' She thought for a minute, then gave me a sharp look. 'What *was* going on that day in the kitchen?'

'Nina's hand?' I was ready for this one. 'I only just arrived a split-second before you did and was I glad to see you? I can't stand the sight of blood.'

'Champagne, at that time in the morning!' she said. I could see it all pass across her face as she considered whether to believe me or not and I think she did. 'And now she's trailed off after him,' she went on. 'Fay was all for him going, you know. Before he met Nina he'd had the plan, well you'll know all about his ornithology, I've got a bird table myself. Then this bird-warden job came up just when he needed it.

'Where?' I said.

'Didn't he say?'

'I haven't wanted to intrude.'

'Ah, that's a mistake people make, dear,' she said. 'If he's your friend you jolly well *should* intrude, go so far as to make a nuisance of yourself so he knows he's got the support. Better too much than not enough.'

'True,' I said, 'you're absolutely right.'

She sighed. 'It has such a romantic ring, doesn't it? Orkney. Mind you, I'd rather go somewhere hot. Fay and I had a little daydream . . .' I could tell by her voice that she was getting into her stride now so I got up and looked at my watch.

'Better be off.'

'Sure I can't tempt you? I've got a lovely bit of cake.'

But I was out of there.

*

I started awake in the night from a nightmare, a hollow inside me that never can be filled; a black circle in the dirt of my mind. Only a dream, only the dream. Didn't know where I was till against the window I saw the silhouette of Fay's urn. Light moving, moonlight tattering – a migraine coming. The pills in my bag but couldn't move, Charlie's leg heavy across mine. Didn't want to wake him, peaceful now, breath rasping quietly in and out like waves.

I tried to get my mind in order by going back through the day: taxi, train, plane, plane, plane. And now I lay beside him and he slept and I didn't know what next, what to do. There was nothing. I may have left some complications behind but the migraine was right there with me, squatting on my head. I had to wake him. He fed me pills and water. When the sun rose he got up and closed the curtains. He came in and out during the day.

'What a waste of your visit,' he said. 'What a shame.'

Bruno put his head round the door.

'Need anything?' he said.

I mumbled that I'd got my pills. I just needed to keep still and quiet.

'It's a bugger, migraine,' he said cheerfully. 'Give us a shout if you need anything.' He was whistling 'Summertime' as he

194

hammered down the stairs. I lay and listened to the voices of people, birds and sheep, and the wind bundling itself against the building, until late afternoon when the worst was over. Charlie brought me tea and biscuits. He opened the curtains as a flock of white birds shrieked past.

'They're getting worse,' he said. 'Or you're getting more. I wonder why?'

'The accident,' I said. Gingerly, I hauled myself up to sitting and it was all right, the nausea was passing off. I nibbled the edge of an oaty biscuit.

'Toni says her mum gets migraine. She takes feverfew.'

'I'll try it.'

'Lots of people coming tomorrow.' He sounded almost nervous. 'The place will be full. We'll have to move out of here . . .'

'I'll be OK tomorrow.'

'Back to the byre,' he said.

'I don't want special treatment.' I sipped my tea. 'I was thinking,' I said, 'of maybe staying.'

'What?'

'I could muck in. I could serve dinners and answer the phone and that. There's nothing hard, is there?'

'*Nina!*'

It made me jump the way he said my name. 'What?'

'I'm a volunteer. Where's the money going to come from?'

'It's yours now, isn't it?'

'What?'

A sharp crumb of biscuit stuck in my throat and made me cough, made my eyes water. I had to drink more tea before I could continue.

'The house, the whole house. You could let it and live off that. Or even sell it. If you sold it we could buy something else.'

The way he stared at me, I could tell he had not even thought of that.

'We could even buy a house up here,' I said. He picked at the frayed cuff of his sweater. There was dirt ingrained in his fingers and one of his nails was broken. I reached for his hand and stroked it.

'What have you been doing today?'

'Fixing a fence.'

I could hear the thin bleat of a sheep. 'Or anywhere,' I said. 'We could start again.'

'Things have conspired to cut me free,' he said.

'*Conspired?*' I said, and then, 'That's what I mean.'

'I've got to go and help,' he said. He looked at me, eyes soft with their starry lashes. There was stubble round his mouth and I felt the prickle of it as he leant in and kissed me on the forehead, the way I think a father might kiss a child.

The following morning started pale and grey. After breakfast, I watched Charlie ringing a bird that had been caught in a trap. The trap was a long tunnel of mesh that ran along a fence so that the bird would creep inside but be unable to find its way out. It was a stonechat, Charlie said. Grey feathers with a dash of black across its wings. He held it with the wings folded firmly against its body, and with a device like a pair of pliers snapped the ring on. I flinched; the sound was like the snap of a tiny bone. The bird's wiry claws clutched his finger and stabbed at it with its beak.

'OK,' he murmured, 'off you go.' He opened his hand and the stonechat flitted away light as a spark.

'Fancy a walk?' I said. 'You can show me round.' But he had to wait for the plane in order to pick up the guests.

'I'll catch you later,' he said. 'You'll soak up the atmosphere better on your own.'

'I wandered into the kitchen where Ruth and Toni were chatting and rolling pastry. Too hot and bright and peopley in there. I walked up the track, away from the observatory, and tried to imagine belonging, even living, here.

The sun shone the fields to lemony green and sizzled on the old-fashioned hay stooks. Birds shrieked and cried in the distance and chirruped and snicked from the tall weeds at the edges of the track. A crow hopped on to the road ahead of me and jabbed its beak into the corpse of a rabbit. It was all so open, nothing hidden, the air bristled with living sounds, the bleatings of the sheep travelling up from the beach.

I stopped to watch the little plane come in. It was low enough for me to see the shapes of heads through the glass. I imagined them peering out for their first glimpse of the island, and seeing me, bright yellow in my borrowed cagoule, seeming to belong.

Across the fields the sea was almost motionless and I realised that there was not a breath of wind. The sea was stunned into such metallic stillness that the clouds were mirrored. That was why the sounds were so sharp, a voice now, someone shouting, and the bellowing of a cow, maybe miles away.

I heard the plane fly away again and saw the Land Rover when it was still distant, like a Dinky toy sliding along the road towards me. As it grew closer I could make out two figures in front, Charlie and Bruno. I stood and waited till they drew level. Charlie rolled down the window.

' 'Fraid we're chocka,' he said. 'You OK walking? Bruno's just finished surgery.'

'How many patients?' I asked.

'Two today. Quite an epidemic!' Bruno beamed, his red cheeks bunching up above his beard. 'Feeling better?'

'Fine,' I said.

'Enjoy the fresh air.' Bruno leant across Charlie and peered at me. 'Best medicine,' he said.

Charlie smiled. 'Enjoy yourself then. See you later.'

I watched them drive away. The back of the Land Rover was crammed with people; there was a rare bird everyone had been raving about over breakfast, Siberian blue robin or something. I lifted my arm to wave but it froze in the air. Rupert was in there, face against the glass, smiling.

The sun was warm. I was clammy inside the fleece and cagoule Charlie had made me borrow. The air smelt of hay and seaweed and a faint flowery something from the roadside weeds. I needed to cool down and I needed to breathe. Of course it wasn't Rupert. How could it be? I took off the cagoule and unzipped the fleece so that the air could flow in and cool my skin.

I climbed over a gate in the dyke and walked fast along the hard white sand. A flock of the wild little sheep scattered and trotted off, strings of seaweed draped from their jaws. The sea made quiet, contented sounds like a baby suckling. My feet swapped over and over in the sand and I was lulled by the soothing rhythm. The beach was longer than I'd thought. I stopped to catch my breath and looked back at my footprints. The heels of my shoes had dug regular little pits along the wavy trail of my walking. I needed some proper boots. There was a uniform up here: boots, jeans, cagoules, wind-chapped cheeks and tangled hair.

At the end of the beach the sand gave way to rocks. I almost tripped over a seal – a pup, though it was huge. I don't know which one of us was more startled, but I remembered what Charlie said and backed off slowly, sat down on a jut of rock. The seal stared at me but I looked away. You're not supposed to look animals straight in the eye, they see it as a threat and I know what they mean.

I gazed into a triangular rock pool, clear water magnifying the stones and shells, a floating strand of weed, a colourless crab scuttling. The seals were the same shades as the stones. Once I'd seen one I saw that there were many more. I could feel their eyes on me, gentle and wary. Sleek black masks lifted from the water to peer. As they shifted, the basking seals made little personal grunting sounds. They moved like people inside sacks, heaving and lumping themselves about. The pup closed its eyes and began to snore, nostrils fluttering open and shut. I went into a kind of dream, soothed by the blubbery softness, a lovely, solid, gentle company. But when I got up to move they panicked, humphing and galumphing off the rocks in a commotion of churning water.

My legs ached as I walked back along the curve of sand; I wasn't used to walking so far or so fast. The tide had come in and was lapping at my footprints, smoothing them back down. The sand glittered as if there was light inside every single grain. I pocketed a couple of tiny shells: hinged in the middle like pink butterflies. There was a splash – one of the seals swimming along beside me. I stopped and it stopped too, put up its doggy head and stared. The peaked roof of the observatory gleamed in the distance. Of course it wasn't Rupert. I was getting paranoid.

I resolved to go back and help. If I wanted to stay I'd have to get stuck in, show willing. I could strip beds and fry bacon, hang washing on the line. I could be useful, part of a team. I could live in tattered jeans and grow my hair. If that's what it took, I could do it. I could work up some interest in the birds. I'd already learnt a new one today: stonechat.

Toni and Charlie were hanging sheets on the line. I stopped to watch. She was slightly taller than him, her hair tied up in a high scruffy ponytail. When she raised her arms to peg the sheets, her T-shirt rode up to show a slim tanned midriff. Charlie laughed at something and she pushed him. A playful push. Her hand rested for a moment on his arm. He poked her, one finger in the middle of her chest. I heard her voice, 'Hey, watch it, buster.' And then they resumed their pegging. White sheets and blue sheets cutting up the view of sky and sea. Sometimes they vanished behind the sheets. I heard Charlie laugh and it was a sound I hadn't heard since I don't know when.

They walked back on the far side of the line, I caught glimpses of them between the slabs of white and blue. Toni carried a red plastic washing basket under her arm. When she saw me she lifted her hand.

'Hi Nina, good walk?'

'Lovely,' I said.

'Make the most of the weather. Gale forecast,' she said. I looked disbelievingly at the mild milk of the sky.

'How far did you get?' Charlie asked as we walked towards the house.

'End of the beach. I saw scals.'

He began to say something, then Toni touched his arm. 'Hey . . .' She pointed.

It was only a bird, a middle-sized brown bird. But they went in fast to get their binoculars leaving me with my feet just where they were.

Ruth was alone in the kitchen when I went in. She was scribbling something on the back of an envelope, phone scrunched under her chin. Her pale hair was a rat's nest and there was a pencil stuck behind her ear that I'm sure had been there ever since I'd arrived. She nodded at the kettle and mimed drinking.

'Saturday, then, look forward to meeting you.' She put down the phone and winced, stretching her neck sideways till I could hear a ratchety click.

'Tea or coffee?' I asked.

'Hang on. Tea.' She opened her laptop, squinted at the screen and keyed something in. She looked up at me. 'Nice walk? Did Charlie say, you two are in the byre tonight, if that's OK?' She snapped the laptop shut and laughed. 'Or even if it isn't.'

'Fine,' I said.

She leant back in her chair and squinted at me. 'How long are you staying?'

'I wanted to talk to you about that,' I said. 'Teabags?'

She nodded at the cupboard in front of me.

'Fire away,' she said. 'I'd better get the lamb out.' She got up, groaned and rubbed her hip. 'Bugger. Wonder if I'm getting sciatica.'

'I was thinking about staying,' I said. I couldn't look at her. I put my palm on the hot side of the kettle, kept it there until it got too hot. It was a chrome kettle, smeared, a warped kitchen, with me in it, reflected in its curve.

'You mean here?'

'If that's all right.'

'Does Charlie know?' She scratched her head and the pencil fell out. 'He never said.' She opened the door of the freezer and brought out a bag of frozen meat. 'I'll stick you on the rota then,' she said. 'We could do with another pair of hands.'

'Really?'

The calm warm feeling that had started with the seals welled up in me as the kettle boiled. I poured water on to the teabags and squashed them against the sides of the mugs.

'How are you at peeling spuds?' Ruth said. 'Fifteen for dinner tonight.'

'Brilliant.'

'Steady on!'

I put her tea on the table. Amongst the clutter was a dead bird on a saucer. Tiny and brown, stiff claws clutched the air.

'Wren,' she said. 'Daisy found it.'

She opened a giant biscuit tin and pushed it towards me. I dipped an oaty biscuit in my tea, took a sweetly softening bite.

'Yes, these are good for dunking,' she said. 'Just the right consistency.' She ran a hand over the paperwork on the table. 'Been catching up with the admin,' she said. 'Well, catching up's putting it a bit strong.' She laughed. The phone rang. 'You see my problem?' she said.

There was a picture on the table, DAISY written in felt tip on the top. It was a house done in bold wonky paint: a house with a chimney and smoke, a smiling sun and trees. There were no trees here, no square houses like that with chimneys in the middle. It was just the happy home of everyone's dreams that even a child could draw.

Toni came in. 'I'm putting some of last night's grub in the mike for Charlie and me. Join us?' she said.

'Not me,' Ruth said, patting her belly. 'I'm on the biscuit diet. Oh by the way, Nina's staying.'

'Staying?' Toni widened her eyes. 'How come?'

She turned away and began foraging in the fridge. In the gap between her T-shirt and jeans was a tattoo of a bluebird.

Ruth went out and I watched Toni tip a sticky heap of casserole into a bowl and push it in the microwave. She turned to me and cleared her throat but Ruth came back in. 'There are folks in the bar,' she said. 'Why not go and serve them, Nina? Prices on everything. It's more or less self-explanatory.'

I went through. The family man came up to order Coke and crisps for the children. They were sitting at a table squabbling over a board game. I asked their name and wrote the amount on their account as I'd seen Charlie do. It was easy and felt good to be behind the bar, in charge. I looked round at all the different malt whiskies. I didn't know that there were so many. I began to read the labels: Glenfiddich; Glenlivet; Glenmorangie; Glenmore. Someone came into the bar and I turned round, a smile starting on my face. And it was Rupert.

'Which do you recommend?' he said.

Charlie came in then. He stood beside Rupert, half a head shorter, red-faced, his hair rough and spiky. The lunatic white thread in his eyebrow curled down over one eye.

'Could you recommend a malt?' Rupert asked him.

'I'd go for Highland Park,' Charlie said. 'That's the local one.'

'Highland Park it is then.' Rupert nodded to me. 'Have one

yourself. Been here long?' Rupert asked, as I turned away to struggle with the optic.

Charlie came behind the bar and showed me how to work it. 'Press up like that,' he said, hand over mine. A sharp and peaty scent was released into the air. I had an urge to knock it back in one hot gulp.

Rupert took the drink, swirled and sniffed and sipped it. 'Mmmm,' he said, 'smooth. How old?'

'Eighteen years,' Charlie said.

'Practically a lifetime,' Rupert said.

'A very short one!' Charlie said.

'Yes.' Rupert looked at me, sleek-eyed. 'What brought you here?'

'Dunno,' I said.

Charlie frowned at me. 'What about you?' he said.

'Oh . . .' Rupert took a slow considered sip. 'Curiosity. Someone I knew came here.' He lifted his glass. 'No doubt I'll see you later.' He walked off and settled himself by the window, the profile of his smile sharp against the glass.

'You'll have to be more friendly than that if you're going to stay,' Charlie said quietly, 'which Ruth has just informed me.'

'I know,' I whispered. 'Charlie, sorry but it just came up, Ruth said she needed another pair of hands and—'

'You *keep* doing it,' he said and though he was trying to keep his voice down it rose in pitch and the little girl stopped shaking her dice and looked up at us. I lifted the corners of my mouth at her. I don't know what was the point of coming all this way to sit in a bar and play board games. A sudden gust of wind hooed against the window.

'I'm sorry,' I said. 'I'll go if you don't want me here.'

He went out, banging the door behind him. Rupert had opened one of the bird books that were lying around and was turning the pages steadily and smiling. The dice rattled in its cup. 'That's not fair, Dad, she's cheating,' said the boy. The sky was darkening; not that clouds were gathering, it was more as if something thick was soaking through the blue.

The father got up and sauntered across to the window. 'Looks like we're in for it,' he remarked to Rupert, and to me. 'Mind if I switch on the light?'

'Go ahead.'

Rupert came across to the bar.

'Another.' He slid his glass towards me.

'How did you know I was here?' I said.

'I might be here to see someone else,' he said. 'Charlie, for instance.'

'Your turn, Mum.'

'No,' I said. 'Look . . . we'll speak later.'

'Oh yes?' he said.

Toni came into the bar behind me, wiping her mouth on her hand. 'I'll take care of this, Nina. Ruth says you should get your stuff over to the byre. We need the room.'

'One Highland Park,' Rupert said to Toni and as I left the bar I heard him say, 'And one for yourself.' 'What a gent,' she said and then the door swung shut. I stood in the hall with my heart thudding. I saw then one of the drawbacks of being on a small island. There's nowhere to run. I did not know how to move until Charlie came out of the kitchen, my bag over his shoulder.

'Come on then.'

'Charlie . . .' I said.

'What?'

'I'll go if you want.'

'Since when have you cared what I want?' he said.

'What?'

'Come on.' He pushed open the door and the wind lifted my breath away from me. A plastic football fidgeted about the yard, dribbled by invisible feet. I followed him down a slope towards the byre. The sheets were snapping and straining on the line. I wondered if they ever blew away.

We went into the byre, a converted building that smelt of raw wood and fresh paint. He opened a door into a room with four bunks and switched on a buzzing neon light. A pair of green velvet jeans dangled from one of the top bunks.

'There's someone in here,' I said.

'Toni,' he said. 'That's her bed.'

'We're sharing with her?'

'It's where the volunteers sleep.' He put my bag down. 'It's OK really. Good shower just next door. So.' He indicated the bunks. 'Top or bottom?'

'Can't we squeeze in together?'

He shook his head. 'I think that'd be a bit . . . you know, with Toni here.'

'But she knows we're together.'

'Still. Top or bottom?'

'Don't mind,' I said and sat down on the bottom one.

'I'll go on top then.' He laughed. 'So to speak!' It didn't sound like him, the way he said that, it sounded like the influence of someone else.

'Not much privacy,' I said.

'It's not that sort of place. You can put your stuff in here.' He opened a narrow cupboard, already crammed with his clothes. 'I'll leave you to settle in.' He went for the door.

'Charlie,' I said.

'What?'

'I won't stay if you don't want me to.'

He turned and looked at me.

'But I can make myself right for this.'

'What?'

'I just need new clothes, that's all. Walking boots and everything.'

He spoke quietly. 'Do you really think it's as easy as that?' He went out. The concrete floor was muddy; I thought how horrible to walk on that in bare feet. There were dead flies on the windowsill. Through the window I watched him open the door and go back into the observatory.

I climbed the ladder to look at Toni's bed, a jumble of messy duvet, grubby T-shirt, box of tissues, dent still in the pillow, book half under it. I pulled it out: *Shrikes Around the World*. I checked inside and it was from me to him. *To Charlie, Happy Christmas, with all my love and more, Nina* and about a hundred kisses.

I removed the book, tidied up Charlie's things and put mine in the cupboard beside them. I put my toothbrush in the shower-room where the floor was even muddier, and wet. On the toilet cistern was a packet of tampons. The shower plug was snarled up with long toffee-coloured hairs and some of Charlie's caught up in the wet trap they made. A horrible kind of intimacy in the mixing of those hairs. I knelt and scooped it all from the plughole, pulled out a long gloop of soap scum, skin cells and hairs and flushed it down the toilet.

I looked out of the window and saw the visiting family come out, dressed as if for a climb up Everest. The Land Rover pulled up and Bruno jumped out. Despite the howling wind he was wearing a T-shirt and I could see the muscles in the thick tops of his arms. He gave the trickling football a kick and scratched his bum as he started in through the door, then he stopped to make way for someone – Rupert on his way out. Rupert stood looking around as if wondering which way to go and then Charlie emerged and they began to talk. I went out.

'I'm giving Rupert,' Charlie nodded to him, 'a lift to the top of the island.'

'Mind if I tag along?'

'You can show me the sights,' Rupert said.

'It'll be the blind leading the blind,' I said, freezing my eyes at him.

'Jump in,' Charlie said. 'But, Nina, you ought to borrow that cagoule.'

We drove along in silence, the wind buffeting us sideways, Charlie's knuckles whitened on the steering wheel. As we approached the lighthouses, a silver confetti of gulls swirled against the dark sky. Charlie stopped in the lighthouse carpark.

'You need to be back by about five, Nina, to peel the spuds. You'll have to walk pretty fast.'

'OK.' I got out and the wind almost knocked me off my feet.

Charlie laughed. 'You're crazy walking in this! Look . . . if you need picking up just ring, someone'll come and get you.'

'Thanks,' I said. Through the window I squeezed his hand and he squeezed back. 'Don't get blown away.' He drove off. We stood and watched him diminish until he was just a speck.

And Rupert and I were left on the edge of the world. The wind rattled and whined in the signal tower; a scutter of rubbish danced a crazy circle in the lighthouse yard. I pulled up my hood to protect my ears.

'Bracing,' Rupert said. He jammed on a black fleece hat and smiled.

'How *dare* you come here!' burst out of me.

But he just looked mildly down at me, and lifted his shoulders. 'Didn't you promise to get in touch?'

'I was going to.'

'You said a week.'

'I was going to.'

'Oh yes?'

'Yes.'

'How's your hand?' He reached out but I shoved it in my pocket.

'So,' he said. 'Here we are. Shall we walk?' We leant into the wind and made towards the sea. The grass was shrunken to the salty ground, scattered with rocks, shells, bones, animal droppings. It was hard to walk against the gale on the littered ground in the wrong sort of shoes with legs still tired from earlier. Why had I come? This was stupid. Small rabbits, startled by our feet, flashed their scuts and flipped away.

Some of the rocks had been built into circular walls, like roofless igloos. These were plantycrews that Charlie had told me about, meant to shelter plants from the wind but the only things growing inside were a spindly straggle of weeds. In one, a couple of the runty little sheep were sheltering, chewing, vacant-eyed, like teenagers with gum.

We walked right to the edge where waves lashed up against the rocks. I stared out into the distance, the wind whisking tears from my eyes. The next place you'd get to would be Norway if you were mad enough to set out from here. The wind sucked its teeth between the leaky stone shelters and there was a wailing, maybe mammal, maybe bird or maybe it was just the wind.

We clambered over some rocks and it was hard in my stupid shoes with their slippy soles. He stopped, hands shoved in his pockets, face lifted as he gazed out to sea. Lost for a moment. If there was a cliff I'd push him off it, I thought, and then everything would be all right. But there were no cliffs.

We saw the afternoon plane bouncing in. Charlie would be at the airfield waiting, one foot on the bottom rung of the gate, delivering the board-game family, picking up the next lot.

I was suddenly struck by how weird this was: me and Rupert together in this desolation. How had we got to here? I almost wanted to laugh: him so incongruously handsome and perfectly dressed, he could have been a catalogue model in his green waxed jacket, conker boots; even the hat, pulled low on his brow, suited him.

'So . . .' I began but it was too windy, my voice was torn away.

'Let's get out of the wind,' he shouted and we set off walking, bent almost double. Despite the hood my ears ached and the toggle at the end of my hood string lashed about stinging my face. We stumbled over what seemed to be a golf course, littered with sheep and their droppings and pitted with rabbit holes. A forgotten flagpole rattled madly, a bandage of flag unravelling in the wind.

We climbed back over the dyke and dropped, suddenly, miraculously, out of the wind and on to a flat and shining beach. The light was pearly grey now as if everything – the peaks of the buildings on the horizon, the curve of the stone dyke, the wheeling birds – were all etched on the sheeny innards of a shell.

A smile unfurled on Rupert's face. The wind had made his eyes water too, eyelashes spiky black. It came back to me then: him in the hotel lobby; his smile, his eyes, his velvety voice, the way he drew me in like some luscious bait. And I took the bait. I can't blame anyone else for that.

'I want you to come back with me,' he said.

'I'm rotaed in now. I'm staying. They need me.'

'They don't need you,' he said, 'but I do.'

Need?

'This is not you,' he said, looking down at me, seeing through me, in a way that seemed almost tender.

'What?'

'This . . . setting.'

'How do you know what's me and what isn't?' I snapped. 'You don't know me at all. Can't you see I'm trying to make it work with Charlie?' My lips were numbed by the wind and it was hard to make the words.

'You'd be better off in a city,' he said. 'Somewhere *anonymous*.'

'What do you want from me?' I turned away and looked back the way we'd come. Two sets of footprints now and both filled with shining water. The wail again, like the call of a spook. I think it was a seal.

209

He put a finger under my chin but I flinched my face away. 'We both know how much you have to lose. *Karen*.'

Something went loose in my legs then, knees buckling as if they wanted to bend backwards. He put his arm round me in a tight grip that held me upright. He held me against his chest as if I was his lover, the waxy smell of his coat in my nose. Anybody could have seen. I pulled away and started to run, but there was nowhere to run. I slipped and twisted my ankle on a rock. I was back in the wind again. I sat down with a bump and let out some tears, just a few, and they were whipped straight off my face.

He came and hunkered down beside me.

'How do you know?' I said.

'Come back with me.'

'No one's meant to know.'

'No one else does. Yet.'

'What do you want? Money?'

He shook his head.

'Sex then?'

'Did you think it was that good?'

'What else is there?'

'What a reductive view of life you have,' he said, straightening up. He looked down at me. 'Money and sex, that's sad.'

I took a deep breath. I had to keep it all together, to concentrate. 'That's not true. It's just . . . I can't think what else you could want.'

'It's very simple,' he said. 'I want revenge.'

I stood up and stared at him. 'Who are you?'

He smiled, the long dimple slanting in his cheek.

I looked down at the water forcing itself up through the sand under the weight of my feet. I bit my lip and brushed the wetness from my face. My cheeks felt raw and chapped.

'You're shivering,' he said. He took off his hat and put it, warm from his head, over my aching ears. The warmth soaked painfully in.

We began to walk; my ankle was only twisted, not too bad to walk on. The waves were growing and in the dark shine between them sometimes the head of a seal popped up, sometimes the white bob of a gull. The sky had gone to charcoal but pierced with shafts of yellow light like something from a bible story. Above the dyke a man on a tractor sat looking down and smoking. I wondered if he'd seen us. People run to islands in search of freedom but this felt anything but free, it was criss-crossed with lines of sight like trip-wires and you couldn't not be known.

'Let's phone and get picked up,' Rupert said. 'It'll take hours at this rate.'

'No.'

We walked without talking, until at last we rounded a headland on to the beach where I'd been in the morning. The storm had landed great stalks and ribbons of mustard-coloured weed, almost as big as trees, and pocked the sand with the glassy cushions of jellyfish. As we climbed up off the beach and on to the track that led to the observatory, I saw that the Land Rover was coming towards us. I looked at my watch. I was late.

Toni stopped and leant out of the window. 'They sent me out to find you,' she said. 'You OK? Want a lift?'

'Thanks.' I climbed in beside her. Rupert got in the back and slammed the door.

'There's a heap of tatties back there with your name on them,' Toni said, jerking the Land Rover into gear.

Her thighs were long and slim in the blue jeans, her hands rough on the wheel, a silver puzzle ring on her thumb.

'Good walk then?'

'Interesting,' Rupert said, leaning forward between us. 'Wasn't it, Nina? *Or Karen?*' he whispered in my ear.

'Cold,' I said, 'for June.'

*   *   *

I was late but no one noticed, or mentioned it, at least. I went straight into peeling the spuds, stepping over Ben doing his floor puzzle right in the middle of the kitchen while Daisy wobbled about on a pair of roller-skates, grabbing at people's legs. The radio was blaring out the news; Ruth stirring a vast casserole; Bruno sipping wine and bellowing good-naturedly into the phone. Toni came in to collect the cutlery.

'Pretty breezy out there, eh?' she said.

'You should wear a rubber glove over that.' Ruth nodded at my hand.

I couldn't look at her. I peeled and peeled, muddy spud skins in the cold, muddy water, scraping my own skin with the peeler.

'Hey . . .' Ruth came and put a hand on my shoulder. 'Calm down, Nina. You're peeling them to nothing. Let's put a glove on that. Come on.'

She took my hand. 'Silly thing,' she said and I could almost have cried at the soft scrape of kindliness in her voice. 'Let's have a look.' She pulled the old plaster off. The scar was withered from the water, one end weeping.

'Glass of wine?' Toni breezed past with a bottle. I nodded and she sloshed some in a tumbler.

Ruth was gentle, bending her snarly head close to mine, holding my cold hand in her warm dry one. She tugged the backing from a new pink Band-Aid and smoothed it down.

'There,' she said. 'Good as new.' Daisy came crashing past on her skates. 'Mind how you go, honey.'

'How did you do that?' Daisy said, bright eyes zeroing in. She picked the corner off a slice of bread and chewed it, waiting.

'Fell over.'

'Can I have a plaster, Mum?' she said. 'Right here.' She pointed to her knee. Ruth raised her eyebrows at me and found her a little round one to stick on.

I put a rubber glove over my bad hand and went back to the potatoes; little ones so there were hundreds, crusted with scabs of mud. Orkney tatties, Ruth said. She had to help me in the end, there was a muddy mountain of them, shrinking too slowly, and dinner was already going to be late.

The guests gathered at the table with their wine or their beer, swapping bird and life stories, and I must have seemed like part of it to them, distributing bread baskets and water jugs, giving them their plates of lamb, spinach and mashed potato. It was only Rupert sending me his sleek-eyed look that made me clumsy and self-conscious.

When I sat down it was at the only place available: across the table from Rupert, beside Charlie. Toni was opposite Charlie as if we were a foursome. Rupert almost ignored me, chatting easily with Toni, and though I studied Charlie from the corner of my eye he didn't look at her particularly. I didn't see anything to mind. He asked about our walk.

'I had to lend her my hat,' Rupert said.

'Didn't expect to need a hat in June,' I said.

'I've got a spare,' Toni offered, 'I'll dig it out for you. But there's always lost hats and stuff lying about, a whole boxful in the office.'

'Ta.' I took a mouthful of the chewy iodine-flavoured meat but it had gone cold. I put down my fork. I went out into the kitchen and watched Rupert lean across to Charlie. He could wreck everything with a sentence. He saw me seeing that and gleamed. I stared back, searching my mind for who he might be. Whoever it was he knew me. He was the only person here who knew the truth, who knew that old name. *Karen*. Just the sound of it changed the shape of me, the way I stood, the way I breathed.

I realised something else as well as fear was stirring up in me. Curiosity. I needed to know who he was. I needed to know how he knew. I needed to know what he wanted. I couldn't go

on any more with him in the background. I *would* go back to
Sheffield; not with him, I knew he wasn't on tomorrow's plane
and that it was fully booked. I would try somehow to get away
first and I would wait for him. And he would come to me. And
we would somehow finish this.

Ruth had come into the kitchen to dole out plates of
chocolate cake and ice-cream. She waved a hand in front of
my face. 'Wakey, wakey,' she said, 'give us a hand with this.'

'Sorry.' I reached for the ice-cream scoop.

'Could you be up for breakfasts tomorrow?' she said.
'About seven?'

'Aye. Thanks to you, *I* get a lie-in.' Toni grinned as she went
past, carrying a stack of dirty plates. There was a bit of spinach
caught in her snaggly teeth but when she smiled the corners of her
eyes tilted upwards, like blue-green boats sailing across her face.

'He fancies you,' she whispered.

'Who?'

'Rupert. He's watching you like a hawk.'

'Is he?'

'He's fit,' she said, 'despite the poncy name. I wouldn't
chuck him out of bed.'

'Wouldn't you?'

I stayed in the kitchen, making a start at loading the dishwasher and peering through at the dining table from time to
time. Toni was telling a story, waving her hands about and
laughing, stopping to swig her bottle of beer, and both Charlie
and Rupert listened, their bodies inclined towards her as if she
was the sun. Rupert looked up suddenly to catch me watching.
I turned back to the dishwasher.

After dinner most of the guests went out for a walk. Clouds
raced across the sky, lemony hints of sunset shivering on the
waves. Ruth and Bruno took the children off to bed and to go
off-duty in their private part of the observatory.

Toni fetched a bottle of Famous Grouse and four glasses.

Charlie came in with a plate of shortbread. I got the feeling that this was their after-dinner ritual.

'What do you do then?' she queried Rupert, sloshing out drink for everyone.

'Ah ha.' He touched the side of his nose with his finger.

'Something secret?'

Rupert poured a drop of water into his glass and swilled it round. 'You could say that.' He brushed me with his gaze. I looked down into the amber drink and took a tiny sip, just enough to heat a sliver of my tongue.

'Well, well! Slàinte!' Toni knocked hers back.

'It means cheers,' Charlie explained, as if that wasn't obvious. 'Slàinte!' He knocked his back too. He never downed Scotch at home like that.

'Give us a clue,' Toni said to Rupert.

'Hush-hush.' He brought his finger to his lips. I saw a flare go off in her eyes. No one could look at his lips and not think they were beautiful.

'Fair dos. What brought you up here then?' she asked.

'Call it curiosity,' he said. 'You?'

'Came here on holiday with my folks when I was wee,' she said, 'always fancied coming back. If there was a vacancy at the school here . . . but there's only seven kids! Bliss. I finish here in August – looking for teaching jobs now. Guess it's time to settle down. I'm nearly thirty. Tick-tock.'

'Plan to have kids then?' Rupert said and I saw the way his eyes penetrated hers, the same golden gleam in the brown that had got to me, and she blushed.

'Oh hundreds,' she said. 'But there's the wee detail of a man, first.'

I watched very carefully and she didn't look at Charlie when she said that.

'What about you, Nina?' Rupert turned the gleam on to me, but I was immune.

'No.' I took a bite of shortbread.

'No?' Rupert looked at Charlie.

'I wouldn't mind a kid,' Charlie said and the shortbread dried in my mouth. I swigged my whisky and the heat of it brought tears to my eyes. Charlie banged me on the back.

'I'll finish clearing up,' I said when I'd stopped choking. 'Charlie?'

We went into the kitchen and left them with the whisky bottle. Charlie suggested a walk but my ankle was throbbing.

'Get Bruno to look at it,' he suggested but I didn't want to make a fuss. We went across to the byre. The wind was dropping though it still whooshed through me, swayed me on my feet.

'You told me you weren't bothered about having kids,' I said.

'Well you never know, do you?' He turned away and pulled his sweater over his head. We showered together but it was too cold to be sexy. Afterwards we cuddled damply together in the lower bunk. I thought of him lying here at night, chatting to Toni. Both in bed. Intimate murmurings and whisperings about shrikes, godwits, Siberian robins. In the time I'd been with Charlie I could have got interested. I could be an expert on kingfishers or herons by now. Of course they would get on well with their shared interest in ornithology. You could almost call it a passion. But I could still learn. It was not too late, stonechat, whimbrel, arctic tern, but why did it have to be *birds* with their cold feathers and scratchy little feet?

I kissed him, enjoying the unfamiliar whisky taste in his mouth, another bird, a famous grouse. At first he didn't respond but I kept on kissing and tasting, ran my hands down his damp back, stroked them over the rough texture of his buttocks, pushed my lovely breasts against him, he always said they were lovely, I squashed them against him, kissed his neck, moved down to suck him, difficult to manoeuvre in the narrow bunk, and eventually he started to respond. And when he pushed inside me it all made sense again, it all fell into place like a key in the lock, locking us tight together, his heart thumping against mine, the shower's moisture turning to sweat on our skins. It was hard and passionate, *this* was passion not some shared interest in birds, this was us, Charlie and Nina together making love, and I didn't care if Toni came in, I wished she would. I wanted her to see us together like this, to see this demonstration of our love. Even though he clamped his hand over my mouth and tried to hush me, my voice came out loud enough for anyone who might have been near to hear and no one could mistake that sound, the passion in it, the utter love.

Afterwards we lay still, close, stuck together, our hearts slowing in unison.

'Are we all right?' I whispered.

'Okey-dokey,' he replied right away, no hesitation. 'Only I must pee. You stay put.'

He got up and pulled on his jeans. I heard him in the shower-room, the toilet flushing and then the bang of the outside door. I got up, put on his shirt and tiptoed across the cold floor to the window. He was standing at the top of the slope staring across at the sea. You could hear the quiet steady roar of waves. The sun had gone and the sea and sky were the same silky grey. A bird cried out, probably an owl. Owls are not so small and scratchy. Maybe I could become an expert on owls. He stood there staring and he must have been freezing with his feet bare and no shirt. *I* was freezing, my feet gritty with mud from the floor. I got back into the bed, messy and damp but still warm, and I switched on the lamp. Eventually Charlie came back in and sat on the edge of the bed.

'Look.' He cleared his throat. 'This doesn't feel right, does it?'

'Of course it doesn't,' I said. I put my hand out to him.

'Charlie, you're grieving. Nothing will feel right, not for a while.'

I heard the breath suck into his lungs. He shivered.

'Get back in,' I said, 'I'll warm you up.'

He didn't move. 'I mean you being here.'

'I know that,' I said. 'I'm going back.'

'What?'

'I'm telling you first this time,' I said. 'See, I can learn. I've got to go back and sort things out, my job and everything. And then . . . I don't know . . . Get in, you're shivering.'

He took off his jeans. 'I'll get in the top,' he said. 'We'll both sleep better.'

'But we're not going to sleep yet!' I said. 'Come on.' I held the duvet up and he lay down with me. His feet were like wet ice. He turned over and I spooned myself round him, tucked my knee between his thighs.

'When are you leaving?' he asked.

'Tomorrow if I can. Hope Ruth's not too mad at me. I'll do breakfasts first. Do you think she'll ever have me back?'

'Dunno.' He was quiet, then said, 'Nina, do you know that Rupert guy from somewhere?'

My heart made a sudden painful scramble, loud enough for him to hear. 'What?'

He waited.

'No.'

'Nina . . .'

'What? We chatted quite a bit while we were walking,' I said, 'so I got to know him a bit.' I was talking too fast. 'Hey, he and Toni were getting on well, I wonder if they—'

'No.'

'Why?'

'He's too smooth. A bit weird, I thought. There's something about him . . . he's sort of . . . implausible.'

'What?'

'Implausible.'

'How do you mean?'

'Hush-hush!' he said sarcastically.

'Toni said she wouldn't kick him out of bed,' I said.

'Did she? Oh well, there you go then.'

My heart was calming down. 'Warm now?'

'Mmmm.'

We lay quietly for a while and then, just as I was starting to drowse, he pulled himself up.

'I'll get in the top before she comes in.'

'She wouldn't mind.'

'Still.' His chilly penis brushed my thigh as he got out. I watched his legs go up the ladder. The bunk above me creaked and groaned as he wrestled himself into a comfortable position. I switched off the light.

I was almost asleep before Toni came in. I heard her brushing her teeth and the toilet flush. She opened the door quietly, creeping, saying nothing. She brought with her the raw smell of the night. In the watery light I could see her strip off her jeans and sweater. There was a crackle as she ripped the elastic band from her hair. She put her head down to shake it out and the air stirred with a faint smell of smoke. She climbed the ladder, long legs bare. I couldn't say if Charlie was awake.

∧

I was so pleased with the progress, and tired out from the wind, that I lay on my bed and took forty winks before I showered and went down. Karen was limping in and out of the dining room putting the bowls of food on the table but never deigning to give me a second glance. I sat down and talked to Toni, taking in the waves in her long hair and the scrubbed face, not a trace of make-up, you could see she was going for the natural look. There was obviously something going on between her and Charlie. You could sense the chemistry.

Toni chatted away, laughing at her own jokes but in a way that made you smile too, infectious you might say, and she could certainly put away the beer. Afterwards, when the clearing up was done, she brought in a bottle of Scotch and four glasses and started quizzing me about what I did.

'Hush-hush,' I said, giving Karen a look to make her blush. Then I turned it on Toni and you could see the spark of interest starting up. It was like a normal gathering, the four of us, drinking and talking as if we'd known each other since the year dot – it was only Karen that spoilt the atmosphere, acting like a wet weekend. Toni gave Charlie one of those oh-deary-me looks as she took a swig of her whisky. Karen got up suddenly and called him as if he was a dog and he trotted out after her. It made me laugh, she was so obvious. Toni stared at me a minute and I stopped the laughing.

'What?' I said.

'You OK?'

'Why?'

She shrugged, finished her drink and got up.

'Fancy a walk?' she said. 'The wind's dropped.'

To tell you the truth, I'd had enough fresh air to last me a lifetime but I went and got my coat. We walked fast down the lane, her legs nearly as long as mine. Though it was late it wasn't properly dark yet, but very shadowy with birds floating on the water as if they were asleep. The edges of the waves showed up very white against the sand. She walked close and the ends of her hair flicked against my face.

'Fancy a smoke?' she said.

'I don't.'

'Shame. Nice wee bit of grass,' she said and I was taken aback, not thinking her the druggy type. I was disappointed, thinking better of her than that.

'Don't mind me,' I said.

We sat together on a rock while she puffed away. She put her head on my shoulder.

'Just look at that moon,' she said, 'the way it shines on the sea.'

I looked up and along with the thin bit of moon I saw stars coming through as the sky got darker, more and more until I felt dizzy. I wondered if I'd been affected by her smoke. I looked down at the waves. I'd never watched the way a wave unrolls before like something coming more and more undone.

'So, what's with you and Nina?' she said.

I took a breath then, thinking do not leap in, thinking how Rupert would deal with this.

'I don't know her from Adam,' I said.

'If you say so,' she said.

'Why should I?'

She finished off her joint and ground the end into the sand. 'Don't you fancy her?' she said.

'Not my type.'

'What is?' she said but I didn't answer that. We sat without speaking for a while, hearing the sea and the sound of something wild calling out or it might have been a sheep. I thought, this is about as far from Mexico as I will ever get.

'What about you and Charlie then?' I said in the end.

'You noticed.' She laughed.

'A bit of chemistry?'

'Aye,' she said, 'yeah, but then Nina turns up.' She sounded quite choked up but pulled herself together. 'You can't win them all.'

We walked back and she chatted on and told me a thing or two of great interest. How she and Charlie had met the year before and had what she termed a fling. They'd lived far apart, her in Inverness, him in Sheffield, but kept in touch and had a plan to meet up at North Ronaldsay and see where it went, is how she put it. This was in the offing when he met Karen and before he'd had a chance to blink she'd got her feet under the table and Toni was dropped like a hot potato.

We stopped outside the byre, a kind of barn where the workers slept, and heard the unmistakable sound of sex. Toni gave a sort of gasp. 'Fucking hell,' she said and stomped off. I followed her in and we got stuck into the whisky. It was the shock of hearing them together, I reckon, that led her into telling me the rest.

'I don't know what the fuck he's up to,' she said, pouring the whisky and knocking hers back. 'After everything he said. And considering what he knows about her.'

'What?' I said.

'He's meant to be finished with her – though you wouldn't think it from that carry on, would you?' She laughed in that way that shows no amusement in the least.

I reached for the bottle to top her up. 'What does he know?'

'It doesn't matter.'

She looked at me this level way, not like your usual girl. You could tell she was a straightforward type even with the drink inside her and the smoke. 'You won't go blethering?'

'Mum's the word,' I said and that made her laugh though you could see her eyes were sad and stoned-looking.

'See, he found something out. Something about her. Something big. No, I shouldn't say.' She clammed up for a bit then, staring into her glass.

'Like an affair?' I said.

'Bigger than that,' she said.

I kept hold of the Rupert cool, watching my face in the glass, counting my breaths until she spoke again.

'Promise?' she said. 'Only I feel like I'll explode if I don't tell someone.'

I gave her a look as if to say it was no odds to me.

'Well, she had a wee accident and was in the hospital and while he was looking for stuff to take in to her he found something.'

'What?'

'A bit of paper.' She leant forward and whispered though there was no one to hear. 'She's not who she says she is and . . . she was in prison, he doesn't know what for but it must have been big . . . She was in for *life*.'

'Life?'

'*Life*.' She sat back and gave me a long look of significance.

'Does she know he knows?' I said.

She shook her head. 'He can't bring himself to tell her. See, he was wanting to finish with her anyway but . . .'

'Yes?'

'He thinks she's a wee bit . . .' She pulled a face. 'Well he's worried what she might do but he should just come straight out with it, don't you think? The longer it goes on the worse

223

it'll be, for both of them. I think it's cruel. It's being kind to be cruel.' She nearly spat that and then shut up. We sat there for a while longer and she knocked back another drink, then she yawned. 'Well, I reckon they'll have finished by now,' she said. 'Night night.'

My plane was in two days' time. The plan was to get Karen on it with me, if there was room, or else get her booked on as soon as possible and I'd be at the airport to meet her. She was not getting out of my orbit again in a hurry. I went down to breakfast ready to tell her my plan. I didn't see her but it wasn't until breakfast was all cleared away and no sight or sound that alarm bells began to ring.

I went into the kitchen – it's so free and easy anyone can go in there at any time – and asked the woman in charge where she was.

She looked up from the paperwork she was doing on the table. 'Bruno had to fly off to Kirkwall with a prem labour this morning. Didn't you hear the plane? She took a lift with him.'

'She's gone?'

'She has that. And left us in the lurch.' She frowned. 'Why? Do you know her?'

*

I unlocked the door and stepped inside. I'd only been away for a few days but already the air in the hall smelt thick and stale. I put down my bag and stood listening. Nothing. I picked up the pile of letters and catalogues from the doormat. Fay got a lot of junk: Damart; Lakeland; free this, free that. I wonder how much mail is sent to the dead each day?

It was *too* quiet. There was no cheeping coming from the kitchen. Charlie Two should have been cheeping. I opened the door and went in. I went to the cage and he was on its bottom. I thought he was dead. His wings were a quite beautiful blue. I forced myself to put my hand into the cage and lift him out, and to my relief he was alive. He struggled feebly, pecked at my finger and opened his beak but no sound came. Cool and light, he just fitted the palm of my hand. 'I'll save him,' I said to Fay or to the air.

I found an eye-dropper and put a slosh of brandy in a glass. I turned him on to his back. His underside was white and fluffy and round his bottom the feathers were stuck together with droppings. I forced his beak open with the tip of the dropper and squeezed a drip of brandy into his mouth. The effect was amazing. He sneezed and shook his head. I got one more drip in but he was struggling more strongly now. I let him go and he hopped on to the table. Galvanised, I thought. I'd heard of medicinal purposes but this was ridiculous.

There was a packet of Trill on the table. I was sure I hadn't left it there; still, I tipped some out and he started to peck at it, swaying drunkenly. Soon the only sound in the kitchen was his beak busily shucking the seeds. And there he was. A little blue bird brought back from the brink. Good as new.

Something soft and painful opened inside me like a bud. I drank the rest of the brandy myself and then had another slug for good measure. It was warming, certainly medicinal. I filled the kettle, took off my coat and looked through the post again. Amongst the junk were a couple of sympathy cards for Charlie – a spray of roses, a misty view – and there was a good-luck card to me from Christine. Good luck? I couldn't think what she meant. Good luck for what? On the front of the card was a cute cat sitting in a horseshoe. Inside she'd written: *Dear Nina, Sorry you went off without a send-off. Get in touch and we'll go for a drink? Chrisxxx*

Which meant, I guess, that I'd been sacked.

The bread in the bin was mouldy. The milk smelt bad, the lettuce in the bottom of the fridge had turned to mush. Charlie Two flapped back to his cage. I filled his feeders with seed and gave him fresh water. He was unsteady on his perch, maybe drunk. I wondered if I should do him a little coffee. He started a sudden raucous cheeping and then said, 'Charlie-boy. Davy.' I put the cover over his cage to let him sleep it off. I would have to give him to someone. Christine? If she'd look after him till I'd got everything sorted out with Rupert, till Charlie and I were settled again. He could hardly object to that.

I saw in the mirror that the colour was already wearing off my hair. It was all pale and faded at the roots. The salon would still be open. I could have got my money back but I was too weary – early plane, all the turbulence and the long views of the islands like maps in the blue and green, then airports, trains; tedious waits and changes. Amazing that after all that it was still only four o'clock.

I'd been lucky that morning, if you can call it lucky. Charlie and I had gone over to the kitchen early to make a start on breakfasts and Bruno had already been there, slurping down a coffee. He'd been called out to a woman in premature labour and had to fly with her to Aberdeen. I asked if I could have a lift. Charlie had looked at me with surprise. 'Sure,' Bruno had said, 'but you'll have to get a move on.' So I'd been able to leave without having to see Rupert – though I knew he'd be with me soon enough. And without having to face Ruth. It was a kind of good luck – but I was left with a sensation inside me like something ruined.

As well as all the junk and cards there was the letter from Charlie. It must have arrived the day I'd left. Whatever it said would be out of date now we'd been together again. I didn't want to know what it said. I tore it up and chucked it in the bin with all Fay's junk: You've Already Won a Valuable Prize; Free Oven Chips For Life.

I phoned work praying that Christine would answer but it was a new voice: 'Angela speaking, how may I help you?' My replacement. You see how easily you can be replaced? I asked if I could speak to Christine and she said, 'May I ask who's calling?' Mind your own business, I thought. 'Nina,' I said.

'I'm sorry,' she said, 'could you repeat that?'

'Nina,' I said so loudly that I startled the budgie.

'Oh!' she said, voice sharpening out of its telephone manner. 'Nina who was here before me? You left loads of stuff . . . hand-cream and that.'

'Keep it,' I said. 'Can I speak to Christine?'

'Ta very much,' she said, 'and there's a pair of tights. Not my normal shade but I'll put you through.'

'Nina!' Christine sounded like she'd won the jackpot. 'Have a nice time? Get my card?'

'Thank you,' I said. 'Meet me for a drink?'

'OK.'

'Don't tell anyone.'

I met her in a wine bar on the other side of town, away from anywhere people from work might go. She was already sitting at a table on her own, half a glass of white wine in front of her. When she saw me, she rose from her seat as if she was about to give me a kiss.

'White or red?' she said.

I hadn't meant to drink, but her wine looked refreshing in its huge glass. I let her buy me one and ordered some stir-fried prawns and noodles. I was starving. She couldn't eat because of her diet. She slid a Slim.Fast bar out of her bag and nibbled at it. I told her about North Ronaldsay and the seals; she filled me in about my replacement.

'Angie's not a patch on you,' she said. 'Well she's all right. She said you said she could have your hand-cream, is that right?'

My meal arrived on a gigantic white plate, a mound of food big enough for five. 'Want some?' I said.

'I shouldn't.'

'Soak up the wine. Or you'll get drunk,' I suggested and a smile bloomed on her face.

'You're right. I better had.' She wobbled off on her heels to get a fork. I shovelled some of the noodles and a rubbery prawn into my mouth. I was so hungry. Then I saw a shape go past the window that looked like Rupert and although it couldn't be him, he wouldn't be back till tomorrow, my stomach scrunched miserably round the food and I put down my fork.

'Yum.' Christine took a mouthful of noodles and chewed with her eyes closed. 'Spicy,' she said.

'How's your love-life?' I asked. She told me about Don and the holiday they'd booked, her suspicion – or wish – that he'd get down on one knee on a beach during a sunset, how she was getting broody.

'Doesn't really matter that he's not good-looking, does it?' she said. 'I mean he's nice-looking, the more I see him the better looking I think he is. It's all in the eye of the beholder, isn't it?'

'Yes.'

'Not like that guy Rupert. But you could never trust someone that looked like that, could you? He'd only have to click his fingers.'

'No,' I said.

'How about we make a foursome?' Christine heaped her fork.

'What?' I swallowed some wine down the wrong way and coughed.

'Don and me, you and Charlie? We could have a drink, a meal maybe?'

'Maybe. Has Gary – or anyone – asked about me?'

She speared a prawn and a sliver of red pepper. 'He said did I know where you'd gone. I just said no.'

'Thanks. Another glass?' I went to the bar to order more wine. There was a mirror behind the bar and while I waited I watched a stream of reflections from the street outside. Anyone could be walking along there and anyone could come in at any moment.

When I got back to the table she was scraping her fork round the dish.

'Ta,' she said, finished the drop of wine in her old glass and pushed it aside.

I smiled at her. 'Chris – would you mind our budgie?'

'Budgie!' She spluttered a laugh, then put her hand over her mouth. 'Sorry. Just can't see you with a budgie.'

'He was Charlie's mum's,' I said.

'Oh, sorry.'

'We've been looking after him only now—'

'Actually, that would be brilliant,' she said. 'Don's dad's got an aviary. He's got all sorts, finches, canaries. If I had a bird it would be a something in common sort of thing, wouldn't it? A talking point.'

'Do you want to come and get him now?' I said.

'Now . . . but . . .'

'I'll pay for a taxi so you can get him home.'

She sucked a point of her hair as she thought. 'Don't know what Mum'll say – but if the worst comes to the worst we could put him in the aviary.'

'Come on then . . .'

We took a taxi back to Chestnut Avenue.

'I didn't know you lived up here,' she said, when she realised the direction we were heading in. I remembered that work still had the address of the bedsit, my official address.

'This is Charlie's mum's,' I said.

'Don could fix that.' She nudged the broken gate with her foot. 'He's hell of a handy. Shall I get him to pop round?'

'Don't worry.'

'Lovely house.' She wandered about touching things, the curtains, a cushion embroidered with flowers. Charlie Two was huddled in his cage, feathers fluffed out as if he was cold. Maybe he had a hangover.

'Pretty colour,' Christine said. She leant closer to look. 'Is he OK?'

'He's been a bit off.'

'Well Don's dad'll know what to do.' She made squeaky kissing sounds at him. 'God, I'm bursting. Can I use the loo?'

'Upstairs, first door.'

I stood stiffly listening to her feet on the stairs; the closing of the door; the slide of the bolt; a pause; a flush; the running of the tap. Surely Fay would understand that this was the best thing? I picked up the phone and called a taxi. I put the remaining Trill and budgie stuff into a carrier bag.

'I don't know what Mum will say when I waltz in with a

budgie!' She giggled as she came back into the kitchen. 'But then she thinks I'm totally loopy anyway!'

There was the tooting of a horn as the taxi stopped outside. I carried the cage out to the car for her.

'I charge extra for livestock,' the driver said as I reached for my purse but he laughed. 'Just having you on, love,' he said.

'Bye, Charlie Two,' I said to the trembling clump of feathers. 'Bye, Chris.'

'Keep in touch,' she said.

I watched them drive off round the corner and stood in the sunshine for a moment. I saw that Fay's ceanothus had sprouted some bright new shoots. Maybe next year it would be the picture that Maisie had promised. There were messages on the phone. One of them was someone called John, asking Charlie to phone him urgently and giving a mobile number. I was about to delete it – Charlie didn't need to hear anything urgent from anyone called John – but instead I rang the number.

'John here.'

'I'm Charlie's girlfriend,' I said.

'Oh.'

'There was a message saying urgent.'

'Has he gone north?'

'Yes.'

'Could you give me his number? I need to give him a bell.'

'Are you John Smith?' I said.

'Hardacre,' he said. 'I've got a pen.'

'If you tell me the message, I'll pass it on,' I said. 'We have no secrets.'

He hesitated. 'I'm sure you don't, love, but it's about work.'

'But he's left.'

'I know.'

'If you tell me the message I'll get him to ring you.'

I could hear him sighing, a kind of shrug in his voice. 'OK.

Tell him Bart wants him back – another 5K and four extra days' leave.'

'What?'

'His replacement's a fiasco.'

'I thought the place was running down,' I said.

'What?'

'Why was Charlie sacked then?'

There was a pause. 'You got hold of the wrong end of the stick there, love. He wasn't sacked, he walked out.'

'Are you sure?' I said.

'Left us right up the swanee. Will you pass on the message? Are you still there?'

I rang Charlie. Toni answered. 'Nina?' she said. She sounded amazed but then she rescued herself. 'Good trip? You want Charlie?'

'Please.' I could hear the kitchen noises that had grown so familiar; with my eyes closed I could see the messy table where the phone was usually left; I could hear in the distance the booming of Bruno's voice.

'Nina,' Charlie said. He sounded breathless.

'Did you get made redundant or did you walk out?'

There was a pause so long I thought we'd lost the connection but I could just make out his breath and then he said, 'I had to get away.'

'But it was a lie.'

'That's rich,' he said.

I wondered if Toni was there beside him, ears flapping. Would she be gratified to hear the roughness in his voice? Not like Charlie's voice, it was the bad influence, the distance. He never used to speak to me like that.

'Has anyone . . . said anything about me?' I asked, thinking of Rupert.

'Ruth had plenty to say. But, Nina, have you got the letter?'

232

'Yes.'

'Have you read it?'

'Why should I? I've just seen you.'

'Read it.'

'I got a card from Christine. Just met her for a drink.'

I could hear the surprise in his silence. Meeting people for a drink was not something I did. It's good to be able to surprise your partner. Never be predictable or the excitement dies.

I decided to let him off the hook. 'I'm tired, Charlie. I need an early night.'

'Read the letter,' he said. 'Please.'

'Night night,' I said and put the phone down.

Although I was tired I had to do something; there was no way I could relax in front of the television, no way I was going to sleep. I went into the bathroom, plastered dye on my head and started cleaning the house. I vacuumed up every last feather and bit of fluff and chaff. Everybody tells lies. When I was small I thought people were the same colour all through; if you cut through a leg or an arm it would be smooth inside like marzipan. I didn't know then that everyone, however beautiful their skin may be, is packed with tubes and bile, blood, bacteria, gristle. No one is beautiful inside, just as no one is purely good. Charlie comes as near as it is possible to be but even he has a bad thought sometimes, or tells a lie. So what?

I felt strange, on the verge of ill, bones hollow and achy. I tried to do the Sufi breathing I'd been taught. Count seven on an in breath, pause, seven on an out breath, pause. It's supposed to calm and clear the mind but all it did this time was make me out of breath, and in the pauses I became aware that Fay was hanging just at the corner of my eye. I tried to smile to let her know I knew she was there but every time I moved my head she slid away and left me grinning like an idiot at nothing.

233

It was so quiet. I was almost sorry that Charlie Two had gone. I could still feel the cool weight of him in my palm, lying across the scar, still feel the fluttering inside. The sensation of a little life cupped in my hand. A life that I had saved. I sent a wish to him in Christine's house, wherever that was, that he would recover. The fear was not of *him*, I realised now, it was that in my fright I might beat him off and kill him, not that I would mean to, but that I'd kill him all the same.

I opened a tin of rice pudding taken from Fay's kitchen, and ate it cold straight from the tin. Its sweet grainy creaminess comforted my stomach as it arrived there, soft and cushiony white, though the comfort stopped short of my nerves and brain.

In Charlie's room the shelves were crammed with bird-books. I ran my finger along the spines: *RSPB Handbook*; *Raptors of the World*; *Flight Identification of European Sea-Birds*; *Redpolls, Twites and Linnets*. I picked up the *Field Guide to the Birds of Britain and Ireland* and carried it downstairs. I made myself a mug of hot chocolate, added a slug of brandy, drew the curtains, and sat down with the book. Fay settled into a fold of the curtain. I made myself stare at the place and of course there was nothing. 'I'm not afraid,' I said to the shadow and the curtain swayed in the way that curtains do sway, nothing very strange in that. The more of the chocolate I drank, the more brandy I added till I nearly was relaxed.

I flicked through the pages of the book: wheatear; whim-brel; corncrake; snipe. In the margins Charlie had written notes, numbers, dates. At the bottom of each description was a map showing distribution and a phonetic rendering of their songs. I tried them out and it made me laugh. Cawing and tweeting to myself, crowing away in an empty house.

I was studying the curlew; its freckled wings and the long curved spine of its beak – the sound it makes: *coor-lee, coor-*

lee. There was a clipping from a magazine about record numbers of them in Norway and a postcard, a photograph of a flock feeding in a grassy field. I turned the card over:

Hiya Charlie,
    Well I got here and it's really great. V. beautiful island, inspiring, and the obs. comfortable, nice folks. A good place to be bird-wise and otherwise. Hope you can come. I'm sure it would help you get things straight.
    So great to meet you, hope we get to do it again!
    Love
    Toni xxxxxxx

I stared at the card, turning it over to look at the birds, turning it back to read the words, birds, words, birds, words, absurd birds, absurd words. Couldn't make out the date. My teeth were clamped together and my knees, my scalp was strange and tight. Do it again? Get what straight? Do it again? Get what straight?

I closed my eyes and breathed. It could be innocent. It could be. There are exercises you can do when you are wound up, physical and mental. I drew myself up as tall as I could, spine straight right from the top of my head to my coccyx, and then scissored over from the hips, hands dropping to the floor, but the chocolate scalded through with brandy ran up my throat and squirted through my nostrils and my eyes ran just like I was crying. That's an exercise you shouldn't do if you are the least bit pissed.

I got out Dave's *I Ching*. I could see how if you were alone with no one to turn to it would be tempting. Some of the pages were stuck together. The coins were so heavy and smelly and dark. Victorian hands will have held them, they will have weighed down so many different pockets. I tried out the throwing, just once, to get a feel of it. Dave's hands touched them the most, though, all the times he threw them in this house and alone in his bedsit. Alone.

The trigram I got was SUNG. And the judgement for that said: *It will be advantageous to see the great man; it will not be advantageous to cross the stream.* And what is that supposed to mean? No wonder Dave topped himself trying to figure that stuff out. I threw the book down and the coins rolled across the floor.

Fay tittered and I went into the kitchen and put my foot on the pedal of the litter bin, flipped it open. A smell like sour breath puffed out. I should have emptied it before I left. Under the rice-pudding tin was the mail I'd dumped in there. You Have Already Won; Oven Chips; Free Calculator from Damart and a letter screwed and torn.

I looked up and saw myself in the black kitchen window, a tight helmet, my hand went up – a crust – I was still plastered in the dye. No wonder my head felt strange. The dye was almost dry. It stung and itched. How could I have forgotten that? Upstairs I rinsed my head. The dye came off in scabs like grainy blood. I knelt and held the shower-head in one hand and rubbed and rubbed, till I saw the water running clear. The dye had been on for more than two hours when it was supposed to be twenty minutes. I looked at the box: Morello Cherry it said. How had that happened? I thought I'd picked up Maple Brown.

I took the torn scraps from the torn envelope, flicking off some swollen maggots of rice. I pieced the letter together as best I could, a bit of it missing and some illegible due to a smear of pudding, on the table:

Dear Nina,
    I'm sorry to do this in a letter . . . impossible to talk to . . . I've tried but . . . I know it's cowardly telling you like this but . . . I know all about . . . How could you not have told me?

*There's no point you coming to Orkney. Of course
you can stay in the house till . . .*
I'm sorry.
All the best,
Charlie.

All the best? A horrible thought struck me then. I'd assumed
that of the four of us only Rupert and I knew about what we
did in Blackpool. But what if Charlie had known all the time,
what if Toni knew too, what if we'd *all* been play acting,
Charlie and Toni smirking behind my back?

Fay's medicine cabinet was crammed full. She didn't mind
me going down and looking. Behind the shampoo, Vaseline,
corn plasters and denture cream were lots of little bottles with
chemist's labels. *Mrs F.A. Martin. One to be taken three times
a day with meals. Do not exceed the stated dose.* I searched
until I came across one that said: *One to be taken at bedtime
only.* I took three with a slug of brandy and put the telly on
loud until the room began to melt around me before the
question I'd been keeping from Nina got through. Had Rupert
known when we first met? Had he sought me out? I sent my
memory back to the hotel, and to all the other times, the
strawberries and the sandwiches and the drinks. All the talk of
goodness and connection. Was this all some long game for
him? But why? Who was he? Why? It was too much. Nina
couldn't deal with things like that. And Nina was so woozy
from the drink and the pills, she only just made it up to bed.

It was a shock in the bathroom, the sun slanting on my
crimson head, smudges of dye on my forehead and cheek,
one ear stained deep brown. When I drew the curtains in the
sitting room Fay fluttered out and hovered over a red stain on
the back of the sofa. It looked like someone had been shot
through the head.

I was hungry but I couldn't go out. The pills, whatever they were, had knocked me into space and now I couldn't get back; I floated round the house protected from all the things I had to think about by a layer of foam. You are so pretty when you smile. Did someone once say that? It was nice, floating with Fay; she was my sort of mother after all. We shared some molecules at least.

The phone rang and I looked at it with surprise, something from the outside splintering through.

'I'm outside,' he said. Fay shrank away. The kitchen sprang clear and real around me and I shivered. There was Charlie's letter on the table and it all came crashing back. I wished I'd taken all Fay's pills not just three, and then together we could have ghosted about in the thinness for ever, none of this rudeness or interruption or human difficulty any more.

He came round to the back door. I saw his outline through the frosted glass like a target at a shooting school. I opened the door and noticed that it was chilly. He stepped in and dumped a carrier bag on the table. He looked different. I saw it at once. Raw and unkempt, unlike himself, dark stubble on his jaw and lip.

'Did you tell him?' I said.

'Tell him what?'

'About us.'

'Us!' He raised his eyebrows at me. 'I should think that's the least of your worries.'

I looked down at the scraps of letter. How could Charlie write that and send it – and then make love to me the way he did? It wasn't *just* me, it *wasn't*. It wasn't just me kissing – he kissed me back and pushed into me. He did it to me. Why, why, why? Was he really such a coward that he could not face me and say no?

'Does it matter now?' he said.

238

'What?' I said, trying to force a clear line of reason through the muzziness in my head.

'About Charlie and Toni.'

'What about them?'

When he hung his head his lashes were stupendous black fans and dimples slanted on the planes of his cheeks. The stubble suited him. A fleck of memory opened a circle in the dirt. I leant on the table. He was looking at the letter. The air was too hard and real, the sun too bright. I stood up straight.

'Charlie's the only good thing in my life,' I said. 'If you've smashed that . . .'

'If *I've* smashed it?' He fingered the bits of torn paper and looked at me, something brimming in his eyes. I made myself think: get through this, get through that, then handle whatever next.

'Well here we are,' I said. 'What do you want?'

He swallowed. I saw the Adam's apple slide in his throat. We stood through a warp of time till my legs went soft and I had to sit down.

'You need to eat,' he said, 'and so do I.' He brought sparkling wine and a carton of orange juice from his bag. 'Buck's fizz,' he said. 'Can you do an omelette or something?'

'*What?*'

'Breakfast.'

'Are you mad?' I said.

He paused as if honestly considering this, then found a couple of glasses. But he was right. Eating weighs you down, body and mind, and stops you flying off. There's a fine balance for birds, Charlie told me, between not eating enough to fly and eating so much they can't.

'What is it with you and champagne?' I asked.

'Not wasting the real stuff on you any more,' he said. His voice was rougher, no more of the suede.

'But there's nothing to eat.'

He peered into the fridge at the tub of margarine, something under clingfilm, the dead salad and a single dubious egg.

'I thought you'd have food,' he said. 'What's in the freezer?' He opened it and pulled out a lasagne. 'This'll do,' he said. 'You having one?'

I shook my head. I poured some orange juice. It was freshly squeezed; at least the label claimed it was, thick with flecks, sweet and sharp.

'Not very domesticated, are we?' He popped the top of the wine and made two glasses of Buck's fizz.

'I'll stick to juice,' I said.

He shrugged his shoulders. I picked up the lasagne, pierced the film and shoved it in the microwave.

'Your hair's an interesting colour,' he said with a sort of snigger.

Through the door of the microwave I watched the rectangular box revolve, the plastic on top billowing in the blast of heat and Fay in there waving. 'Did you know your ear is brown?' he said. The kitchen filled with the smell of hot cheese. 'You should have kept your hair the way it was. Long, blonde. That was pretty. Angelic was how they put it, remember? Coffee? Didn't they let you keep it long inside?'

I filled the kettle. 'No milk.'

'Did you get real coffee in prison?'

His eyes followed me about. The microwave pinged and I tipped the slimy oblong of meat and cheese on to a plate.

He pushed the glass of fizz towards me and I took a sip. The orange flecks had risen in the foam to make a fruity scum.

'You said revenge,' I said. 'I don't . . . who are you?'

He held his hand up as if to say wait and ate his way steadily through the lasagne, chopping the slippery pasta with the side of his fork. I watched the red fat seep out and run over the plate.

He looked up and met my eyes. 'Not bad,' he said. He got

up, found the cafetière and made coffee. Strange to see him moving about in the kitchen. There was a feather stuck to the top of the coffee jar and he held it between his fingers, stroked it the wrong way so that the filaments stood out and set my teeth on edge.

'I see you've offloaded the bird. Or did it die? Or did you . . .'

'A friend's got him,' I said quickly, a catch in my voice on the word 'friend'. I thought longingly then, and I never thought I could have longed for this, to be sitting at my desk at Green's Robotics with Christine nattering away beside me, back in what already seemed like a golden age of safety.

Rupert stretched out his long legs, faded jeans, grubby at the knee. The same jeans he'd been wearing when we were hundreds of miles away. The first time I'd seen him in anything that looked less than brand new. He pushed down the top of the cafetière, looked at my waggling foot and said, 'Can't you sit still?'

I scrunched my toes in the woolly socks and felt all the muscles tense in my legs right up to my neck and skull.

'Who are you?' I said again.

He poured the coffee. 'The name's Mark. Mark Curtis. And yours, as we know, is Karen Wild.'

I picked up a spoon and flipped it back and forwards, watching the reflection, a warping Nina rolling over and over in the smeary steel like someone falling through the sea. He told me he'd been eleven when Isobel, his eighteen-year-old sister, had gone missing just before Christmas. 'Imagine that Christmas,' he finished and then, 'Put that down.' I did put the spoon down and saw that there was dye in my nails as if I'd clawed someone to death.

Fay listened from the lampshade, a wisp of cobweb like a question mark, as he told me how his mother's heart had broken when Isobel's body was found; how she'd been housebound ever since. 'I have to make it up to her somehow,' he said. He got up and went to the window; I think to hide his face. His back was rigid, I could hear little sounds in his throat as he struggled to get himself under control. I stroked the numb ridge on my hand. Noticed a wet drop of orange on my dressing gown. Life is so messy. Even the simple things like eating and drinking.

'I'm sorry about what happened,' I said. And I meant it. There's an expression 'my heart bleeds for you' and though it is a cliché it is so accurate, the flowing leaky feeling in the chest, pure empathic sorrow.

'I feel for you,' I said and then he laughed and it was not like him, it was as if something inside him had flown apart. His arms flailed, his hands flapped, his face cracked. It was like a shameful private act and I looked away until he'd finished. It was not Rupert's laugh. There was a long silence, soured by its ugly echo. Fay shrivelled up and vanished.

'Rupert . . .' I said; I could not think of him as anything other than Rupert although that laugh had not been Rupert's.

'Yes, *Nina*?' He went and stood behind me. It chilled me when his shadow fell across me, almost as if it was cold.

∧

I put my hands on her shoulders from behind, like a lover would. You could feel the flinch go right through.

'What do you want?' she said.

'I want you to come with me.'

'Why?'

She made no attempt to escape from my hands. I could have slid them down and touched her up. I could have done anything. She was only wearing the dressing gown with not much under as far as I could see.

'What's the matter?' she said.

'What?'

'You seem different.'

Of course I laughed at that. Different! She didn't know how right she was.

'Don't,' she said.

'Don't what?'

'Laugh like that. It's scary.' Of course that only set me off again.

She curled herself forward on the table, head in her hands, then she said, all muffled, 'Please tell me what you want.'

'I told you,' I said.

'Why?' She sat up and twisted her head round towards me. 'Not unless you tell me why.' I put my hands on her shoulders again and, almost of their own accord, they moved together round her neck. It was small and soft in my hands. The natural instinct was to squeeze. I could feel the life flowing and beating in the tube of her neck. After a moment I let go and she gasped in a gulp of air.

'Coming then?' I said and you could tell she'd got the message loud and clear, the way she nodded. Not that she had any choice. Her face was red and there were tears standing in her eyes but I didn't look. Having a sister teaches you about women and their wiles. It was not in the original plan but I had to tie her up.

'I won't go anywhere,' she said. She didn't cave in easily – you have to give her that. She went on trying to make out she'd wait for me while I got the car but I wasn't born yesterday. I tied and gagged her, dressing-gown cord, hankie stuffed in her mouth, put her in the cupboard under the stairs while I went to fetch the car.

I hailed a taxi back to Peerless View. There was her room all waiting for her. I did some finishing touches to be hospitable. The cupboard smelt damp so I folded the things on a little table, neat piles like in a shop. I put the picture of Charlie by her bed. A nice detail, I thought. As I arranged her nightie on the pillow, I had the strange idea I was preparing a room for a bride but it was only that the creature comforts might make her more likely to co-operate.

When I locked up and went out down the dark and oily stairs it was with a kind of thrill in me, knowing that next time I came in it would be with her. I kept catching myself laughing with the uproar of it all. Not like a birdwatcher, more like a fisherman about to land a big 'un. I should have waited, had a coffee, a shave, a bit of a sober up, but there was the thought of her in that cupboard. She couldn't get out herself, I was sure of that much, but there was the chance someone else might turn up. How did I know who had the key?

So I drove straight back in the car – and got stopped. I don't know what drew the attention to me, first thing I knew a police car was passing me, flashing and indicating pull over. 'Licence, sir?' the policeman said and asked me the number plate of the car. It took the smirk off his face when I rattled it off and produced my licence.

'Have you had a drink this morning, sir?' he said.

'Absolutely not!' I said and, 'Chance would be a fine thing!' I was cursing the stubble, the scruffy clothes, not changed since I left Orkney what with all the stress, which is not like me, personal hygiene is normally top of my agenda.

'In that case, sir, if you wouldn't mind stepping out of the car?' It was going to be a breathalyser. I was going to be stopped from driving. And then I remembered Dad saying the police were after me. Now they had the licence with my name. I did something I never thought I'd have had the nerve to do. I put my foot down. It was like TV, the car chase through the streets, heads snapping round to look, and there was a kind of thrill in it, making me laugh. It was more like TV than real life but then so much is these days. I remember lights and a bump of some kind and I don't understand entirely how, but I gave them the slip. I drove down a street that may have been one way and had to leave the car, climb over a wall and run through a garden, a kid on a swing screaming her head off. Over the wall and back out on the street, forcing myself to walk not to draw attention and heart going like the clappers. Made it back to Peerless View and in and got the door locked behind me.

It was panic stations and I didn't know which way to turn. I was running with sweat and sick with the excitement of it and got to the sink just in time. When it was all out of me I ran water to clean the sink. One of those rubbery things on the end of the tap like at home so you can direct the water where you want. All the lumps of sick stuck in the plughole and the water wouldn't make them go and that nearly had me heaving again.

What I wanted was to pull myself together and have a shower but there was no shower, only the big stained bath that made me think of coffins. The flat was dark what with the boarding on some of the windows and the dirt on the rest. I ran a bath and got in there, head under, until I'd calmed down then had a coffee. I shaved and dressed in my Rupert finery. My fingers were shaking when I did up the buttons. I rubbed a clear place on the mirror and practised the voice and smile. He was growing fainter, outgrowing his usefulness. Just this one last go.

I went through the options. One was just to leave her. Most likely no one would come. How long she'd last without food or drink, I didn't know for definite. Three or four days? It would be a long and drawn-out death and fitting, to be shut in a cupboard, similar to the way Isobel died. I decided on that. The easy option. I went to the pub for a sandwich but I couldn't settle. The feeling of her life between my hands would not go away, it was a kind of flowing. I changed my mind. There was the room ready for her for a start. It would be an anticlimax after all the planning and anticipation. And there was the chance that she'd be found and the police would be involved. I went cold when I realised another mistake I'd made: telling her my real name.

I thought of Mum then, thinking what it would do to her if I ended up inside. I could picture her sitting up in bed in her usual way, magazines, TV, biscuit tin, and then the phone ringing, or perhaps the police would make a personal appearance at her bedside. It did not bear thinking about. I had to get to Karen and bring her back. Now I had no car but it came to me that there was his car, which would be the perfect thing, not a car anyone would be looking out for. I'd noticed the keys when I was going over the house and I could picture them now, on a row of hooks in the hall. It was a risk going out again at all with them looking for me. I would wait till dark, keep my head down going then drive back with every care. If I was stopped it would be all up for me, but why should I be stopped? Stone-cold sober, cleanly shaved, well spoken, well versed in all aspects of the Highway Code and driving an old black Audi. Not the type to draw attention.

The more I thought about it, the calmer I became. Calm and decided would be a way of putting it. It made me smile to think that I'd been envisaging hordes of police with roadblocks and suchlike but what had I really done? Had one too many before I drove and then made a dash for it rather than blow into a bag. Hardly the crime of the century.

I was worried about having left the house unlocked all day. I had to be watchful. If she'd been found they'd be lying in wait. I walked up and down Chestnut Avenue a few times just as dark was falling and no sign of anything, not a light, the curtains still open. I took the bull by the horns and walked straight up to the door like any innocent caller.

When I was sure the coast was clear, I put on gloves and went round the back and into the kitchen. When I put on the light it was like the *Marie Celeste*, all just as we'd left it, dirty plate and glasses on the table, a chair on the floor. Her mobile was on the worktop. I had a look and there were four missed calls. They were all from someone called Rose, who must be her probation officer. They said where was she? What happened at work? She'd broken the terms of her licence and could expect arrest. So the police were after the pair of us now.

'Karen?' I called. I stood there in the dark looking at the little triangle of door under the stairs. I switched on the light. Silent as the grave was the phrase that came to me. I could have done with a bit of reassurance from her, a knock or a grunt. The keys were just where I'd pictured them. I went outside to start the car.

On the front passenger seat was a box of jellies. It was like a sign to me from Isobel and the sweetness of it made me strong.

I opened the box and took one, red – when she was in charge she would have the red and black ones and only let me have the yellow and green. The sugar melted round my teeth as I turned the key. If it hadn't started I don't know what. It took a few tries but then it went. I backed it as close up to the front door as possible. I sat in the car a minute, wanting in a cowardly way to drive off out of it. But I could not do that having come this far. If she was dead then she was dead and I didn't know what, but I could not afford to be seen by any neighbours sitting in that car. I left the engine running and the back door open and went inside.

I steeled myself to kneel down and open the triangular door. It was pitch black in there and I could see nothing. I put a hand in and got hold of a leg, bare and cold. I jerked my hand back wondering if this was the famous chill of death, but then she groaned. I pulled her out of there, floppy as they come and not quite with it and she'd also wet herself which was an unpleasantness I hadn't counted on.

After a check for passers-by, I lifted her into the car, got the door shut and – this comes from watching TV crime which is like a training course for the criminally minded – went round with a J-cloth and wiped my prints from every surface I might have touched that morning.

It was simple then to drive back, pull the car into the yard and lock the gates. The wall at the back has glass in it like shark fins for that added bit of security. I carried her out, up the stairs and into her new room.

She soon came round when she saw her new abode. I offered her Pot Noodles as well as a drink but she'd got the hump and wouldn't answer. I took her in a Horlicks with some digestives and locked the door. I had put a bucket in there, in case she was caught short again.

It left me all on edge, the upset of it all, took away something of the triumph of the moment. I paced up and down the hall outside the locked door, listening for a sound. I could hear nothing. There had been a bit of rough handling in all the kerfuffle. I was like a new parent must be, wanting to check all the time that she was still breathing, but I didn't. I was so restless I went out and found a pro. This one had ginger hair and tits like bags of frogspawn. I tried to keep from nudging up against them but they were everywhere and in the end I had to pull away.

'It's all right, darling,' she said, 'it happens to everyone,' giving me a look of understanding that if I'd been a weaker man I'd have wiped right off her face. But I was not letting any other trouble come between Karen and myself and so I paid up in full and left. If nothing else it had passed an hour or so of the night.

*T*he night of the twelfth of December, the day that Jeffrey had sent her away, the day she'd heard the posh and cosy voice of his new girlfriend and smelt the cake, Karen went for a cigarette walk. She had changed so much in this new life, at this new school: no sex, except with Jeffrey; no swearing, or hardly any. She had very nearly become a nice girl, the sort of girl she used to envy and despise. She'd changed the way she spoke, opening out her northern vowels; she'd watched the body language of the girls at school and copied it. She was a good mimic and could fool almost everybody but she couldn't fool herself. And smoking was the one habit she couldn't, or wouldn't, kick, her one last little trace of before.

Roger gave her pamphlets about giving up and Joan said nothing, but left photographs of lungs lying on the kitchen table: airy pink butterflies and filthy clogged-up lumps. They forbade smoking in the house. If not for that rule she may not have gone for a cigarette walk that night . . . if not for this, if not for that . . . the ifs snag at my mind like the barbs on a wire fence.

She walked through the dark streets, inhaling smoke as she peered in at the Christmas-tree lights in the windows. Sugary brightness dazzling in the frost. She went down to the sea front, to the Spa Gardens, leant on the railings, gazed out beyond the lights of the promenade to the black glitter of the sea. Waves broke with a regular sigh and the shingle rolled and grumbled. On the horizon she could see tiny points of light, a ship in the distance.

Since seeing Jeffrey and hearing the new girlfriend's voice she had kept her mind trapped in a cage of physics and maths: graphical solutions to simultaneous equations; resultant force and terminal velocity. But now it broke loose and stretched its wings. On the promenade below her was one lonely figure, small and huddled, and a trotting dog. She ground out one ciggie and lit another; the match flame catching and singeing the fake fur round her hood.

She walked towards the place where the well was, not with any intention at all, simply that is where her feet carried her. It was too cold to stand around. She remembered Jeffrey's words, 'I always thought when I have a girlfriend I'll bring her here,' and the ludicrous blooming of pride within her when he'd said girlfriend, a word that signifies love and belonging, arms around you. The smoke deep in her lungs on the freezing air was delicious and she felt it in her veins. She rose above herself, feeling powerful and detached. Friction causes wear and heating, she thought, speed equals distance/time.

She reached the gate marked PRIVATE and went through. Frost gleamed on the leaves in the orange streetlight and scraped off on her coat. She felt the snag of a barb on her sleeve, a tiny rip in the fabric. Inside there was very little light and it took her eyes a moment to adjust. Before she could see, though, she could hear. She could hear voices coming from below her feet, an echoey giggle and murmur. She saw the black smile in the sparkly ground. She heard the sounds of people making love.

She stood for a moment listening and looking, her breath catching the little light there was, making long feathers in the air. She rose above, amongst the vaporous feathers, and *watched as she took off her coat, flicked it with her lighter, waited for the snarling sound of flame on cloth and dropped it in the well. There was an immediate shriek, a male voice saying, 'Christ, Christ,' a flash of the tops of two heads as she pulled the lid across, closed up the hole in the ground. Her foot scraped the earth and leaves and twigs across just like Jeff had shown her. And then, the cold striking through her school blouse and sweater, she ran home, slipped in without the doctors noticing her lack of a coat.*

They were watching the Messiah *on TV and she sat numbly between them. 'It's starting to feel quite Christmassy,' Joan said, 'next week, we'll get a tree. It's so nice having a young person with us, isn't it, Roger?' They were drinking sherry and nibbling Cheeselets from a wooden bowl. It was the sort of evening she would want in her adult life, cosy, civilised and safe.*

'I lost my coat,' she said at bedtime. 'Sorry. Someone nicked it from the cloakroom.'

'But you've been out.'

'I wore my blazer, it was freezing.'

'You can borrow one of mine,' Joan said, 'and you can ask about it at school tomorrow. But don't worry; we can always get you another one. You could choose one for Christmas if you like.'

'Thank you,' she said. 'Goodnight.'

'Goodnight, dear . . . oh by the way, Jeffrey called round this evening. He said he'd see you tomorrow.'

'Jeffrey?'

'Yes! Jeffrey! What's the matter?' Joan laughed. 'She looks as if she's seen a ghost, doesn't she, Roger?'

'When?' she said. 'I mean how long ago?'

'Not long. You just missed him.'

'Was he OK?'

'Looked OK from a medical perspective!' Roger said. 'Off to bed now, there's a good girl. School tomorrow.'

She lay awake for a long time. Maybe Jeffrey stamped out the flames and climbed out? There couldn't have been much fire, anyway: combustion requires oxygen. Maybe no one was hurt at all? But he wouldn't have had time to get round here before she did. Maybe it wasn't Jeffrey then. No, don't think that, don't think that. There was no one down the well at all. Of course. She wouldn't do a thing like that! It had been a hallucination. Yes, that was it, a sort of waking dream. She breathed out a long smoky sigh of relief. Put the lid on a stupid het-up memory of a stupid dream revenge she didn't take. Put the lid down tight.

∧

In the morning I got spruced up before I went in. This was the first day of the new life. I had a feeling almost of being cheerful, what you might term optimistic. The culmination of fifteen years. I thought to offer her a bath and she could get dressed. Outside the sun was shining and the road roaring as per usual. I opened the door and went in. It was all gloom in there with thin stripes of light from between the boarded windows. I put on the light and there she was hunched up on the bed looking like a dog's dinner. It was a let-down. In my mind's eye when I'd pictured this day I'd seen the young Karen and I know that's ridiculous but such is man. And here she was with her thin white face and her dyed hair all up on end like a hedgehog – and also, to my nose, a little high which I know was not her fault.

'I'll run you a bath,' I said. 'Cuppa while you wait?'

'This is pathetic,' she said, looking up at me. 'Just let me go.'

It takes your breath away that a person in a position of such weakness could have such cheek. I went out and locked the door. I had this over her of course, I had the power to come and go as I pleased. Pathetic is just the sort of word Isobel would use. Not all the memories are good, of course not, sometimes Isobel was a bitch to me. Would she even thank me now, after all my trouble?

I went in half an hour later and told her the bath was ready. I noticed that she'd put the picture of Charlie on her pillow.

'You've been in my house,' she said.

'*Your* house?' I said.

I had her there, you could see, and even more so when I took the life licence out of my pocket.

'Does Charlie know about this then?' I asked.

The expressions that went across her face then answered any question of whether she knew he knew. She put out a hand to grab it but it was a weak gesture and not really meant.

'By the way,' I said, 'I've got a message for you from Rose.'

You'd think I'd touched her with a cattle prod the way she sat up at that.

'Just to say you've broken the terms of this,' I shook the licence, 'and the police are on the case. Oh don't worry, you'll be safe here.'

'How do you know Rose?' she said in a little voice.

I could have made out she was a personal friend or some-such but didn't have the stomach to string it out any longer.

'I listened to your messages.'

'Have you got my phone?'

'I left it. Come on,' I said, 'you'll feel better after a wash and brush-up.' She looked at me then in such a way that I realised I was talking as Mark not Rupert and at that moment I decided to drop the pretence. She was mine. No further need. We could be Mark and Karen – no more Rupert, no more Nina – we could just be ourselves.

I took her to the bathroom and stood outside while she bathed. I could see through the crack in the door if I wanted but to tell the truth I had no interest. I took away the cold Horlicks from her room, put it in the microwave and drank it myself.

I went back and listened to Karen splashing away. I did take a peep just to see what her progress was. Seeing her naked and unaware, something rose inside me. It was the white skin of her back, the wet hair clinging to her skull. It came to me that she was only human and I felt the pity rising up again.

She was mine, she was mine, she was mine.

The genuine Karen Wild.

I stood in the kitchen flicking through the scrapbook, remembering what all this was *for*, till she called out that she was freezing and I got her back to her room. I let her get dressed and took her a cup of tea and biscuits. She was wearing a skirt and one of the blouses I'd brought over. It was good to see the co-operation, a bit of respect in her eyes.

'I'll leave you to look at this,' I said. It was the scrapbook. Not the original, I'd photocopied everything in case she took it into her head to spoil it. But I thought a spot of reminiscence would do her good.

When I got back, she'd drunk the tea and the scrapbook was on the floor beside the bed. 'Did you look at it?' I said but there was no movement from her face.

Then she said in a way as if to a child, 'So, Mark, what is it that you want?'

Hearing my real name on her lips like that gave me a start. There were no lines to say then. I had what I wanted. I had her. But then what and then what?

'What's this for?' she said and reached over to the corner of the bed where I'd left the items of restraint. I'd forgotten they were there. They'd only been in case of need. An impulse buy from the sex shop – handcuffs padded with fake pink fur. They had caught my eye by the till, the look of the fur I think it was, the colour of bubble-gum. You'd think having seen them she'd have kept quiet. They'd been tucked under the edge of the mattress and no need for her to go ferreting around like that.

I would have left it at that for the time being but the hoity-toity sound of her voice got to me. I got hold of her and forced her hands together. She kicked at me but her feet were bare and she bit me on the arm but I was not letting go and I did not let go until I'd got the cuffs on.

During this her nose started to bleed all on the new mattress, which would mean scrapping it and mattresses do not come cheap. She was all twisted over with the pink fur round her wrists. Her face had a look of pure hatred and blood running down her mouth. I didn't want blood getting on the fur, which had a pretty effect with the silver cuffs and the pale skin. I tried to dab at her nose with a hankie and she spat at me. Well I was not having that. I backed away and left the room, locked the door, left her to stew in her own juices.

There were teeth marks on my arm and one place where the skin was broken. I went into town to buy first aid. A bottle of TCP and plasters and suchlike. The woman in Boots gave me a funny look. 'Are you all right?' she said. She was that motherly type. 'Only bitten by my girlfriend,' I said and the face on her then made me laugh and I knew I had to get that under control.

The smell of the TCP was so much like childhood, and all the scraped knees and cut fingers and the chewy edges of sticking plasters, I had a strange moment of such strong remembrance that, standing in the kitchen with its big stained sink and all, I wasn't even sure where I was or why.

I had her though. I had her. I was revving myself up with that thought. After everything all the years, and Mum in her chair and Dad in his pathetic jeans, I had her. I had to keep thinking that.

On the way back I'd bought another bottle of tequila and I poured one and swigged it back with salt on the rim like they do. Had to keep the hate. It was revenge. I could not go soft. That could not happen. It was up to me to put right the wrong of years. I had her where I wanted, but the white skin, the little skull under the wet hair. A feeling of pity would be the start of a disease, like a virus caught from somewhere, and next thing you know it'd be all forgiveness and happy-clappy this and that and sailing off into the sunset. I drank the tequila fast.

I *had* her.

~

O n Christmas afternoon, leaving the doctors and their real children dozing in front of the TV, she went for her ciggie walk. It was dark and the streets were quiet. It was mild and wet. She wore her Christmas present, a pink duffel coat with white toggles. The drizzle sat on the surface of the wool like grease. She let her hair get wet. She wandered through the streets looking through lighted windows at other people's Christmas afternoons: fairy lights; TVs flickering; a man asleep with a paper hat over his face – but in one, a woman with a grim face, ironing.

A man walked towards her, his dog skittering along ahead of him. 'Happy Christmas,' he said. She took a deep drag of her cigarette. 'Same to you,' she said in smoke.

She walked to the Spa Gardens, through the PRIVATE gate and pushed through the wet bushes. It was too dark to see the black circle on the ground. She crouched down to listen; she couldn't kneel and mess up her brand-new coat. There was no sound, of course. There was nothing. She smoked another cigarette, there in the triangle of darkness, and then, spooked suddenly by a fluttering in the bushes or maybe it was within herself, she stamped out her cigarette and hurried back to the doctors.

The night before Jeffrey went back to university his parents were out. She went round and they made love on the sitting-room floor. They hardly spoke, she hardly looked him in the eye, but the sex went on and on in every way she could think of until she was bruised and sore with carpet burns on her knees and elbows.

'You're incredible,' he said when she got up to go home. 'I'll miss you.' He promised to be home the weekend after next.

She walked fast back to the doctors' house and stood outside looking at their windows, the light through the curtains, her own room with the lamp left on, wasting electricity. 'You're incredible,' she whispered to herself, 'I'll miss you.'

She heard nothing from Jeffrey for a few days and then there was a note on a torn-off bit of A4:

Dear Karen,

Working hard. Party last night, didn't get to bed till five, so yawn, excuse short note, essay and practice and a concert later. Can't come back for weekend as promised, too much on. I've been thinking that we're too young to be tied down. How about we consider ourselves free during term times but still get together in the hols? Let me know what you think.

Love Jeff

She didn't bother to reply.

Λ

I got myself together, went back in to have a look. I went to have a feel. With her chained up like that I could have looked at anything I wanted and take my time. But it was her and she was wrong. The face was wrong. I unbuttoned the blouse and she squirmed and to tell the truth I wasn't interested in more than a token way. She looked nearly middle aged and at the same time like a child.

'I'm sorry,' she said.

I stood back from her.

'I did do it,' she said with a choke in her voice. 'I'm sorry. I'm so sorry.' She stopped herself then before she could say Rupert. 'I'm so sorry, Mark.'

It went through me when she said my name like that, what with her bitten nails and the way she was plucking at the cuff. You could see all the nerves she had stored up inside her. Fifteen years' waiting and all for that one word *sorry*! Did she think that was enough?

'Sorry?' I said in a kind of mimic and my voice came out so loud it rang.

She hung her head and started on the story of it in a small flat voice and to do her credit it was the same story she'd trotted out in court. Her voice going on like that made me realise I was tired. It had the feeling of a bedtime story. I sat on the end of the bed. She told me about the doctors who took her in and how they wouldn't let her smoke in the house, which is fair do's in my book. But if not for that, she said, she wouldn't have gone out that night, she would have stayed home and had a ciggie in her bedroom and it all would have turned out different.

'You trying to put the blame on them now!' I said.

She looked right through me. 'No,' she said, 'but don't you think it strange . . . if not for this, if not for that, how the most seemingly tiniest ifs can have such huge consequences?'

I had no opinion either way. I let her carry on. She was jiggling her foot about as she spoke and hitting her fingers on her open hand as if she was counting, this, then this, then this.

'I walked through the streets looking at the Christmas-tree lights in the windows. I went down to the Spa Gardens. I listened to the sea, waves rolling in and out, the rumble of the shingle. It just goes on and on, doesn't it? Doesn't care.'

No arguing with that.

'Since seeing Jeffrey with the girl I'd sort of kept my mind in like a cage of physics and maths, which was a safe place for it. But once I was out with the smoke and the night and the waves . . .' Her voice shook with the next bit about how she walked to the well.

'I remembered what Jeffrey told me,' she said, 'how when he had a girlfriend he'd take her there. And then a horrible joke he made once afterwards, once he'd started university and gone all cynical. Pussy in the well, he said. And it kept going round my mind, *Ding dong bell, pussy in the well*.' She half sang that bit and I held my hands under the edge of the bed then to keep them from shutting her up. Thinking of Isobel down in the well, thinking of pussy, thinking of Isobel.

'It was all dark and frosty and I could hear voices down there, in the well, before my eyes adjusted. When they did it was like a smile in the ground, where the lid was partly open. I could hear the sounds of . . .' her voice sucked in, 'it was the sounds of Jeffrey and – I thought it was Jeffrey – and the posh girl, having sex.'

'But it was Isobel,' I said.

Her eyes flashed up and met mine for a moment, then she was looking down again, gnawing her thumb. I waited, just watching her foot going and going.

'I didn't know what to do,' she said. 'It was a moment of . . . you won't believe me, Mark, I can't expect you to believe me. But it was like it was not *me* for a minute, like I lost myself, it wasn't a thought or a decision. I . . .' but she stopped.

'Say it,' I said. I had to hear the end of it then. It was like an itch and all her talking was scratching at it, scratching and scratching but not hard enough. I had to hear her say it.

She was silent. I put my hand out and pressed down her leg, the jiggling was doing my head in.

'Say it.' I squeezed her knee. 'Say it.'

When I squeezed harder I could feel the tremble going right through her body and travelling up my arm. I took my hand away. 'Say it.'

'I . . .' She shut her eyes. 'I took off my coat, lit it with my lighter and dropped it in the well. Someone shouted, then I didn't know what . . . a scream . . . I pulled the top shut.' Her voice had gone nearly too quiet to hear. 'Then I ran home. They were watching the *Messiah*. They didn't notice the missing coat at first. They were talking about Christmas and how nice to have me there.'

Tears were racing down her face now. 'They were eating Cheeselets and Roger poured me out a ginger wine. I was between them on the sofa and it was like it could be. Like it could have been. A sort of life I could have had. I wanted to tell them. I couldn't tell them. I nearly ran away that night. But then I thought maybe somehow, maybe by some miracle, it would be all right. Maybe they'd get out, maybe . . .'

Her voice trailed off as I put my mind back to that same night. Mum and Dad had gone to the pictures and Isobel was meant to be staying in with me, but she went out. She bribed me with a bag of chocolate limes. If Isobel had not gone out that night . . . if Isobel had not been such a slag . . . I had to stretch my tongue far out of my mouth to get away from remembering the chocolate limes. *Ding dong bell*, I thought, *pussy in the well*. Karen was watching me with her face all streaked. I had to get out of there then.

~

*I*n mid January, on the evening after her chemistry and physics mocks, she was sitting on the sofa between the doctors, eating strawberry ice-cream and watching television. There had been a programme about a family of lions in the Kalahari. The news came on. After the headlines Joan turned to her.

'What's the story with Jeffrey then?' She smiled at her husband as if they shared the same amused but tolerant attitude to the antics of the young. But Karen didn't answer, her attention captured by an item on the news. The bodies of two young people, Steven Spencer and Isobel Curtis, had been discovered in Felixstowe by a council workman in a disused well. There had been previous reports that these two were missing but because of their ages – both over eighteen – it had been assumed by some that they'd run off together. Their partially charred remains had been in the well for some weeks and, said the newsreader grimly, with a picture of a grinning young couple of strangers hovering on her shoulder, foul play was suspected.

'Oh my Lord,' Roger said, switching off the television. There was a long moment of clock ticking, flames flapping, sharply drawn-in breaths.

'Should I ring Barbara?' Joan said.

Karen's mouth was dry. She put down the cold bowl she'd been cradling in her lap. There was a roaring in her ears. Something inside her fell and fell away until it disappeared. She gathered her voice carefully to say, 'Do you know them?'

'Isobel's parents, yes, golf club . . .'

'They've got that problem boy.'

'Lord above.'

The phone rang. It was always ringing; it always does in a house of doctors. Those days it was never Jeffrey, but this time it was. His voice was almost squeaky with importance: 'Did you see the news? Steve. He was my mate. Fucking hell.'

She pushed the sitting-room door shut with her foot and sat on the stairs in the hall. She felt very tiny and cold and weary like someone who doesn't belong. 'I didn't think anyone else went down there,' she said.

'Must have been for old times' sake sort of thing,' he said, 'like us. We always said we'd take our girlfriends down there when we had them. But they never would have shut the lid! I reckon I should ring the fuzz, don't you?'

'I don't see what help you'd be,' she said, but weakly.

There was a pause. In the background music was playing. Karma karma karma karma karma chameleon. 'Did you get my note?' he asked. 'You didn't answer.' She said nothing. 'Will you be there when I get back?'

'I doubt it,' she said and put the phone down.

She nearly went that night. She started to pack a bag, then unpacked it again, not sure what was hers to take. She lay awake all night and tried to cry but it's hard to cry for people that you never knew. In the darkness she stared in the mirror. She looked young and sad and lovely and very like the girl she was trying so hard to be. The tears that did come were for herself and she clenched up against them in disgust.

Along with the bodies, the remains of a burnt coat had been found in the well. It was initially supposed to belong to Isobel

Curtis, but since she was wearing her own coat, that made no sense. It took a surprising amount of time, almost a week, until, on the day of her final mock exam – English lit. – the coat was identified by the Merriams as Karen's and she was taken away.

∧

O n the way to the pub I met a dog on the street that was
maybe a stray looking up at me with those dog eyes. It
followed me to the pub and I fed it some tortilla chips. I only
had one pint then back to Peerless View.

The look on her face when I went back in. 'I didn't mean it,'
she said. 'Please believe me, Mark.'

She turned the waterworks back on, bringing the fur,
already smudged with blood, up to wipe away the tears
and so on.

'Don't,' I said, 'don't muck them up.' She looked scared but
she held still and let me wipe her face this time, tilting it up to
me like a baby's. I looked up then and saw something I hadn't
noticed before. The corner of one of the hardboard sheets was
coming away from the window.

'What's that?' I said.

'What?'

I went over and pulled and the nail fell out.

'You've been mucking about,' I said.

'How could I?' she said, holding up her cuffed hands.

'Before,' I said.

'No,' she said.

'Liar.'

Shows how I'd let my guard down not to notice that before.

No way it could have come loose with how I'd hammered it home.

'Bitch,' I said. 'Your whole life is a lie.' I went to have another drink of the tequila. I was getting quite the buzz and purple flashes in my eyes. The salt was crusting round my lips, sore in the corners. The look on her face when I went back in with the hammer!

I swung it down on one palm, a fleshy clump of sound. It was good to see the terror in her eyes.

'I need to pee,' she said. I gave it a bit of thought and it was true it had been a long time. I know there are some who take pleasure in the toilet habits of others but I am not such a one. 'If you don't undo me and let me use the toilet I'll have to wet myself,' she said.

I wouldn't have put anything past her, to try to get away, to launch herself at me, but at the same time I did not want the unpleasantness, so I unlocked the cuffs, pulled her out of the door, holding tight round her wrist, and pushed her into the lav. I stood outside with the hammer; it gives a man an extra swagger about him, a heavy tool like that to hand. When I heard the flush I shoved her back along the hallway and into her room. Not surprisingly there wasn't any fight left in her. You could see her eyeing up the hammer.

'No need for the cuffs,' she tried when we were back again.

I laughed, giving a meaningful look to the window boards.

'I didn't do it,' she said, which continued my amusement. I cuffed her by one hand to the bed head this time to keep her away from any further mischief. I put the hammer at the other end of the bed well away from her clutches but where she could see it. We both looked at it.

'Do you believe how sorry I am?' she said, in a trembly little voice.

I didn't dignify her question with an answer.

'Do you remember when you said about the possibility of goodness?'

When she said that it was like remembering something from a film. Ducks quacking, champagne and broken glass.

'Well I've been thinking about it and I do think there is a possibility,' she said. 'Even for people like me. Or you.'

She was trying to lump us in together now! I laughed in the way I try not to laugh because it causes alarm but then what did it matter any more if I did cause alarm? Alarm was the effect I wanted.

She huddled herself up and waited till I'd stopped, then she cleared her throat. 'I know I did the most terrible thing,' she said, 'and I know you can never forgive me. I don't know why I did it. If I could go back and change it . . . but we never can go back, Rupert, Mark.' She picked at the cuff, fidgeting about. Her eyes looked into mine and the blue had gone to black. 'If there was any way I could undo it. But there isn't. I wrecked my own life too.'

'What a shame,' I said.

I looked down at the hammer and then at her. One swipe on her head and I could be out of there and Mexico here I come. Or I could have more fun with it first on other parts of her anatomy. Or maybe not use the hammer at all. Maybe it would be more fitting just to leave her here to rot. There were sirens, not unusual on that street, but more sirens and coming closer.

In the kitchen there were blue lights flashing through the muck on the windows. I picked up the tequila and swigged it. In Mexico there'd be a worm in the bottle but not in good old GB. The police had stopped outside. Two cars. No way they could know I was here. No lights on, car hidden in the yard round the back, gate locked. Another siren and an ambulance. Ambulance? What did they think . . . And then I saw it and I laughed. I laughed and laughed. There was a crash down there, a couple of cars tangled up together, and now another siren, another ambulance. Nothing to do with me! It struck me as funny that there they were all outside and here we were. I stood and watched, drinking the tequila. It was like a God's-eye view of a disaster, the little people scuttling about, a woman crumpling down in a faint. They covered her in a blanket. The boys in blue darted about like blue-arsed flies and that thought made me laugh. Blue, blue, blue. I stayed there riveted, watching all the time as the street lights started to come on. It was like TV. Like it was all put on for my benefit. A van came and they cut the car, sparks flying and a screech of tearing metal. The top of the car peeled open like the lid of a tin and inside was a dead mashed man. I drank away and watched.

*

The hammer was on the end of the bed. I stretched and stretched until my toe touched the cold head of it but all that did was nudge it further away. More and more sirens. At first I thought they were here for him, for me, for us, but it was something else going on out there, something that was making him laugh. I tried to wrench my hand from the cuff but couldn't get it past the knuckle of my thumb. He stayed out there laughing. The door was open, first time he'd left it open. I could see into the dark hall. I pulled at the cuff but careful not to pull too hard or clank the bed. The head of the hammer was the darkest thing in the room, an iron head, clawed at one side, a pale new wooden shaft. Of course it would be new. A heavy iron head, black with two long sharp claws.

The laugh again, scattered, like a mind falling apart or starlings startled from a tree. I brought the handcuff close to my eyes, stupid tacky silvery thing, you wouldn't think it could hold me but it did, the lock held firm and the key was in his pocket. *Warning. This is not a toy*, it said in tiny letters and there was the twist in my stomach that sometimes comes before a smile but I was not smiling.

Without the thickness of the fur, I thought, I might be able to work my hand free. I began to tear at the fur with my teeth. I pictured a fox in a trap that will chew its foot off to escape. Bits of fur came off and caught in the back of my throat and made me retch, but I gnawed and pulled at the edges until it began to come away. I spat out rubbery nubs of glue until at last the thick and wettish strip of fabric came off and my hand slid out.

He was coming. I reached for the hammer and stuffed it under the pillow behind me and shoved my hand back in the cuff just in time. I was bleeding where the metal had scraped. I let him see me working away at it with my teeth.

'It's a crash,' he said, 'a crash! Police out there and here we are!' He began to laugh again and laughed at me chewing at the cuff. 'I ought to let you have a look.'

'It's all right,' I said.

I could smell the alcohol on him. He swayed, looking at me, then he sat on the bed. If I could only twist round I could get the hammer and then, I don't know, he was still so much taller and stronger, I would have to take him by surprise. Stupid, stupid, to put the hammer under the pillow. He would see me turn.

'It's time to . . .' he began and looked at me, then at the foot of the bed, then back at me. 'Where is it?' he said.

'What?' I said.

'The hammer.'

'I don't know,' I said. 'Did you take it out with you?'

He gazed at me, his eyes had a sad sozzled look. My heart was slamming against my ribs.

'I'll fetch it later,' he said. 'Afterwards.'

He got up from the bed and went to the wardrobe; I couldn't reach behind me without taking the cuff off again. I began to twist, just to make sure the hammer was completely hidden, but he turned back to me.

'Pussy in the well!' he said and giggled and started humming the tune. He opened the wardrobe door and, from the top shelf, he took a carrier bag. 'Props,' he said.

'What?'

'*Props.*' There was a gleam in his smile and just for a moment he looked so handsome, the slant of his dimple, the slope of his jaw. He was like an actor, a beautiful film star playing a baddie, but then he laughed again and that impression flew apart.

'Ding dong bell,' he sang, 'pussy in the well.' He stopped. 'Now.' He pulled a bundle of hair from the bag – a wig – blonde. He came towards me holding it and I let him put it on my head. 'There,' he said, 'that's better, that's pretty.'

∧

Her eyes opened wide but she kept her mouth shut and held still while I put it on her. The hair was much too thick, her own had hung down silkier, but still it was long and blonde. The blouse she had on was white and the skirt navy. She could have been dressed for school. I pushed up her skirt and down her knicks and had a look and a feel. I've got her. *Pussy in the well* went on in my head like background music in a film while I was thinking about Karen Wild, the schoolgirl, all the headlines: *Teenage Whore Turned Cold-Blooded Killer. Devil with an Angel's Face. Evil in a Gym Slip.* And always the same photo underneath with her eyes looking straight out at you like butter wouldn't melt, long hair fair and smooth, face smooth, smooth smile but it wasn't right, all the times I wanted to do her when I was a boy, do her and get her and make her pay, but it wasn't right, I couldn't get geed up properly, it wasn't right and then I saw what it was that was wrong. I'd got it wrong all the time, it wasn't the blonde I wanted it was the dark, the dark, the dark hair in my mouth and round her throat and I ripped off the blonde and I shoved on the dark and she was struggling now and she was a tight girl and that was better and I was hard, hard more than I've ever been and that dark hair in my mouth and in my hands and round her neck and she was twisting and struggling and the more she struggled the . . .

*

I did make sure it wasn't the claws, even in the struggle with the hair in my mouth and tightening round my throat I couldn't bear to smash the claws against his skull. It was the blunt side and not with all my strength. His eyes opened and he gave a sort of choke like surprise, almost like a laugh, and then he fell. My face was wet with spit and blood. It was mine and it was his. He fell off me, out of me and folded down, head on the bed, legs on the floor, jeans round his knees, hands dangling soft now, hairs tangled round the fingers, blonde and black.

I took off the wig and put the hammer down. It had gone quiet outside. No more sirens. Nothing but the night. The lino was cold on my feet. I stepped over his legs and put on some trousers and a sweater. I was shaking and it was hard to get my feet into socks and shoes. I kept my eyes on him all the time and he didn't move.

When I was dressed I picked up the hammer and then I went to have a closer look. The sleeping bag was darkening with blood but he wasn't dead. I could hear his breath. It sounded peaceful, almost satisfied. I lifted the hammer. One more blow. The eyes were closed, long dark fans of lashes, smooth lids. The mouth was slightly open, quirked at the corner as if in the beginning of a smile. A trail of drool ran out and soaked into

275

the sleeping bag. His face was like an angel's. I lifted the hammer again but I could not hit him. I didn't want to kill him or even hurt him any more. The hammer was heavy, the long shaft of it in my right hand, the black head resting on my left palm. Though the hammer head was painted black, the undersides of the claws were gleaming naked metal. One blow.

But it came to me like a blast of light that I couldn't do it. A smile broke painfully across my face but the chattering of my teeth was getting so loud I thought he'd wake. It was hard to get the key from his pocket with his trousers down. His penis dangled in space, sorry little thing now. He groaned and twitched but I was ready with the hammer if I needed it to scare him, but he didn't wake. I got the key, picked up the dark wig, my picture of Charlie, went out of that door and locked him in, as he had done so many times to me. I left the key there in the lock.

I found the kitchen and turned on the light. There was a sofa with his sleeping bag, a suitcase with his clothes. On the table an empty tequila bottle, Jesus on the label. The table was scattered with salt. There was the scrapbook with the pictures of Karen Wild and Isobel and Steven. There was his phone. There was his brown leather jacket on the back of a chair. Inside the jacket was his wallet with some money. Also Karen's life licence. I looked in the suitcase, lovely clothes, hardly worn, all folded neatly, and underneath an envelope with money. I'd never seen so much money, not in cash. It was thousands, no time to count. I took the hammer, the life licence and the scrapbook and put them in a bag. I put on the dark wig and smoothed the tangles out. I picked up his phone and dialled 999 for an ambulance and then I went out and down the oily smelling stairs.

Outside the road was closed, there were bollards, streams of orange tape. There were police around but they didn't see me coming out. I walked smartly away from there, expecting a shout or a hand on my shoulder but there was nothing. I walked to the canal and I threw the carrier bag in. The hammer made it sink. I stood and watched the glossy night-time water until the ripples died. I looked at the picture of Charlie, the calm blue of his eyes, and then I dropped it in the water and watched him float away. The money was a thick wad in my pocket. I heard a siren, the ambulance for Mark, I hope.

And I hope he'll live.

Nina Todd has gone and so has Karen. It's late. I'll walk to Novotel and get a room. I'll have a bath. My name, I think, is Lauren Field. Do you like that? I have a gut feeling about Lauren Field. She will not be perfect, but she might be good.

A NOTE ON THE AUTHOR

Lesley Glaister teaches a Master's degree in Writing at
Sheffield Hallam University. She is the author of
ten previous novels including *Honour Thy Father*,
winner of the Somerset Maugham Award and the
Betty Trask Prize, *Easy Peasy, Sheer Blue Bliss* and,
most recently, *As Far As You Can Go*.

A NOTE ON THE TYPE

The text of this book is set in Linotype Sabon, named after the type founder, Jacques Sabon. It was designed by Jan Tschichold and jointly developed by Linotype, Monotype and Stempel, in response to a need for a typeface to be available in identical form for mechanical hot metal composition and hand composition using foundry type.

Tschichold based his design for Sabon roman on a font engraved by Garamond, and Sabon italic on a font by Granjon. It was first used in 1966 and has proved an enduring modern classic.